FOLLOWING CHRISTOPHER CREED

FOLLOWING CHRISTOPHER CREED

CAROL PLUM-UCCI

HARCOURT

HOUGHTON MIFFLIN HARCOURT

BOSTON   NEW YORK   2011

Harcourt is an imprint of Houghton Mifflin Harcourt Publishing Company.

www.hmhbooks.com

Text set in Minion Pro.

Library of Congress Cataloging-in-Publication Data
Plum-Ucci, Carol, 1957-
Following Christopher Creed / Carol Plum-Ucci.
p. cm.
Summary: Legally-blind college reporter Mike Mavic hopes to get a story
about a body found in Steepleton, believed to be that of long-missing teen Christopher
Creed, but finds something odd about the town, including
Justin Creed's obsessive drive to learn what really happened to his older brother.
ISBN 978-0-15-204759-7
[1. Investigative journalists—Fiction. 2. Reporters and reporting—Fiction.
3. Missing persons—Fiction. 4. Brothers—Fiction. 5. Emotional
problems—Fiction. 6. Blind—Fiction. 7. People with disabilities—Fiction.
8. Mystery and detective stories.] I. Title.
PZ7.P7323Fol 2011
[Fic]—dc22
2011009600

Manufactured in the United States of America
DOC 10 9 8 7 6 5 4 3 2 1
4500301559

TO STEFFI

ONE

I**T HAPPENED ON A DARK AND STORMY NIGHT.** I'm a sucker for stories starting like that. I like it even better when it's true. I said as much to my girlfriend, RayAnn, as she cut the engine, and we were left with the sounds of drumming raindrops on the roof and a surge of wind through the forest. Finally she leaned over me and opened the passenger door of our borrowed car.

"I'll stay here," she said.

I heaved my backpack over one shoulder, trying to size up the distance between us and a couple of flashlights bobbing in what appeared to be a crowd.

"Thought you wanted to be an *investigative* journalist," I lectured.

"Can I write about a bank robbery before I do a dead body?"

I got out, saying, "You can do anything you want. *God bless America . . . land that I—*"

Lanz, from the back seat, started panting and whining. I patted his head.

"Stay," I told him as I stepped into the rain and slammed the car door.

The forest trail was wide up to the crime scene tape holding back a group of people with flashlights. I stooped under the tape and kept going. The last ten yards were treacherous—uphill and full of bramble, which, fortunately, kept me from skimming backwards. I crept up to a second crime scene tape surrounding a gaggle of orange ponchos where portable floodlights beamed onto the ground. We were maybe a quarter mile behind Torey Adams's house, I knew, from the map on his website.

Adams launched ChristopherCreed.com four years ago, about a year after Chris disappeared during their junior year at Steepleton High School. They hadn't been friends, but Adams needed to make sense out of Chris's disappearance. Creed hadn't had any friends. Since its launch, lots of visitors have become site fans, including me and RayAnn. Adams is a budding musician in L.A. now who doesn't post much anymore and doesn't respond to interview requests.

I haven't been a reporter for long. In fact, some would say that because I write for a college newspaper and I'm only a junior, I'm not actually a reporter. I'm a *pretend reporter,* that's what they would say. *Whatever.* I know a good potential story when I hear it. I've been following this one for four years. I know when it's finally time to sell my laptop to buy a plane ticket.

I had already won my blowout with Claudia Winston, our editor in chief, a first-year grad student and equal parts bluster and brains. This morning she tore around the office demanding to know why I was stupid enough to bail on covering the Spring Formal, which would force her into it because all the other reporters were going, and I know she hates dances. She reminded me loudly that the newspaper has no budget for replacing laptops of imbeciles who sold them to report on crimes that have nothing to do with Randolph University or our newspaper, the *Exponent.* I told her that if she prints this holy mess, Associated Press will buy it, no question. My name and "of the *Randolph Exponent*" will be in every paper across the country, and she'll be famous as my editor. Like I said, I know what I'm doing.

I think.

It took the cops a couple minutes to realize that I was

not one of them, because I also was wearing an orange police poncho, which an Indiana state trooper gave me last fall when I was covering a car accident in a blinding rain storm. It explains why nobody stopped me, nobody bothered me. Finally an officer noticed my backpack. It says RANDOLPH on it in bright yellow letters.

"No one past the crime scene tape but FBI and Steepleton law enforcement," he snapped, and I tried to pull my eyes from the neon skeleton to look at him. A spotlight shone on it. The skull was less than half uncovered, the angle telling me the head had been turned to the side when the dirt was thrown on top. One eye socket gazed nowhere and everywhere, and muddy teeth were bared in a forever-silent scream. No raindrops were hitting it, and I realized that we were under a tarp. The skeleton was still buried from the waist down, with one visible arm extended out to the side slightly. An officer was digging carefully—sweeping, in fact, making short, patient swipes. The arm bone appeared to be wrapped in muddy, leafy, woodsy remains of some sort of fabric. The officer was nowhere near the feet yet. Torey Adams said in four different places on his website that Christopher Creed had always worn Keds. I looked down where the feet might be, and, seeing only the mud of a homemade grave, laughed at my uneasiness.

I took off my glasses, reached under my poncho, and rubbed the raindrops off them with my T-shirt, biding for time. I put them back on my face and took one last glance at the corpse, even as I turned my polite grin to the officer, because my dark glasses allow me to do stuff like that. My eyes can pick up a lot when bright light is shed on something in the dark.

"I'm Mike Mavic. Reporter. I called this morning." I stuck out my hand for the officer to shake, but he only glared into my dark glasses. I was used to stares and let my polite grin remain. "I called and talked to, um . . ." I reached nervously into my pocket, pulled out a piece of paper where I'd written down the name, and held it out.

He snatched it up and held a flashlight deep under the tarp so rain wouldn't devour the ink. "You talked to Chief Rye?"

"That's right. This morning. I've interviewed different police officers over the past six months. Rye said I could come."

The officer moved away toward a hulking poncho holding an upside-down shovel that looked to me like the staff of Moses. The figure was on the other side of the corpse. I kept my head high but my eyes lowered. I could see a lot in this light. I saw the chest coming clean—four rib bones, and I heard curses as little pieces of fabric kept getting stuck in the broom utensil.

Chief of Police Doug Rye had a booming voice, despite his whispering.

"Some legally blind guy . . . college paper somewhere near Chicago . . . just some friendly geek . . . stay, so long as he doesn't . . ."

The officer eventually walked back around the body and spoke close to my ear. "He can't talk to you right now. He wants you to stand where you are. Don't move, don't come any closer to the remains."

"Sure. Thanks."

I waited patiently as the broom picked up mud but managed to leave a mangle of that fabric on the bottom rib.

I'll tell a truth here that could get me in trouble if people knew, because not even my boss Claudia realizes this: *Legally blind* is a huge term, and it basically means I don't see well enough to drive and I can get scholarships for blind people. *I'm not as blind as I make myself out to be.*

I lost most of my vision when I got cracked in the head with a baseball my first week at college, playing in a dorm scrimmage. Most people's vision, including frontal and peripheral span, runs about twenty-five feet, side to side. After two failed corrective surgeries, my entire vision screen is seven inches wide. About four inches of that is in black and white, and I lose everything for two to three seconds if I turn my head too fast. If I don't wear shades, I see "twinkles" outlining things, so I wear them almost always. Funsville. But I make sure to count my blessings every day, because I could be taking meals through a tube while examining the back of my hand all day and finding that amusing. Life is excellent or life blows, depending on how you look at it.

I can actually see well enough to navigate around campus without Lanz, but I like Lanz. We understand each other. I usually take him for the fun of it, but when I don't, I'm in no danger of walking dead-on into a tree, though I've done it to get politically correct girls to feel sorry for me. I can't always see whole faces in one close-up frame—*but I can see eyes.* I can tell by people's eyes whether they're smiling or happy or depressed or judgmental or sober or high—whether drug-infested people are on uppers or downers. Light reflects in eyes, and when that's all you can take in at once, they tell you a lot.

This officer's eyes told me he felt sorry for me and wanted to help out a blind college dude who's pudgy enough to get winded climbing a small hill and who smiles even in the rain. If I were some sobering *New York Times* reporter, he'd have told me to can it and go wait with the local goons.

Don't get me wrong: I'm basically an honest person. But I want to be a journalist like any good Roman priest wants to be pope, and the truth is, people tell you more when they think you're a blind reporter. I don't know why that is, but I'll take every advantage I can get. I live to get that goddess of a story. Soon, I want to send one of my crime pieces to Salon.com and have the editors say, "Move that piece of garbage off the homepage and make room for Mike Mavic. The guy's so talented it's scary." I will be a happy man when my words make people laugh and cry aloud.

"You came pretty far pretty fast," the officer said.

"I've been following this story since the beginning."

"One of those, huh?" he said, letting out a short laugh. "You relate to Chris Creed or something? If so, you're not the first college student to show up here wanting to write about him."

That was deflating, but not enough to give me pause. "Chris and I were born in the same year. I also ran from an unhappy home, leaving younger siblings, and I was picked on in school by the 'pops.' That's short for *popular kids,* back in my hometown." I think the runaway part was what got him staring. Most kids who related to Chris and wrote as much on Adams's site had been picked on. A few were runaways also, but not many.

"Jesus, I didn't know there were that many Creed-type families out there," he said, sidling up to me and saying in a low voice, "or, off the record, that many Sylvia Creeds to run from."

"Actually, there are thousands of mothers like that," I said, grinning slightly wider. He'd have known that if he read all the posts on the ChristopherCreed site. "Walmart could market voodoo dolls of the Mother Creed and make a bloody fortune off sons born to some unfortunate likeness."

"The Mother Creed?" He snickered. "That's what you Web fans call the poor woman?"

"Actually, that's a personal ID. You like?"

"Not bad, for a writer." He yawned and didn't try to hide it. "We just found the body this morning. I've been standing here ever since, guarding, waiting for the FBI to show up for this dig, which didn't happen until four. Wish I had duck feet. How'd you hear about this corpse so quickly?"

"Luck," I said. "I checked Torey Adams's website again today. This is the first update he's made in five months."

"Mmm . . . his parents must have called him."

I turned and looked back at the flashlights of onlookers. "Do you think they're part of that crowd back there?"

"I doubt it. Not the types. Chief Rye will call Vic and Susan Adams when he gets back to the office, and a few choice others. Those back there are . . . the folks with nothing better to do, you know?"

"Yeah." I laughed soberly. "I know."

That's not something he would have confessed to a *New York Times* reporter.

I heard yelling behind me. It was a woman's voice—loud, unhappy, unintelligible, and voracious. It sent chills down my back, dark memories of my own little hells.

"Speak of the devil," he groaned.

"Think she's drunk?" I asked. Some local college dude posted last year that Sylvia Creed had turned into a drunk in the four-plus years since her son had disappeared. Adams posted that he feels sorry for her. Sometimes.

"Why don't you go interview her and find out?" the officer asked. He'd grown tired of me. He was unburying a corpse. I could understand. But I would rather interview him, and this is one thing most people don't understand: The interview starts when the reporter identifies himself, not when the reporter shoves a pad or recorder in your face.

"Do *you* think this body is Chris Creed?" I asked.

He took a moment, leading me to think he had nothing to say, until, "I would love to think so. This town has an open wound. It just keeps bleeding."

That was a Quote of the Decade.

"But you really have no opinion," I urged him on.

He laughed uncomfortably. "There have been a couple copycat disappearances in the years since Chris left town. This could be one of them."

Dumbfounded anger jolted me. The police I interviewed never mentioned copycat disappearances. My inexperience was frustrating. *Have I ever* asked *if there had been copycat disappearances? Has Torey Adams ever* printed *such on his website? No, and no.*

I tried to think through my anger how such a fantastic news item would not have been posted on ChristopherCreed.com. First of all, Adams hadn't updated it much in the last couple years. In the last entry he posted five months back, he said he probably wouldn't be updating anymore, as he wanted to get on with his life and he felt that almost five years is enough to give to a missing kid he had never actually hurt, beyond punching him in the face once in sixth grade. Adams had never allowed me to interview him, even though I sold all six of my iPods to go see his band play a concert in Anaheim last year. The manager was letting some press backstage, but I made the mistake of saying why I was there. Adams sent word out that he had nothing further to say about his website or Chris Creed, and I never got backstage. Adams's band had a debut album coming out. Heaven is a great distraction from hell, I guessed. I couldn't blame him.

I reached down, feeling for the recorder in my backpack. I hit Record and made sure the officer could see it. That's journalism ethics, but I didn't make a big deal of it.

"How many copycat disappearances are there?" I asked.

"Two. Only one of them showed up again, two weeks later. So if this is not Chris, it could be the other copycat."

"Okay . . . who's the other copycat?"

He didn't answer right away. A band of fabric that I couldn't make out rolled across one rib, which the FBI diggers/sweepers were pulling out of the ground. The agent sweeping was female—speaking unintelligibly to the agent behind her.

I kept smiling, trying to distract from my uncomfortable shuffling. The officer finally softened to it.

"The one who showed up two weeks later was a Renee Bowen."

I knew that name well enough to do a double take. "The teenage girl who was known to be kind of mean to Chris Creed?" I asked. "She was a gossip hag in Adams's web tale . . ."

He nodded. "She's not a teenager anymore. She's twenty-one. Has a recent history of drug use and run-ins with the law. She left a note very similar to Chris Creed's about wanting to 'be gone. Therefore, I AM.'"

Chris Creed's letter scrolled slowly on the opening page of the website. I knew it by heart. Renee had been somewhere close to the front, a pretty-faced antagonist. Adams had made me dislike the girl, and on top of that, plagiarism guns my hate engine.

"There was a lot of press, a lot of local stink, until someone found Renee sleeping at a friend's house. So much for that one."

I nodded, trying to conceive of Renee Bowen using all her strength to be Chris Creed. Problem: He'd been missing for nearly five years, and she couldn't even make it out of town.

"Guess her family was relieved," I said. "And who's the other copycat?"

"Justin Creed. Chris's younger brother."

I let this one sink in without moving, though I felt like I was falling. All I said was "Wow." I might lie by omission about my ability to see things, but I'm not such a prick that I couldn't understand how Mrs. Creed might turn into a drunken wasteland.

"He hasn't shown up?" I asked numbly.

"He just left two weeks ago."

I glanced down at the bones being uncovered in front of me and let my gaze bounce up again immediately. "So . . . this couldn't be Justin."

"Not unless he was burned. There was a brush fire out here last week. The jogger who noticed the protruding portion of the skull this morning said she thought she smelled kerosene. Can't smell anything now. Not in the rain."

I forced my mind on to stupid details. *How would a burned body have gotten into a shirt? Or is the fabric around the body a blanket?* I decided not to ask. I realized I'd been swaying when the officer's hand came down on my shoulder.

"Are you okay?" he asked. "Maybe you should stand back from the corpse. If you're not used to seeing them—"

I moved slightly to snap out of my sudden desire to get away from the corpse. "I'm fine. I'd just . . . been hoping to get an interview with Justin Creed when I came out. It's been at the top of my list, and it had never occurred to me he wouldn't, you know, be here."

I dived into the memory of having tried before, back

when RayAnn and I first met and I was testing her commitment after she'd asked to assist me on bigger stories. I had her call the house either to get Justin on the phone or get his cell phone number, but the Mother Creed answered and told her to cram it when she identified herself. The woman said we could talk to her, but not her child, then proceeded to question RayAnn for five minutes instead of the other way around. RayAnn finally hung up and took two aspirins. It was nuts.

I looked again at the neon bones and this muddied blotch of fabric the agent with the broom kept fishing for. She finally brought it up.

She held it up for the cops.

"Bra," she said. "I suppose that means we've got a female. What the hell, Rye. Do you have any missing females?"

"No missing females, Jenna. Not at the moment," he boomed, then cleared his throat.

The officer made some remark about hoping I wasn't too disappointed, but this would probably not be a career-making story on finding the body of Christopher Creed.

"Walking into the corpse of Chris Creed would be a gold mine for any reporter," I confessed. "But I can live with the situation, no matter who it is. It'll write, either way."

That caused him to stare. He probably thought like Claudia Winston, who was expecting me to show up on Monday with the Corpse of the Hour angle or there was no story at all. I had the start of a great story—complete with two winning Quotes of the Decade, the second one being "No missing females, Jenna. *Not at the moment.*" It's as if this town of Steepleton had descended into Stepford-wife numbness and people were responding to death-in-the-woods in the same easy way you'd respond to that No Smoking sign on your cigarette break.

"So then, what exactly brought you here?" he asked.

The corpse, obviously. But I'd just said I didn't need the corpse. I could understand his confusion. I was slightly confused—but also at peace with my choices.

"Gut instincts?" I took a stab at wording. "I don't know if being blind has anything to do with it, but I have very good gut instincts. I fall into stories that write themselves all the time."

"And a dead body didn't hurt anything, I suppose." He finally laughed a little, probably at my seemingly compulsive ways of spending my time and money. But he worked more with corpses than concepts, being a cop instead of a writer. I let him laugh.

Steepleton had been my interest, my story brewing for months—the people of a small town like this, people who are left when the dorkiest kid in town takes off and nobody can find a trace of him. There are no remains. The people *who remain* become *the remains* . . . I figured I'd have to play with that line, but the point was in it. Adams had left enough hints on his website for me to gather that the people had become withdrawn, bitter, distrustful gossips with little weird streaks. Adams wrote that after Chris disappeared, his weirdnesses started coming out in others. I think it was that line that hooked me to his story, to the idea that I wanted to come here if the moment ever was ripe.

It's always about the people. It's never about the facts. I forget which of my success gurus wrote that, but I've never forgotten hearing it. Hence, any great story on Chris Creed's disappearance would always be about Steepleton. This corpse was a nice sidebar—if you can forgive my sounding callous—one that would provide the impetus for showing how weird people can be. I wished the officer well in finding an identity, recorded his name as Tom "Tiny" Hughes, and walked back to see if I could hear what the Mother Creed was saying about this.

I stuck the recorder in my pants pocket under my poncho and sucked in air silently. I wanted to hear this woman babble without approaching her, without seeing the torture in her eyes. All my college material reads that serious journalists should not try to interview a drunk. It seems like a chance to get some really good intrigue, but there's no telling whether it's the truth. Drunken quotes are almost taboo among reporters, and I was glad of it at the moment. I just wanted to see what it was like to stand fifteen feet from the Mother Creed. A legend to me. A firestarter. An enigma. I wasn't certain I shared Torey Adams's belief that the woman deserved some compassion, though I admired him for it. I moved toward her voice, but in a staggering, dizzy way.

TWO

ON CHRISTOPHERCREED.COM, TOREY ADAMS responded once to a horribly mean "domineering mothers" post. He wrote, "People like Mrs. Creed, who overenunciate every sentence, are usually very unsure of themselves on the inside. They're not speaking with conviction; they're speaking with abject terror that nobody will listen to them." I like Adams's little twists of wisdom, most of which he credits to his mom, and I tried to remember that as I heard the Mother Creed spitting her cacophony of syllables to the little crowd surrounding her.

". . . good to have the *FBI* finally take notice of our *little* existences. It's a *shame* we have to *wait* until *five o'clock in the afternoon* for them to get with the *program*. Are they a*sleep* up there or just *dozing*?"

I made a sharp right, down toward a group of people hovering behind the other end of the crime tape, remembering Adams's tale from five years back. The Mother Creed had tried to implicate one of Adams's newer friends when Chris disappeared, a backwoods guy named Bo Richardson. But it hadn't worked out for her—less to do with Richardson's only half-strong alibi than with her lack of credibility, I think.

It was hard to focus on her lack of clout when she kept blasting remarks. I found myself haunted instead by Adams's memory of hearing her voice on the other end of the phone the night he and Richardson cooked up this scheme to get her and her husband out of the house so Richardson could search it for Creed's secret diary. They thought something written in there might lead to him. The Mother Creed's voice alone had made Adams piss his pants.

I sympathized, as my pisser muscle was retracting strongly just by my getting within ten feet of her. I wondered if she would ask who I was, and that thought made me think of the warmth of the car and the easiness of RayAnn, who was as naïve and unscathed as Tinkerbell. But it turned out the woman was too busy discrediting law enforcement to realize that I had come up.

I flipped on my tape recorder again. Good backdrop noise for my story.

The rain had slowed to a drizzle, and someone had lit a cigarette and said to her with plaster of Paris vocal cords, "If it's Chris, Sylvia, then you can lie him to rest in peace."

Miss Cigarette was dead wrong, but I just kept staring at the blackness above the tarp. Mrs. Creed went on and on about how her lousy ex-husband had told her that she had no class, but actually *he* had no class or he would be down here bothering with the rain. She went on about how he and his new wife *read novels* to each other, and hearing her voice was like having your ear right up to a train track when a steaming locomotive breaks. I figured I was up to my nostrils in this story and my nausea was a personal reaction, but a girl behind me seemed equally moved.

"Will somebody just kill that swamp creature? Why can't it be her body lying out there?"

Ah, teenagers to interview. A distraction. I turned and gave two girls my credits.

"Why are you here," I asked, "on this dark and stormy night?"

One of them glanced over her shoulder at the Mother Creed, then said to me softly, "Because we feel bad for Justin.

We're his friends. Despite that he's got a drug problem. I mean . . . he was a druggie when he left here, said he wanted to straighten out his life and all, but he felt like he had to start out fresh."

"Like Chris did?" I asked.

"Sort of. Only it's not the same. Chris didn't have any friends. He had no one to rely on, so he left without telling anyone."

"So . . . Justin told you that he was leaving?"

"Yeah. That's not his body. It's gotta be some . . . stranger's." She was staring at my dark glasses. This thing about people telling you more if you're blind—it's generally true, but this was my first run-in with high school girls.

"Can I ask . . . why you're wearing shades?" She giggled. "It's, like, totally dark out here."

I went with my gut instincts. "It's a . . . temporary injury. I can actually see you."

Everything is temporary. I lifted the glasses and smiled into her pupils. Little twinkles showed up around her eyes, and it was good that I couldn't see her clearly. I sensed I'd see eyes full of mean teenager judgment. My own eyes look normal, unless you're really into pupils—then you might notice that mine are flower shaped from scar tissue instead of round.

"Oh. I thought you might be . . . you know . . ."

Blind. I would ignore that.

"What are your names?" I let my shades fall down again.

"I'm Taylor Hammond and she's Mary Ellen Noyes. So . . . you came all the way from . . . where is it? To write about Chris?"

"Randolph U, in Indiana. I got addicted to Torey Adams's website a few years back," I admitted.

"Mr. Famous. I heard Torey Adams posted this news about the corpse today. I doubt the corpse will bring him back here. Nothing's brought him back."

"Maybe the local gossip has something to do with that," I suggested. "Wasn't it flying around among the locals that he helped kill Chris? That could hurt a guy's feelings, especially a nice guy like that."

"Only the biggest gossipers in town still like to say that," Taylor said, laughing. "Most of that died down years ago. Now that he's a rising star, the gossip is that he'll say he was born and raised in Oregon or somewhere and we won't get any of his glory."

"It's always something," I noted, and didn't get a laugh.

"I read the whole site once, maybe a year ago. I saw all the posts from people like you . . . from all over. That's weird. People from Anchorage and Arizona and Florida posting about a kid from Steepleton. Wow."

"A lot of people relate to Chris," I said, which was the understatement of the year in my case, but it wouldn't work to my advantage to spew my personal horrors from grade school and high school all over my interviewees. "The story is dying away too fast—my humble opinion. It was helping bullied kids."

"I don't see what the big deal is about Chris Creed," Taylor said with cute giggles. "Except that now there's this corpse."

"Except that now there's this corpse," I parroted, leaving aside the police verdict that it wasn't him and my confidence that I didn't need the corpse of Chris Creed to sell the story.

"People still talk about Chris around here," Taylor went on. "Justin thinks he's a legend and tried that disappearing act too, but you know what they say about some middle children and drug addiction. We think he just wanted to go to rehab without having to tote his mother in there, via, *up his ass*. He'll be back."

"Do you actually have any contact with Justin?" I asked.

Taylor and Mary Ellen looked at each other for a long time before saying no.

"Do you think this is Chris's body?" I jumped off a delicate subject, figuring I'd swing back to it when they trusted me more.

"Hell, no," Mary Ellen said quickly. "Justin knows where he is."

My heart skidded into my throat. "Really? And where is that?"

"He won't ever say," Mary Ellen said.

"If he knew, he would have told us," Taylor argued with her. "He reads like a maniac, finds all these self-help books nobody's ever heard of. Quantum thought. That's his latest rage. He thinks quantum thought will bring his brother back to him."

I had heard of quantum thought. It bordered on my favorite subject—the power of *positive* thought—but that's been around since forever. My thoughts could control *me*, could make *me* successful, but quantum thought was something about being able to control others—and things, and places—with your thoughts. A few guys in my dorm were quantum thought cultists, and I'd listened to them apply theoretical math to positive thinking, but if they'd had any results in the real world, I hadn't heard about them.

"One day, his brother's coming back. The next day, Justin's all drugged out and depressed," Taylor said. "He said none of the stuff he reads will really do anything for him until he quits abusing himself. We just want him to come home normal again. He was a fun guy. As for his brother Chris, well, Justin barely mentioned him until right around Christmas of this year. You wouldn't have known he had an older brother unless you were a Torey Adams web fan. We don't know what came over Justin, but suddenly he was obsessed, wanting to find him, denying that he's dead, and all this stuff."

Mary Ellen nudged her. "My mom—she loves to gossip but doesn't mean any harm in it. She says that Justin hit the age that his brother was when he left and it's given him a psychological twitch. A little obsession. Whatever. For Justin's sake, we'd like to know what's up with Chris—alive, dead, where, when, all of that.

"If you guys happen to hear from Justin, would you tell him this reporter from Randolph is his number one fan and would like to talk to him?"

"What are you going to write about Justin?" Taylor asked.

"Just . . . the truth. I feel the world owes him that much." I didn't know if the truth was actually bad or good, but I hadn't lied about what I would write, and the girls took it with pride.

"Definitely. We'll call you. He should call us any day. You got a cell?"

I gave the number to them and watched little lights flash as they bleeped it into their cell phones. I knew they had talked to Justin recently, but there was no point in alienating them by making accusations. I wondered if I should ask them to a local diner or glue myself to them a little better before leaving. I didn't want them to space on calling me. I might be a budding reporter, but high school girls could bring on earth-shattering flashbacks, and I could think of nothing further to say that would make me memorable to them.

I remembered promising RayAnn I would spend more time in town talking to people than studying a corpse. So I left Taylor and Mary Ellen then, drawn back to RayAnn and Lanz like a metal spike to a giant magnet. They were a safe haven while I played crown prince to my own former likenesses—emotionally tormented kids who might also be drawn to Chris Creed, whom I could make understandable to the masses.

That was a second reason I was here, the first being to amuse myself with a great story about Steepleton. I rarely do radical things for one reason only; I'm just too conservative a player. Beyond the great story, my gut instincts were telling me, *Now is the time.* I didn't understand gut instincts very well—which isn't to say I didn't use them. I used them almost constantly.

THREE

THIS GREASY SPOON DINER lay out on the marshes behind
Steepleton, and Adams had talked about its fantastic bacon grease-burgers on his website. It was so small a diner, it
didn't even have a name, but all the locals knew of it and I
wagered some folks in there loved to talk.

We found it after asking a man walking his dog through
the center of town, and he pointed us down a road leading
to the back bay.

The diner had only one couple in it, though RayAnn
said the place could seat two dozen people at its paltry three

tables and three booths. I felt hopeful more would show up, but between ordering and the arrival of our cheeseburgers, I did my usual mental relaxation exercises, which I got from a dozen books and as many websites I subscribed to. If you were legally blind and trying to become a reporter, after obtaining a bachelor's degree from a well-respected university, you would meditate on this stuff, too:

What men can believe, men can achieve. Napoleon Hill.

If the dream is big enough, the facts don't matter. Zig Ziglar.

You're like a teabag . . . not worth much until you've been through some hot water. John Mason.

Then, I said one of my daily affirmations loudly in my head:

I am the star of my own show. My life is my own creation and choosing. On this date five years from now I will be . . . the youngest executive on the New York Times *and will be taking my vacations in Polynesia, sucking back margaritas on a dock. I will. I will. I will.*

As I felt RayAnn's fingers wrap around mine and pull my hands into the middle of the table, I was reminded of how much my daily affirmations had helped me recently. *This year, some woman will love me . . . okay,* like *me* had recently been dropped from my mantra because it had come true.

She cleared her throat and said, " "The ultimate measure

of man is not where he stands in moments of comfort and convenience, but where he stands at times of challenge and controversy.' Dr. Martin Luther King Jr."

I smiled. "How'd you know I was meditating?"

"For one, you just saw a corpse. Logic by default. Second, your lips move when you're thinking emphatically."

"Where'd you find that quote?"

"John Mason's Nugget of the Day this morning, in my e-mail box. I memorized it for you. Rising to challenge and controversy is the story of your life, Mr. Geeky Dweeb."

"Like attracts like, Ms. Dweeb. You went out with me without a gun to your head, if I remember right."

RayAnn also was considered a dweeb at Randolph, but it had nothing to do with her looks. She has swirly, rusty blond hair to her shoulders and so many freckles that you can't find her nose. She's got a shy, squinty smile and dimples, and if she thinks I'm too fat, she doesn't hold it against me. She is to skinny as I am to fat. We both have one foot on the beyond normal line and the other foot on a banana peel.

"If my dad knew I was actually going out with you, he would be upset." She giggled.

"Tell him I was never fat until college. Dorm food, carbo hell."

"You're not that fat, and you know that's not what I'm talking about."

Correct. This is RayAnn's dweeb issue: her age. She'd turned seventeen just two days ago. Yes, I, at twenty, had been going out with a sixteen-year-old, and I'm not even from the bayou. If I'm a cradle robber, Randolph is a bigger cradle robber: They admitted her. RayAnn acts older, so it's hard to remember her age. She had been homeschooled and all that yada yada that goes with homeschooled kids: Got her GED at age fifteen, started Randolph at sixteen. Her parents are liberals, deep thinkers who enjoy fudging all lines of convention. Except they didn't want her roommates or the campus party animals being her introduction to romance.

"Your parents ought to love me. I'm not exactly Joe Rapist, am I?"

"No," she agreed quickly. "I wouldn't say that . . . *at all.*"

Her sarcastic giggling noted, I rubbed the bridge of my nose.

"Our relationship is only a month old, RayAnn. You'll get mad at me at some point and then it will all have become 'statutory rape.'"

"If I get mad, we can talk it out."

"I'm not a therapist. And I don't need a statutory rape sentence dirtying up my future glory."

"We'll work on your trust issues."

"I'm going to write this piece, RayAnn. I'm going to be catapulted to fame and fortune via Christopher Creed . . . *Be he alive or be he dead . . .*"

"Freight train running all through my head . . . Gone, gone, gone in the morning," she sang back at me. It was lyrics from Torey Adams's virgin album, appropriately named *Torey Adams.* The album wasn't released yet, but I'd gotten a pirated download of "Gone" after hearing a preorder clip on Amazon. I knew it had to do with Chris Creed, though it was the only song on the album that hinted at Adams's distant past.

We held hands across the table, and eventually the couple let on to the waitress how they'd traveled around to the wrong side of the woods, so they never found the cops or the corpse. The woman's talking painted a picture: Their son was a rookie cop, and her job as his mother was to bring the squad homemade cider and brownies if a crime or accident scene kept them somewhere longer than a couple hours.

I could sense the couple watching us, and finally the man asked: "Is that couple praying?"

RayAnn and I withdrew our hands to our laps, and RayAnn giggled. Having come from a small town, I know that's how small-town people get strangers to warm up to them. They make you laugh.

"Hi, we're from Randolph State," RayAnn said in her totally friendly way. "My boyfriend, Mike, and I are journalists there. Mike came out to do some research. I'm helping him."

"I didn't know Randolph had a journalism major," the man said. He was well spoken and would have to be educated to know that. "I thought it was an engineering school. Why not go to Indiana U?" the man asked. "That's the state's writing school."

I smiled and simply said, "I like the road less traveled." The whole truth contained a practical side: I could be a desk editor on Randolph's newspaper in another six weeks—after the next editor joined the eighty students monthly who flunked out of engineering. At Indiana, a thousand writers lie in wait for desk positions—too much competition for a job that is coveted but not difficult. I ended with a joke: "We're newspaper geeks, and I can't remember what my major is. I just know it's not dance."

They laughed and quit glancing at my shades, their suspicions about my impaired vision confirmed. They didn't fire any related questions at me.

"I'm Forrest Hayden," the man said. "This is my wife, Annie."

I reached my hand out and they shook it.

"So, what research are you doing way out here in New Jersey?" Mrs. Hayden asked.

I told them my interest in Creed, generated from Torey Adams's website.

"Well, you picked a great time," Mrs. Hayden said quickly, "with that corpse turning up in the woods. They found one almost five years back, but it wasn't Chris. We rather hope this one is. His mother would rest more easily if she had answers."

"Do you mind if I ask you some questions?" I brought my tape recorder out of the pouch in the poncho and held it in my lap. They didn't object as I turned my chair toward them. We'd already had our small talk, so I cut to the chase.

"How would you say that Steepleton has changed since Chris disappeared?"

A long pause was followed by nails drumming on the table.

"*Guilt*," Mrs. Hayden finally said. "There's this underlying feeling of *guilt*. Like we've all done something. We just don't know what. We were a pretty normal town before the kid left and it turned into an unsolved whodunit."

"Guilt. Not a good thing," I agreed.

"But I think *underlying* is the wrong word, Annie," Mr. Hayden put in. "It's not a sensation that *lies under* things. It's in the air. It hangs from the trees. It drifts around on the wind. It's a feeling of . . . general negative . . . something. Negative energy."

I took a shot at accuracy. "Do you mean . . . *bad frequency*?"

"You mean as in *radio* frequency?" Mr. Hayden asked. "That's interesting phraseology."

"It's just the latest term for *bad karma*," I said with a

shrug. I didn't want to put words in their mouth, though *bad frequency* was a term I used almost constantly to describe my own past. It sort of explains concepts such as how the rich get richer and the poor get poorer, and trouble breeds trouble. Coming under bad frequency means you've had a stream of bad luck, one bad thing following after another and another, even though those things seem to have no relationship. It's like you get beat up lots in school, which makes you depressed, makes you less careful with yourself, and so you walk out in front of an oncoming car by accident. Your broken back seems not related to getting beat up in school . . . but psychologically speaking, it's very related. Bad frequency can go on for years with some people, getting worse and worse if the victim doesn't get turned around. It had for me.

"No, I like that. Bad *frequency*. Steepleton has gotten on *bad frequency*. That's accurate," Mr. Hayden mused.

My empathy kept me from bombarding them with another question. I kept a respectful silence during his thoughts on bad frequency.

Mr. Hayden finally went on. "A couple years back the governor was trying to enforce stricter statewide driving laws. An article in the *Press of Atlantic City* listed the top twenty-five New Jersey towns for auto-related fatalities. Steepleton was number one. It's not like we've got a lot of hills or twisty-turny roads. All we've got is Route 9 and a bunch of side streets. No one can figure out why we rank so high."

Raindrops crackled against the windows. I reached my hand back, patted the table in front of RayAnn, and heard her scribble a note. She would look up the article.

"That statistic in itself bothered us a little," Mrs. Hayden went on. "But then, last year, an entirely different news article came out, one on the cost of health insurance in New Jersey. It provided a list of the highest rates of cancer in the state by city. Steepleton also was at the top of that list."

Steepleton had the state's worst cancer rates and car accident rates. I could feel RayAnn staring at me, waiting for me to dance on the table or something. I shifted around. "Yes. I would say that defines *bad frequency.*"

When they didn't add anything, I asked, "But this . . . couldn't possibly relate to Christopher Creed?"

"Obviously it doesn't." Mrs. Hayden laughed nervously. "However, Steepleton is known for three things. Bad driving, the most cancer per city, and being the place where that kid disappeared and nobody has ever found him."

"There is something wrong here. Nobody can deny that," Mr. Hayden said. "Maybe cancer victims and car accidents are just symptoms. I don't . . . exactly know what I'm talking about."

I waited through another silence that finally ended with their meat loaf and our cheeseburgers arriving.

Mrs. Hayden touched my hand. "Eat your food, hon. It will get cold."

I turned and bit into my bacon cheeseburger. The grease ran onto my chin, and I gave a thumbs-up, hoping the waitress saw.

The cowbells rang again, and this time the room was flooded with young voices, laughing and babbling.

"Three girls," RayAnn muttered. "Maybe fifteen or sixteen."

College is a cloister of sorts. It's just you, professors, and other almost-adults. The high school girls from the woods were the first I had been exposed to in at least a year, I realized. Their use of "swamp creature" to describe a destroyed parent revisited me.

"Good. It's all good . . ." I stood and picked up my recorder. The forward motion was to counteract this feeling of reverting back into the accused booger picker of sophomore hell—the guy that cute, giggling girls liked to torture. I'd been tripped at least six times in the cafeteria, the first time washing my face with the inside of a tuna hoagie that nailed the floor a split second before I did. I did not want to go there in my mind. RayAnn does not comprehend school meanness, having never been exposed, and she stood up with me, reading my intentions.

"I ate at the airport and you didn't," she said. "I'll go ask if you can talk to them in a few minutes."

I froze with a huge wad of burger inside my cheek, listening to hear if they were the types who could catch RayAnn up on school meanness in one foul lesson. Fortunately I had reason to feel guilty for the swift assumption. RayAnn was giving them a lowdown of why we were here, and the response was all positive.

"Wow, that is so cool. You guys came all the way here?" They even gathered their chairs around and introduced themselves as Katy, Elaine, and Chan.

Katy was the chatty one, an endless question. "So . . . do you write for a high school newspaper or a college?"

"College," we both chimed.

"Oh! Because you look older . . . but you look really young."

Though it was out of range, I easily imagined the path of her pointing finger.

"Nope, I'm in college, too," RayAnn said quickly and left it at that. Bless her.

"Hey, are you blind?" A hand went slowly up and down in front of my face.

"Katy!" One of them nudged her.

"I just want to know! What's wrong with that?"

"Not entirely," I said. "I have tunnel vision and some color blindness, and if I turn my head too quickly, I've got nothing for about three seconds."

"What a bummer," she said.

"Could be worse." My grin spread as my usual speech filled my head. These were nice girls. I'd forgotten there was such a thing in high school. "It's more annoying at times than anything. For the first three months after my accident, I couldn't see anything, so I remind myself of that, and then I'm grateful instead of starting a pity party."

"So, like, how do you do college? Don't you have to read textbooks and stuff?"

"The college has to provide audio text and Internet audio software for blind students, but I also can see about half of a sheet of paper at a time. I read about the same amount as any other college student. It just takes me longer. I'm like one of those bobble-head dolls. You know, from reading." I turned my head in a wobbly, back-and-forth fashion, and they laughed.

"Is that your German shepherd out in the car?"

"Yeah, that's Lanz. He's a service dog."

"How'd you drive to here so fast from Indiana?" Katy asked.

"We actually flew. But RayAnn has friends online from, like, four continents," I said, jerking my thumb at her, thinking I shouldn't mention the word *homeschooled*. It would be another subject that could take up to half an hour trying to explain how you can sit in your pajamas all day in front of a computer as a means of getting through high school, your "classmates" being in New Zealand or New Jersey. "One friend goes to Rowan now. We paid the girl a hundred bucks to pick us up at the airport and do without her car for a few days."

"Good friend," Chan noted, looking slightly confused. RayAnn stayed quiet. She could have mentioned that she spent a month in Italy with the girl after they'd discovered common relatives for an online class project, but we know better than to draw attention to our own lives during interviews. Between her life and mine, it gets to be a game.

"We're calling it a rental car because it makes us feel official" was all I said. I put the recorder in the middle of the table, trying to jump-start a new subject.

"So you came out here to write about Chris Creed?" Katy said. "Chris was way older than us. We didn't know him except to see him around when we were in middle school. He was kind of dorky, a skinny little bigmouth, supposedly. He's a much bigger deal around here since he disappeared."

"Part of his intention in leaving?" I suggested.

"If that's so, he was really, really smart. He ought to be majoring in marketing, because he sure marketed himself right." Katy hooted loudly at her own comment, and it was clever enough to get chuckles all around. "Only one of us thinks he's dead, and that's Elaine. Chan and I think he's alive, though beyond that, we can't tell you anything about him. Nobody can. Save, maybe, Justin, who is also among the missing."

"Can you tell me about Justin?" I asked.

"He's in rehab. That's what we figure. We know all his friends and what they say gets around, but we don't hang with them."

"They're . . . what? Different, somehow?"

"Yah, they're at the center of everything. But sometimes they can get mean," Katy said. "Justin Creed got mean this year."

"*Definitely* he's popular, but he's got a real mean streak lately." Chan giggled nervously.

I almost collapsed. You hear over and over again how different one sibling can be from another. But I'd always had this image of Justin growing into another Chris—another victim with no desire to get evil. I'd gotten the idea at the crime scene that he had friends, but I wasn't prepared for this.

"Define 'mean streak,'" I said, mesmerized. "Does he . . . get into fights?"

"He never did until recently. Then he got in three last month," Chan said. "He's become a chronically angry person. He smiles, but generally it's when he's doing something to someone. Like this one time, he sat behind Natalee Lange at a basketball game. Natalee is a beautiful girl with this long, long, wavy blond hair. He sat a few rows up from her in the bleachers the whole first half, taking tiny pieces of his chewing gum and flinging them at the back of her hair. She never felt anything. But she went home with like thirty pieces of gum in her hair. Thank you, Justin. Natalee had to get a short haircut, and it will probably take five years to grow back."

"Yeah, that's mean," I agreed, in awe. "Why do you think he's like that? Any ideas?"

They paused, but not with the same enjoyment of deep thought as the Haydens, I sensed.

"Some say it's his mom. He gets in fistfights with her," Chan said. "Sent her to the hospital one night with a bloody nose. She pressed charges. He said a night in jail was the most enjoyable night of his life, so I guess you could say they don't get along."

"I guess not," I said through hapless chuckles. "Wow. So, what's with the rehab?"

"You know, maybe you shouldn't print this, what we're saying," Katy broke in suddenly. "What if Justin saw it?"

I agreed to use fake names if they were that worried about their necks. So, they told us that most of the really popular kids around here partied on weekends, but the "loadies" partied on weeknights or even came to school high. Almost out of nowhere, Justin had started in with coke and Valium. With his fights at school, his friends started to harp on him, saying he was turning into a loadie. And that quickly, he was gone, too.

"And you're sure he's in rehab."

"Well, I don't think that body out in the woods is Justin Creed. Word was starting to get around when we left that the body was female," Chan said.

I didn't confirm it.

"It had something to do with female clothing," Katy took over. "But I think whoever dumped the body could have put that there to confuse things. It *could* be Justin. He could have gotten in a fight somewhere and accidentally been hit over the head. He hung out in the woods a lot. All his friends go to this place called the Lightning Field. It's this field where the woods come all the way down to the back bay without any marshes lying in between."

Chan took over. "The Lightning Field is really just a part of the forest where there was a huge fire four summers ago. It's all flat now, except you can still see the burnt trunks that stick up, some of them thirty feet high. It's eerie. I know. I've been out there."

The note of pride in her voice let me know that this was a place for cool people and these girls weren't exactly on the list of regulars.

"Some people say the Lightning Field is haunted," Katy said. "But don't let Justin hear you say that. He thinks he talks to his brother out there. He's hit people for saying it feels creepy out there. He says it feels wonderful, like a . . . a euphoria?"

I watched RayAnn's shoulders spaz as she shuddered, and I gathered her thought was of Justin so sunk into drug culture that bad things started to feel good. But I wasn't so sure he was totally blackened by his drug use. His friends at the crime scene had mentioned him reading a slew of self-help books, including some on quantum thought, to which I was raw. But one thing Justin and I probably shared was a euphoric feeling when the right self-help authors gave you confidence in facing your life. After I read *The Magic of Dreaming Big*, I was high on life for about a week and a half. It was during that time that I talked my roommate, Todd Stedman, into visiting a cemetery with me late one night so that I could look for some of my ancestors, part of a Personal History class research paper.

I shared that trip with the girls, just as a note of interest. "To my amazement, I didn't feel scared at all. In fact, I wondered, as my roommate read names off of tombstones, if my great-great-great-grandparents were looking down from above, so glad I had taken an interest in them. If you believe in some sort of afterlife, then that makes sense, right?"

"Right," they chimed.

"My belief in ghosts swings with the wind. But my belief that the cemetery felt happy and not sad—I've never changed my mind about that."

"Mike can feel energy that other people can't," RayAnn

bragged. "But he hates when people accuse him of being psychic."

"There's nothing magical about it," I said. "It started with being hypersensitive to people's moods. Comes from living in an alcoholic home, I think. No pixie dust."

"Do you think it has something to do with being blind?" Katy asked.

"I think that helped it along." I nodded, listening through their riveted silence until I swallowed and washed burger back with the Coke. "It got ten times keener after I lost my vision two years ago. Now I can sit in a meeting at the newspaper, and if the reporter next to me begins to disagree with something being said, or loses interest, or becomes angry over an assignment—I know which way his mind just went. The reporter doesn't even have to move."

They all agreed that they had felt the same things, though probably not as strongly. To bring the subject back around to Justin and the field, I asked, "But doesn't Justin believe his brother is alive? Other people told me that tonight."

"Yeah, definitely," Chan said. "He doesn't think he hears his brother's ghost. He thinks his brother's voice reaches across the miles or something. I don't know what the terminology is for that, but that's the word on the street."

"You mean . . . he speaks to his brother telekinetically?" I asked.

"Yeah. Like ESP. He swears to it. He says the Lightning Field is the only place where he's really happy, and when he's there alone, he can hear his brother's voice. He says Torey Adams is wrong. His brother's not in Texas, never was in Texas."

"And . . . this isn't drugs talking?" I asked.

"I don't think drugs helped it," Katy said. "But he's been talking about his brother since right around Christmas. If he was doing drugs that early on, nobody knows about it."

I nodded, trying to put all this together. With the talk about Texas, Katy was referring to a response on Adams's website that had caused a big stir . . . a lot of people posting that the letter might be from Chris himself. I even posted something to the effect of "the letter sounds like him, if you read the e-mail he left for Principal Ames and compare the two," not that many were listening to me in the reverb. The initial letter implied that Chris had run off to Texas to live with one of his mom's two sisters, both of whom hated his mom and would never have betrayed him. Adams himself wondered . . .

I shook the confusion from my head or tried to, having crossed the line between fact and hearsay many times. I was having trouble sorting what was newsworthy and how I would state the rest.

I felt distracted, off-center, pulled slightly toward the shadow behind Katy and Chan, and the distraction was why

I couldn't organize my thoughts. Negative energy, big-time. I'm so good at sensing people's energy, I could have predicted the type of story that came next and would have loved to avoid it, but trying to be the good professional, I went for the trouble.

"Elaine, you haven't said a word. What do you think of all this?"

Her laugh turned over so deeply in her chest that it sounded like a thump. "Chris is dead. I think Justin knows it. He just doesn't want to face up to it. He's got this positive-thinking shit that he reads, and then he says his brother is not dead and he hears from him."

There you go: Someone who puts "positive thinking" and "shit" in the same concept can inspire some serious eye-rolling if you're the type who works at keeping your thought-life healthy. Hooray for dark glasses.

"And?" I asked.

"And he's manic-depressive," she said dismissively. "Any idiot ought to be able to see that. When he's manic, he thinks he hears his brother telling him he's alive. When he's depressed, he just lies there and stares at the stars, tells everyone to shut up, he's got a headache. The truth is, one night when Justin wasn't around, a bunch of kids saw Chris Creed out there in the field. He was surrounded in white light. Like, not as somebody living would appear."

Fortunately, I had just covered a séance held in the dorms as a feature story for the weekend section of the paper. I had experience in not laughing in people's faces. It's not that I don't believe in the supernatural, but there's a difference between believing in an intelligent and affectionate Source behind the universe and believing that dead folks wander around down here, lost.

"Tell me about it."

"A bright light appeared out of the trees and when you looked at it closely, you could see it was Chris," Elaine said. "No question. Just like a holograph. It was definitely Chris."

"Sounds like a third-generation story. A pass-it-down-the-line deal," RayAnn put in skeptically. "Like somebody pointed a flashlight against a tree as a gag, and by the second or third time the story was told, it was a holograph image of Chris Creed."

I could feel Elaine blustering. "That's why I've known ever since that he is dead. *I was there.* I saw it with my own eyes. He came straight at us, staring at us, and then simply evaporated. I can introduce you to the kids who were with me. They saw it, too."

The silence was broken only by a giggle from Mrs. Hayden, and as she picked right up with some sentence about her workout at the gym, I gathered they weren't eavesdropping. I liked the couple.

"But . . . your friends here don't believe you, apparently," I said. Katy and Chan had a rebuttal to this story, or they wouldn't have told me in the beginning that Elaine thought he was dead but they didn't.

"Um . . . they were dropping acid," Chan said. "Don't print that, please. Or if you do, you didn't hear it from Katy or—"

"Acid, schmacid," Elaine said. "So, somebody spiked my soda. I'm not a loadie, okay? I haven't done it since."

"It just cuts into the . . . believability of this tale." Katy turned to me, putting a hand on my arm. "We just don't talk about this. Or, not very often."

This Elaine had a "little" voice, if I had to describe it. Not childlike, not breathy, just with hardly any power. All her energy came from her sarcasm.

"I don't care whether other people believe me or not. Five people saw it. Justin missed the whole thing, then started threatening the screamers in school on Monday."

"I don't suppose he likes people talking about his brother as if he were a, uh, spook. That's understandable," I said.

"Yeah, but people will never stop talking like that around here. And word sure gets around. I don't know who told him. Justin believes what Justin wants to believe. I believe in the truth. Think of it. Acid can make you see things that aren't there, surely. But they can't make everyone see the *same thing,* can they? We all saw the *same thing.*"

The silence broke with Mrs. Hayden's chair pushing back, and her form moved to a funny posture in front of the window. ". . . seeing stars now. I think of those poor drenched officers out there, all day long, and now that their work is almost done, we see the stars."

Mr. Hayden's voice chimed with my own: *"Bad frequency."*

I needed this next move like a hole in the head, but I wanted my fame and writing glory enough to swallow my anxiety. I couldn't think of an educated response to Elaine's suggestion that a mutual hallucination is not a hallucination.

"Can you take us to the Lightning Field?" I asked the girls.

FOUR

OUT IN THE PARKING LOT I gave Lanz the remainder of Mrs. Hayden's meat loaf along with a Ziploc bag full of dry dog food from my luggage. We waited for the three girls to get their takeout order, which Katy said they would eat in my car.

RayAnn seemed less perturbed about going to the field than going to the woods where the corpse had been. She leaned against the car, describing the bright moon as an almost perfect gold circle with one piece sliced off the side. I turned and found it, smiling a little. It was big enough that I couldn't see it all at once.

"I can't think of any way to leave Elaine out of this," I said. "She means no harm. But I'd rather be punched in the gut than go around with someone like that. Take your pain all at once."

"People who . . . are not warm? Who break down your good mood?" she said, trying to vocalize it.

"Yeah, and they're not satisfied until you feel as bummed out as they do. What am I trying to say . . . ?" I reached down to pet Lanz, who bumped his cold nose affectionately into my hand while chewing his food. "She'll try to ram that story down our throats about seeing Chris Creed's ghost out there. I just don't buy that stuff."

"About Chris being dead, or about ghosts in general?" she asked.

"Both, but mostly that second thing," I said. "Put it this way. I think if someone came back from the afterlife, it would be either to say something profound or do something significant. For someone to come back just to scare the crap out of a bunch of tripping, high school ne'er-do-wells . . . that's a problem for me."

"How do you explain them all seeing the same thing?" she asked. "That's a hell of a story. She sounded so . . . adamant."

Rather than bust my nerves trying to answer that, I shoved my mind into another subject, some school reality:

"I'll need to borrow your laptop sometime tonight or to-morrow morning."

"I expected nothing less," she said, but sighed anxiously. "I can't believe you sold your laptop just before you've got a huge research paper due."

"Journalism first, school second," I said, knowing no self-respecting newspaper would care about my GPA if I had a year or two of good published stories under my belt. "Besides, I might get Claudia to publish some of my find-ings somehow. It's a paper that should write itself."

RayAnn knew about my research. I'd actually gotten participants off ChristopherCreed.com by posting in the "Bullied2" forum. She recited the assignment I'd posted for them because it had intrigued her: "Think of times you've been bullied. Then make up a person who is kind, merciful, and was there to see it. Write the story of what happened to you from his or her eyes instead of from your own."

I took a bow with a chuckle. I'd gotten five respondees. Three said things like "This didn't help me. It's too hard to see the world from somebody else's view, especially when writing, which is hard." Two, however, wrote of shifts in their thinking that were "amazing."

One girl said her "kind person" now exists almost con-stantly in her mind, and reminds her how to view a situation every time someone makes fun of her. Another high school senior said it helped him so much that he was going to re-write his entire life from his kind person's point of view. I'll never forget his words: "There is something very cool about writing your worst memories through someone else's eyes. You start to see what happened to you . . . *almost as if it happened to somebody else*. Especially if that made-up person is nice, it's a great exercise because there are many mean people in this world."

The kid had gone on about how we automatically take our self-esteem cues from mean people, which I felt to be somewhat true. But I was transfixed by his statement about looking at your life as if it had happened to somebody else. That was precisely what I'd been looking for, because that was how I'd survived my own break with my family: I viewed it as a *him* and *me* thing. I often said as much to people who knew I'd left an unhappy home life, but most of the time they didn't get what I was talking about. RayAnn seemed to.

"One out of five isn't bad," she said. "You'll write that paper up an hour before it's due and ace it—your usual."

I didn't care about the grade so much. "I'm thinking maybe I could give the exercise to the Psych Department and they could actually research the therapeutic value of it. You can't get the money to form a microcosm for research when you're broke."

RayAnn nodded thoughtfully, supportive as always.

"It's a shame you can't get Chris Creed to contribute. I know you think that's how he stayed away so long."

"That little cuss had it too easy. Torey Adams did the writing as his 'kind person.' All Chris had to do was click and read. Most people are not lucky enough to have someone else do the writing."

"You really think Chris Creed has read Torey Adams's website?" she asked with a glint and a smile.

People seemed to find that concept interesting, though I felt it was logical. "I don't think he's dead or electronically challenged. My question is, how could he *miss* it?"

"Unless he's living in the Congo, with a plate in his bottom lip and spearing fish in the Amazon for his daily intake." RayAnn smiled.

I pulled her up to me by the back of the neck and kissed her. "You're funny. It's one of the reasons I adore you."

"Oh, you *adore* me," she said. She was a much faster mover than I was. She wanted the *L*-word. She wanted to be sandwiched between me and my dorm mattress. I wasn't stupid about that. I was stupider about why I'd been telling myself "tomorrow" for more than a month.

Fortunately the screen door creaked open, saving me from spiraling into the confusion I loathed. The three girls came down the steps, and as it turned out, RayAnn and I didn't have to do anything to lose Elaine.

"You guys are crazy," she announced. "I wouldn't go back out there for a million bucks. Straight or otherwise. Have fun."

"We will," I promised. I held my hand out behind my back and RayAnn 'fived me as Elaine's departing footsteps tromped across the parking lot stones. I can get lucky sometimes.

Chan and Katy said nothing as they piled into the back seat, and I promised them Lanz would neither bite them nor drool on their burgers. Their forced giggles made me suspect they too were having second thoughts. They ate their cheeseburgers and fries in silence as RayAnn drove.

We had to leave the bay area and head up Route 9 another mile and a half, then turn back toward the bay again. I was laying a picture in my head. There weren't a lot of side streets in these woods, and if you wanted to get from one place to the other that was close to the water, you had to either go by boat or drive west to Route 9.

"Get ready to walk," Chan said as RayAnn finally slowed the car and cut the engine.

As I opened the door, the air smelled densely of earth and forest, and the only sound was the *drip, drip* of raindrops still falling from the trees. I figured I would take Lanz this time. RayAnn mentioned that no other cars were parked here.

"No bikes," Chan noticed as the engine went silent. "Unless they're hidden in the brush from cops. But I've heard this about the Lightning Field lately—ever since Justin took off, people are afraid to come back here without him after dark."

"Why?" I asked. *Did he carry a ghost buster shield and a silver stake?*

"They say it's just . . . eerie. When he's back there, talking about how wonderful the place is, people can actually get to feeling that way. When he's not around, people say, it just feels like a vortex. You can't have any fun for being creeped out. The only one I know who enjoys it out here without Justin is Kobe Lydee. He's in our grade. He thinks he's a ghost chaser and he'll make a gazillion dollars off getting Chris Creed's ghost on tape."

I found the moon and paused for a moment, making sure I appreciated what people were saying about Justin Creed. Apparently the kid wielded a lot of influence, and his self-assurance—which may just be a synonym for my word, *energy*—must have been off the charts. Somehow, I didn't feel it was his corpse we just saw, and it was something beyond the female undergarments. Gut instincts, I guess.

FIVE

"WOULD YOU PREFER NOT TO GO?" RayAnn asked Katy and Chan as I got out with Lanz. "Because Mike and I can—"

"We'll go," Katy said, giggling nervously. "I just can't promise we'll go with you all the way into the Lightning Field, or how long we'll stay."

The trail was marked with bright splashes of glow-in-the-dark white paint on the trunk of one tree after another. It would be hard to get lost even if RayAnn's flashlight were to give out. We walked along in silence, and I tried to see something beyond the splashes of neon in RayAnn's flashlight beam. I relied more on Lanz than I ever had before. But he kept going slower than I wanted him to, and after ten minutes, I felt like I was half carrying him by the harness. My arm hurt, and he was whining.

I finally stopped, rubbing my tricep. "What's up, buddy?"

He stood rooted, his legs slightly trembling, so that I could feel the vibes against my thigh. They had said at Seeing Eye that a dog can sense your mood and become nervous simply because you are. But I didn't feel nervous. I felt a little tired, as jet lag was starting to set in, and a little annoyed that RayAnn's friend who'd "rented" us her car hadn't owned a Jeep so RayAnn could blaze this trail. My legs were tired, but my brain was curious. I wanted to get a feel for this place that Justin Creed called holy and everyone else called hellish.

Lanz let out some short whines.

"Can't pets, like, feel everything?" Katy whispered. "He senses something . . . dark. Let's go back."

"He'll follow me." I ignored her premonitions, dropping the harness handle and stumbling ahead. My tunnel vision could get worse in the dark, but I could make out a break in the trees coming up by standing still and moving my head slowly, allowing my brain to process the scene in frames. The large moon now painted a jagged glow, separating the dark sky and the ultra-black treetops. Moonlight struck the wet and shining ground at the edge of the forest, revealing an open space as big as a football field. Sure enough, Lanz came after me, whining and panting, and the girls followed to get closer to him.

We came into the clearing, and I stood there, taking it in frame by frame, not knowing what to make of this place.

"It's . . . full of tree trunks," RayAnn reported to me in a whisper. "There are a dozen or so . . . scorched, pointy, hollowed-out tree trunks."

"They're black?" I asked, and felt her staring at me as I whipped off my glasses, blinking away a dozen twinkles.

"They're kind of, like, petrified, the trunks," Chan whispered. "They turned a grayish white over the summers instead of staying black."

White burned tree trunks? Lanz whined and nudged my hand for comfort, so I dangled my fingers and stroked the top of his head, taking in frame after frame. He wasn't buying into the idea we were safe, probably because we were in a petrified forest. *Will somebody explain that, please?*

"How do burnt tree trunks turn white?" I asked.

"The only thing known to do that is lightning—if they were struck by lightning before they burned," Katy said. "Somebody brought up the question in science class, and that was the only answer Mr. Kingsley had."

I took in the six or seven tall, shimmering trunks pointing jagged fingers up to the sky like skeleton ghosts. "Must have been a hell of a lightning storm."

Lanz did his best to guide me around larger rocks, stumps, and budding baby trees, but his mind was elsewhere. I finally let go of his harness again and stumbled close to one tall, shining trunk. I put my hand out and touched it. It felt like crystal or like wood depending on where my fingers were.

The girls were breathing quietly behind me. "Why did you want to come out here, anyway?" Katy asked. "Can we go soon?"

There was no wind, no movement, no sounds out here except our breathing. I didn't want to leave—not yet.

I could feel an energy here that I couldn't exactly verbalize. I was good at pegging the energy of one *person* at a time, but this was something more intense. Maybe it was nature's energy, or fried nature's energy . . . I could only compare it to what the energy of a thousand souls, with moods and unsung statements all diving through each other, might feel like. I could see how Justin could believe in quantum thought just from spending time out here. I had trained myself to think positively, to have a mental advantage on whatever trials and tribulations I met up with throughout the day. It was pure psychology. From what I read of quantum thought, the authors felt that thought energy could reach out into the universe and actually alter the course of your life in huge ways. I was no quantum physicist and had never given any ideas to my energy reaching out any higher than the ceiling of my dorm room. But out here, it was as if a roof had been lifted off of what I decided was believable and what I thought wasn't.

I lay my hand on the trunk and breathed deeply three times, trying to conjure Justin Creed's presence to this place via blasts of confidence. According to quantum thought, I could bring Justin here if my belief was powerful enough . . . or I could at least get him to think of the place, wherever he was. As I was a skeptic, I decided with a smirk that any quantum energy I possessed would probably bring him here two months from now, and then we could all say it was a co-incidence.

I did this deep breathing/conjuring without saying anything. It's fine to be insane as long as you keep it to yourself.

"My mother will kill me for being out here," Katy tried again.

"Tell her you went with a couple professionals," I said with as much calm as I could muster, despite Lanz's sticking his nose in my hand and whining.

"Do you feel anything . . . weird out here?" I asked the girls.

"Definitely . . . yes . . . definitely," Katy said, and Chan whispered in an equally breathy whisper, "It's bad . . . it's dark. Something evil."

"What's your vote, RayAnn?"

She came silently close to me. I could smell her shampoo. "Would I sound really squeamish if I said . . . I feel that we are not alone?"

I dropped my hand and turned, and then I felt it, too. Someone was watching us. As my heart sped up, Lanz growled, and I couldn't decide if he was sensing my fear or hearing something.

My hearing has improved almost daily since I lost my vision. Now I heard breathing . . . far off to my left. I pointed without opening my eyes. Trying to look at things could be a distraction to me. "There's somebody over there."

None of them moved. I suddenly wondered at the enormity of my stupidity, bringing three girls out here. I had seen a corpse earlier tonight, and the concept behind our coming to Steepleton was that the corpse had been there for years. It didn't occur to me otherwise until I saw an undergarment pulled up intact. It could be a recent murder, and if so, no one knew where that murderer was, or what the motive was. I had never won a fight in my life, and I had no clue how I would win one now, but I made a mental note to sign up for Tai Kwon Do when I got back to school.

I reached for Lanz's harness handle and he moved forward with me, growling louder and louder.

"Who's there?" I called.

SIX

I HEARD MORE WHISPERING. *A lunatic talking to the moon?*
Then there were two sets of whispers.

Suddenly, peals of laughter broke out at the place where
I'd pointed. Not nice laughter. I thought of my high school
cafeteria and tuna hoagies. A form jumped up, then another.
The sound of the voices put them about ten feet away.

"Oh my God, it's a dog!" one girl said, startled.

"It's *five* dogs," another said, laughing. "Wait . . . it's that
guy from where the cops were. Is that a Seeing Eye dog? I
thought you said you weren't blind!"

"I kind of lied," I said, taking two steps toward them and stopping, thinking the better of it.

A form bobbed up close, waving a hand up and down in front of my eyes as Lanz whined over and over. He'd been trained not to bite. If he ever bit, I had to give him back. But I didn't know what he'd do in a situation like this.

"How many fingers am I holding up?" A shot of wild, laughing eyes flashed, a set of teeth. I felt my neck snap and I stumbled backwards dizzily to the tune of "Have a nice trip."

Lanz barked and lunged, not helping my dizzy routine, but I held on to his harness. The girl I spoke most to at the crime scene had been Taylor, and this one was—

"Mary Ellen, is Justin with you?" I asked, trying to pretend that this whole thing wasn't happening. My Ghost of School Days Past told me any threats I made would egg them on.

"I told you, he's gone!" Mary Ellen said, but I could hardly hear it because Chan and Katy were screaming. "Who the hell is with you?"

I sensed there were two people with Mary Ellen, and suddenly RayAnn was beside me, saying, "Get back from us. Do you *like* getting bitten by dogs with teeth six inches long?"

I liked the authority-sarcasm combo. I hadn't known she had it in her.

"Who are you?" Mary Ellen repeated.

"I'm with Mike. We asked these two to bring us out here."

"And who are they?"

"What, do you pay the taxes around here?" RayAnn snapped. "Last I heard, if you own the land, you can ask the questions."

Three voices laughed at her, but nobody came forward again. A male voice cut in. "It's just that we like to know who's coming out here. Ya know . . . cops and all."

Ah, a level-voiced male. I sensed the females evening out, but with disappointment. They could have sucked energy off Katy and Chan's fear and eaten us alive.

"We're the bouncers, me and Helene," Mary Ellen said. "If we don't want somebody at the party, they get bounced."

"Oh, get a job," RayAnn shot back, but I could feel her hands shaking as they clung to my arm. "Can't you flip burgers somewhere? Do something constructive with yourself?"

"Whoa!" I mumbled to her. I wanted our heads to remain on our necks. Frankly, I wanted an interview, too.

"Look, everybody, calm down," I jumped in again. "Nobody is going to touch anybody. We're here looking for Justin. If he's not here, we'd like to ask some questions. If you don't want to answer, that's fine. We'll just leave."

"What kind of questions?" Mary Ellen asked. "Justin left town. I told you before."

"Just about Steepleton, about Chris Creed, that's all.

Our interest is Chris, not Justin, except what Justin might have to say as a brother."

They agreed to talk, but it was a jig getting comfortable. Katy and Chan insisted on going back to the car, but we didn't want to give them the flashlight, so I told RayAnn to take them. She refused, probably defensive about leaving me with volatile people. Mary Ellen's Igor, Helene, said she would lead them back in the dark, that she knew the way. She recognized Katy and Chan, called them by name, and I detected a note of embarrassment in her voice, maybe over Mary Ellen's attack on me. They left with her, which put me and RayAnn with Mary Ellen and the guy. He introduced himself as Kobe, and I assumed he was the infamous Kobe Lydee referenced by Katy and Chan. He was a ghost chaser, they had said, whatever that means.

All four of us ended up lying on this tarp, the three of them staring at the stars as I pretended to. I could enjoy the full moon if I kept my vision turned just the right way.

"What happened to Taylor?" I asked Mary Ellen.

"Grounded. She sneaked out to the crime scene but only stayed half an hour or so. Her dad's off tonight. He's a troll."

"Mind if I tape us?" I asked, pulling my recorder from my pocket and flipping it on.

"Can you write?" she asked curiously. She'd been lying to my left, and I sensed her roll over so that she was looking at me.

"Sure."

"How?"

"Neatly. I can see some things. Taping is easier."

"Were you born that way? Why'd you lie earlier?"

"I had a head injury three years ago, and it damaged my optic nerve center," I answered. "I should have been straight with you. Sorry, I'm learning. Journalists need to be the invisible people who don't get thrust into the middle of the story, if that makes sense. If I said I was blind, I would have had a lot of heads turning to look at me, and it would have invaded the mood."

"A head injury? What happened?" She kept it up.

"I got hit in the head with a baseball my first week at college."

"Yeah? On purpose?" The girl had a way of homing in on your weaknesses, and I wondered if it was habit or unintentional.

"It happened. There's no undoing it, and I'm here on business. Cool?"

She flopped back down again. Lanz was sitting at my feet, but he refused to lie down.

"What are we doing here?" I started. "Why were you back here, lying on a tarp and staring at the moon?"

"We're hoping to get a look at Chris Creed," Kobe said. "*The ghost of* . . . in other words. There have been a lot of sightings lately. Now we have this corpse."

"You're thinking it's him?" I asked, no longer sure about the body being female, having heard theories from Katy and Chan.

"It's not him. I think, maybe, he did it."

Okay . . . My eyes rolled, with a smile that made me thankful for darkness. I'm a polite guy. "He won't show up in a T-shirt that said I DID IT by any chance?"

"Very funny. A lot of people have seen him. Some people are just seeing lights in the woods—weird lights where there should only be darkness. But this one night, this group of, maybe, five kids, saw him. Most of us were at a basketball game. But not a single one has changed their story yet."

"I think I heard about that from other people," I said. "They were tripping?"

"What difference does it make? They *all* saw him. Blond hair, gangly, JCPenney polo shirt, Keds . . . but all lit up in a white light."

Mary Ellen added, "There's only one person around here who wore JCPenney polo shirts to school every day . . . only one kid whose mother was still dressing him in high school."

"You're saying what those kids saw was Chris . . . because the person was wearing a JCPenney polo shirt? And how did they notice the sneakers?" I didn't want to burst their bubble, but it was my job to shovel through the horse droppings.

Mary Ellen said, "No, they thought it was Chris because he was surrounded by white light. As in, he was dead. A spirit. You could see through him. He looked just like he did when he left. The polo shirt was secondary."

A see-through Chris Creed. Witnesses: five. *Did he do a cartwheel or something? Is that how they noticed the Keds?*

I felt like I was tipping into something I would have referred to back at school as a "sewer moment." Last month I covered that séance in Windsor Hall—just for a fun write-up—one of the dorms that a few goth residents swore was haunted by the spook of one Billy Hamilton, who'd killed himself several years back. The fact that Billy committed suicide at home in Kentucky, in his own garage, made no difference. He had been a Windsor dormie, and now he stood over people's beds on the second and third floors and they awoke to find him staring at them and then exiting through a wall.

As a person who is well trained to wake up happy, call daily problems "opportunities," and meditate on future successes, I decided I would never, ever again join hands with people calling up the dark. My mood had seeped sewage for a couple days, which is my best description for battling the feeling that someone was constantly lurking behind me, staring and smiling hungrily. If you're blind, it's an even more unpleasant sensation.

What did you expect? I asked myself. I had known I would run into some of this out here. I had invited it. "So, like, why do you want to see the ghost of Chris Creed? Do you . . . want to communicate with him?"

I was trying not to deliver it in a caustic tone, but I didn't quite succeed.

"You believe he's alive," Kobe said, a note of disappointment in his voice.

"That's what Torey Adams believes. I follow his train of logic, not to derail *your* train. At the moment, I'm a journalist, so let's say I'm neutral."

"Well, we've got our reasons," Kobe said, and I waited for them, but Mary Ellen broke in.

"If we believe Chris Creed is dead, it's not because it's weird. It's because it's logical. Tell me how a kid leaves almost five years ago and manages to stay away," she demanded.

"I think one decent theory was on Adams's website," I pointed out. "Chris stayed with relatives in Texas who couldn't stand his mother, believed she could mess up a kid, and helped him hide."

"What about Justin and Matt?" she asked. "How could Chris go off and leave his brothers? Don't you think he would miss them?"

I had to agree about that. "Leaving your siblings behind

and never getting in contact seems extremely heartless." Matt would now be a high school freshman. Adams had written even less about him than about Justin.

"So, how does Chris do that?" Mary Ellen persisted.

"I wrote a research paper on people who are successful at starting over. There's been studies on some people in the Witness Protection Program and some who ran away from home and never went back. A lot of those successful at 'starting over' have been able to shift their focus, view their old life as if it were somebody else's life. You become a new person."

"Wish I could become a new person sometimes," she griped. I sympathized.

"I suppose in cases like Chris's, that 'new person' thing helps people lose any false sense of responsibility for family members who, truthfully, need to learn to look after themselves anyway. Big brothers can't be at school, watching your back, and they don't exactly want to live at home while going to college. They want to get the hell out."

"You sound like one of those experts on Chris," Mary Ellen said. "They post on Torey Adams's website and leave endless descriptions of all the rotten things that mean kids did to them in school. Are you one of them?"

I caught a click in her voice, like maybe she was trying to be nice but wasn't much good at it. I could have given her a breeze-through of my catalogue of school hells, but I took it up a notch, not wanting her to get on the wavelength again that I was some target.

"Some people post on ChristopherCreed.com because they have been abused terribly by classmates. Others post there because they're runaways. I'm one of the few who have the dubious distinction of being both."

"You ran away?" she asked, studying me with more respect.

"I call it 'leaving home,'" I said. "I was almost eighteen."

"Tell us about it," she said with an excited little hop on her butt. "Where are you from?"

I laughed, feeling defensive. I understood that people were curious as soon as I said I was a runaway. But they didn't understand the caution you need to take. I said, "Are you going to post it on ChristopherCreed.com? *'There was this guy, Mike Mavic, out here who ran away, too, and now he's a reporter at Randolph State!'* I've got a mother a lot like Mrs. Creed—only worse. She used to be a cop, an investigator, in Oklahoma City. She was one of the first officers on-site at the Oklahoma City bombing. But she's still resourceful. I've often imagined her scouring ChristopherCreed.com and other sites frequented by runaways, reading the posts, trying to figure out if one of them's me."

"Well . . . what was she like? What did she do that made you run away?"

I felt RayAnn perk up. Her family was much more fun to talk about than mine—we hadn't actually gotten to this question yet. I leaned way forward with a groan, putting my elbows on the tarp and drumming my fingers. This wasn't exactly the way I had wanted this conversation to go. Not only was it about me instead of them, but it was a difficult question to answer. I probably would have avoided it if Mary Ellen hadn't found my hot button with her next thought.

"It's just that you seem so . . . calm, so . . . together. You're blind, you left your family . . ."

"Yeah, I call that bad frequency," I shared with a laugh. "I was on it for years."

"But look at you. You're in a really smart college, and you're a reporter, and all this cool stuff that a lot of normal kids would not even be. Just tell us how it came about. And I won't bust you on ChristopherCreed.com or anywhere. We've kept Justin under wraps, haven't we?"

I knew my life could be a testimonial that would help others. I was one of those "if I can make it, you can too" types of people who could make a living giving motivational speeches, probably. I was becoming a Zig Ziglar, a Napoleon Hill, I told myself every day. But I had a long way to go.

"Tell ya what," I tried. "I'll answer any questions you want about my past—given you won't bust me—if you tell me where Justin is so I can interview him."

There was a long silence, and one of them swallowed. "We can't. He'll kill us," Mary Ellen said. "But if he contacts us, we can promise to tell him about you, give him your cell number."

"We're leaving Sunday morning," I said. "I really wanted to do a little better than a phone interview from my desk in Indiana with my deadline five minutes away."

"I can pretty much . . . guarantee he will call you by to-morrow" was all Kobe would promise, taking out his cell. "You could say Justin and I are tense toward each other, es-pecially since my secret fave project happens to be his brother and certain people have big mouths. But I'll do him this one and tell him you're looking for him. Give me your number."

As I spat out the last digit, Mary Ellen continued, as if the deal were sealed, "So, what happened at your house?"

I drummed on the tarp some more. This was why I don't tell many people I took off. It's very, very hard to describe. I sighed. "I wish I could say I was beaten, molested, and thrown down into a fruit cellar where the cockroaches could have at it. It was nothing so dramatic."

"She didn't beat you?" Mary Ellen asked.

"Occasionally when she was drinking she would do something violent, but mostly she drank, I think, to drown out the memories of the Oklahoma bombing. She was one of the police who ended up pulling dead kids out of that daycare center."

"My uncle's a fireman, and he pulled dead bodies out of the Trade Center just after 9/11, and he didn't turn into a drunk over it," Mary Ellen pointed out.

"A whole schmear of events actually followed it, if you want to talk about bad frequency." I shuddered but kept my grin. "My dad died maybe a month after that. We farmed corn. He fell off the tractor somehow, got caught under the wheel."

"Wow," she said.

"And ... drumroll ... between the bombing and my dad dying, my mother found out she was pregnant with my sister, Merilee."

"Ohh . . ."

I hoped she'd leave it alone, but she was the inquisitive sort.

"So, what did she do besides drink, if she didn't beat you?"

I just kind of threw it out there, fixating on getting them to bring Justin to me. "It was weird . . . sort of like we were *married*. I don't mean anything sexual by that—she never, like, tried to jump in my bed or anything. My dad died when I was in second grade, and by fifth grade, some kids had cell phones. Kids would always talk on their cells at school with friends. I was always talking with my mother. She knew exactly when the bells would ring. There I'd be, on my cell, talking about the bills or taxes or my little brother and sister. She didn't want me to have friends. She was really possessive, controlling, and if I asked to go anywhere, she would say, 'We've got all this work to do.' *We've, we've, we've* . . . It was never *her*, never *me*, always *us*."

"So, you ran away?" Mary Ellen digested this. I guess it didn't seem like enough. She hadn't lived through it.

"My senior year, I got a girlfriend. Finally. For about a week. That was the last straw. You should have seen my mother carrying on. She said Sydney wasn't a nice girl, she was from a bad family, all this stuff, but the truth was, it could have been *any* girl. Sorry it's not any juicier than that."

"You felt strangulated." She finally got it.

"Exactly. I could see the rest of my life unfolding . . . I would take care of her until I was seventy and she was ninety-five, and she'd still be dishing out orders in her 'once a cop, always a cop' tone. So, in my case, I didn't mind leaving my brother and sister. She never had that sort of relationship with them. Besides, they were scrappy and feisty. I didn't have that nature. I was a peaceful guy. Better to just . . . make like a tree and leaf, before she chopped me down like that . . . *Giving Tree* story." I was stumbling. I hadn't exactly tried this aloud too often.

"And she has no idea where you are?" she asked.

"Nope. But she's still trying. She got my cell phone number once." I chuckled.

"How do you know? Did you talk to her?"

"No. It was last fall. I was walking to campus one morning and my cell rang. I looked down, and there was my old phone number. I jumped nine feet in the air."

"You didn't pick up?"

"It was all gut instinct. Over in a flash. I connected the call so she wouldn't hear my voice on voice mail, and I was walking past this duck pond. I heaved the phone straight into the pond. I cut class, zipped on over to Verizon Wireless, and had a new phone, new number, and a hacker friend destroying the history of my file, all within half an hour."

RayAnn cracked up. She had heard this part of the story. She went on, "A lot of people were walking to campus and saw him throw the phone into the pond. We had just met. They thought it was me, and that I was hot for Mike, which I was. But they thought I was, like, stalking him or something."

I tossed an arm over her shoulder as they laughed.

"Do you have an assumed name?" Mary Ellen asked.

"Mike is really mine. The Mavic I picked up in Tijuana, Mexico, for two hundred bucks, along with a fake driver's license, fake Social."

"Mavic is really not your last name?" RayAnn asked incredulously.

"How could I keep my real last name with an ex-cop for a mom?"

They sat quietly, absorbing all of this, I guess. "So, are you going to get Justin for me?"

"I'll really try, honestly," Kobe said, though I sensed strongly that their inability to get him right now, right in front of me, was bull. I hoped at least they would start punching a cell number as soon as we left.

Mary Ellen shuddered. She noted accurately, "I was such a jerk when you first came out here."

RayAnn laced her fingers through mine.

I supposed that was a Steepleton version of an apology. "That's okay," I said cheerfully. "It's not like I'm inexperienced. Do you mind if I ask . . . Why do you act like that?"

"I don't know." Her head disappeared as she lay flat again with a sigh. "I'm the only girl in a family of four older brothers. I get picked on too."

"But somehow that doesn't make you sympathetic," I said in what I hoped was a journalistically neutral way.

"You would think. I don't know why I hate on people. I never really thought about it before, but I do it . . . because I *have* to. If I sense weakness in another person, it infuriates me," Mary Ellen confessed.

"Why?"

"I don't know. Maybe I'm like a dog. Do you ever watch that show *The Dog Whisperer*? Cesar Millan, the dog expert guy, says that dogs bite weak energy. That's why you should never run from them or show fear."

I loved the show. Cesar Millan talked about energy all

the time. With him in mind, I actually felt Mary Ellen's energy shift from curiosity to fear.

She finally continued. "Wow. What am I? Some, like, *primate?*"

Kobe bolted upright. "She's King Kong! She's . . . a raptor! A fire-farting Tyrannosaurus rex!"

They banged into my right shoulder with their wrestling match, Kobe laughing and pinning Mary Ellen down. Mary Ellen kept demanding that he shut up. I barely heard RayAnn note, "Did you see what he turned into once she got vulnerable?"

Interesting point. He started "biting."

"Fine, Kobe!" Mary Ellen finally yelled louder than he laughed. "I will never tell you anything again! I would love to have some real convo with my friends sometime that wasn't about . . . who's weird, or who's not popular, or who's *dead*. Why do we try to film spooks out here? Huh? For some reason we love being scared and depressed."

"It's not a downer—it's fun," Kobe said defensively, backing away from her on his butt. "I do think there are Others, capital *O*, out here, and I think it's exciting. You didn't have to come, ya know. You could have gone over to Taylor's to play 'I'm grounded' games on her PlayStation. You said you wanted to feel it out here. You wanted to know what I was talking about."

"Fine. I'm lying quietly and looking for a white figure in a JCPenney polo shirt obviously bought by his mother," she said blandly.

"Uh . . . you were saying you had 'reasons' for wanting to draw the ghost of Chris Creed to you," I put in, turning the subject again.

"I'm not saying he would *talk* to me," Kobe corrected me. "I'm not a medium or a spiritualist or anything like that. I'm just a guy who lives in this town and wants to know what's going on, that's all. If I see him out here? I'll know."

"Know what?"

"My uncle just died of bone cancer, and he lived on the Creeds' street. I want to know what's up with the cancer rate. And the car accidents. There are these newspaper articles, and last year they were the talk of current events class, until it boiled over and everyone had put the subjects together: cancer, accidents, and Chris."

I said that the Haydens had told me. "So . . . what do the car accidents and cancer have to do with Chris Creed?"

It took him a moment to say what I would have guessed, though he acted like it was big news.

"I want to know if Chris is behind it. I want to know if he's come back. I want to know if he's getting revenge on all of us for the way Steepleton treated him."

I realized what bothered me out here tonight was the

deadly silence. You would expect trees in forests to rattle and whisper through their leaves, but it was too early in the season. Mid-April meant the trees were budding, and the breeze blew through in silence. Silent woods are unnerving. I cleared my throat.

"Uh . . . I'm no fan of horror movies, but wouldn't an angry spook, like, impale people on fences? I've never heard of a spook giving a body cancer. That doesn't, um, fit the MO."

"But it's happening. Got any better theories?"

"Maybe y'all should shy away from farm-raised fish and hormone-enhanced poultry?" RayAnn tried. It cracked me up, but I smothered it with a cough, detecting that Kobe was not amused.

"And these car accidents," he said. "Betcha Rye didn't tell you that three of them were total fatalities. Nobody was left alive to say what would cause a car to drive off the road into a ditch in the middle of the night. Just . . . the cops driving around in the morning find yet another car turned upside down on the side of some back bay road, a couple of dead people still in their seat belts."

RayAnn had taken out a reporter's pad and was scratching furiously. "Do you have the families' names?"

Kobe was spitting them out to her, giving little details, and I felt myself listening through the quiet, not hearing anything, but turning icy in a hard-to-describe way. It was the same sensation as walking into class and suddenly re-membering you have a paper due that you forgot about. Yet nothing had changed here. Even the wind was momentarily still. *Power of suggestion.*

"I should have brought Tyra out here. She's this goth in school who says she can talk to the dead. I can't stand her probably-tattooed ass, but I don't know anything about that stuff," Kobe continued and turned to me suddenly. "Hey, I saw you touching the trees and breathing deeply when you first came in here, before you knew we were watching. What was up with that?"

"Nothing related," I said, my chill growing deeper.

"Justin's mad at me right now . . . knows I'm among those who think his brother is dead. But I'm cool with his quantum thought theory, which sounds like it could work on the dead, too. Why not? At least, it might work out here . . . This *is* a weird place."

Kobe must have heard Justin describing how it works, because he started breathing himself, in and out, in and out. "I believe I am seeing Chris Creed."

I rolled my eyes but couldn't quite stop myself from looking out into the woods. I persevered through a dozen frames of utter blackness before remembering that people who believe in quantum thought state their wishes in the present tense, as if they have them.

"I believe I have the power to draw Chris Creed to me." He breathed in and out. "I believe that the ghost of Chris Creed is coming out of those woods."

Mary Ellen said, "Stop it. Justin says quantum thought is for drawing happy things. What you're doing doesn't seem right."

"Justin said it will work on anything," he replied, "so you have to be careful. I believe I see—"

Lanz growled, so low that I was probably the only one who heard him.

"Mike, we've got those girls back at the car," RayAnn whispered, her nervous energy jutting into me and obviously not pleasing Lanz.

"I believe I see a white light in those woods that is transforming into the ghost of Chris Creed . . ." Kobe refused to give it up.

"Um, maybe you should study up on quantum thought." I smiled patiently. "You could misfire and bring out some abomination that will fly up your backside and make you howl and sputter—"

"Bring it on," he replied without a laugh. The kid was morbid.

"Fine. You call Chris Creed back from the dead. We're just going to pack it in. Can you be sure to tell him to come to you and not to follow us?"

He ignored me with all his inhaling and exhaling.

I stood up slowly, still feeling the energy darting and shifting around me. I took the woods in frame by frame and saw nothing but pitch darkness. It wasn't until I was standing totally straight that Lanz growled loudly. I realized he had been standing, rooted, not staring out at the dark woods, but behind me.

SEVEN

I JERKED AROUND TOO QUICKLY, and everything went black. But the feeling of facing a human being was so strong that I dropped down again and put an arm up protectively to shield RayAnn.

Kobe finally stopped that godforsaken deep breathing. Mary Ellen fell half into my lap. "Justin, is that you?"

Slow, clomping footsteps moved closer, as if a person a little ways off was toying with us. Somebody wanted to see us squirm. Lanz growled.

"Shine your flashlight, asshole, whoever you are," Mary

Ellen demanded. "Don't make Kobe beat the crap out of you . . ."

"Tell me what this is, please, RayAnn," I managed.

"It's a policeman," she finally said blandly.

The form stepped up and developed a face. A deep, booming voice answered. "I'm on my way home after a long night, but I figured I'd come out here and clear this place of idiots before hitting the hay."

"Chief, you just blew it!" Kobe said. "Creed was coming to let us know he's behind all our bad luck."

The man yawned and didn't try to cover it. Chief Rye was African American, and the little bits I could take in of his skin glowed deep gold in the moonlight. His grin looked slightly amused as Mary Ellen sputtered some apology for inappropriate name-calling, but she got cut off.

"Chief Rye, I'm RayAnn Spencer. Mike Mavic and I are here from the *Randolph Exponent*—" A flashlight shone in my face, and I found my legs and stood up again.

"Mike. I see you're finding your way around the area. Sorry I couldn't talk to you earlier." He shined a flashlight around and it stopped on Mary Ellen's face. She had reddish hair. Kind of pretty. "I can't tell the journalists where to be and where not to be, but this is no place for teenagers right now. I don't have to tell you we found a body tonight."

"Right," I said, hearing the tarp being shaken out. "We were just leaving."

"Turns out this corpse is recent. Four months old, tops. Don't forget your camera, Kobe," he said. "Until we figure out what happened, play it safe. It looks like a domestic squabble turned ugly, but until we're sure, do not be out in dark fields. Do you read me?"

Obviously, Rye had a balanced, friend-foe relationship going with these kids.

"Sorry. I thought it was Chris Creed's body at first," Kobe said. "You know . . . old news."

"No, it's not a Creed . . . not either one of them."

My body flooded with relief. No more fears of needing séances to get my interview with Justin. Kobe and Mary Ellen got their things together and tramped on ahead to the trail. Once they were out of earshot I asked, "Can you say who it is?"

Rye answered in a low voice, "I gave in to the hounding of the *Press of Atlantic City,* so I guess I can tell you too. It's a girl from the Pinelands, another jurisdiction. We'd heard she was missing, but word was out that she and her boyfriend, Danny, eloped to Vegas for a quick marriage license. The mother hadn't heard from her, but that's nothing new. They fought like cats and dogs. She never even reported her missing. Her mother identified the jewelry, so we woke up a Pinelands dentist to verify it's her teeth. DNA will be a formality."

Not a Creed; it's no big deal, I started to tell myself, to ward off bad feelings for some family out there. I could hear RayAnn scratching in the dark on her reporter's notebook.

"What's the deceased's name?" she asked.

"Darla Richardson."

I gasped, and my shock doubled when Kobe and Mary Ellen mumbled, "Who's that?" as if they'd never heard this name before.

"Darla Richardson?" I repeated loudly. "The wild and crazy thirteen-year-old sister of Bo Richardson from Adams's tale? *That* Darla Richardson?"

"The same," Rye said. "Only now she's eighteen. Or was. Let's get moving. It's been a long day."

I spun to them in amazement. Richardson was a "boon," short for "boondocks" and the backward people living out there, and had become Adams's friend despite their differences, yada yada, all this stuff from ChristopherCreed.com. I was slowly coming to comprehend that the website meant less to people in this town than it did to the legion of cult followers in faraway places.

One passage came spilling back to me from Torey Adams's story: He, Ali McDermott, and Bo tried to get Chris's diary out of the Creed house, wanting to see if it said anything about where Chris might have gone. Ali knew Chris's secret hiding place. While Bo and Torey stood on the sidewalk between Ali's house and the Creeds', scheming on how to get it, they had a conversation about Bo's wild and crazy sister, Darla. She was already staying out all night with boys in her neighborhood, Bo had said, and he was always trying to stop her from acting out.

"Isn't she an upperclassman in your high school now?" I asked.

Kobe said something about the high school boundaries being redistributed several years ago so that all the boons went to Pinelands Regional now. The boons had played such a major role in Adams's story, it amazed me to see this new generation hardly acknowledging their existence. People forget fast. Boons had been the backhoe kids at Steepleton High, the kids who gave the place an edge.

"Darla Richardson," I repeated to the police chief. It wasn't funny, so I couldn't understand why I sensed him smiling until I grabbed Lanz and we started walking back to the car together. I realized he'd been eavesdropping.

"Sorry if you're disappointed. Lydee tries quantum thought to conjure up one of the Creeds, and you get the chief of police. You're all short-circuiting somewhere," he teased.

"Kids in high school make for strange interviews." I didn't mention that I had just tried the thing myself when I first arrived here. "You know what quantum thought is, obviously?"

"I don't own any books on it," he said. "But I read the Amazon bestseller lists."

"Do you believe in it?"

"You live around here, you don't *disbelieve* anything. I'd say you're pretty lucky, at any rate. If you're looking to do some updated story to what's on ChristopherCreed.com, your only problem is that you'd have a hell of a hard time chasing down that cast of characters. Bo Richardson is in the military in Kenai, Alaska, Ali McDermott is a senior at Boston U, and Torey Adams we all know about. This particular funeral, sad as it is, is the only thing I can think of that would bring them all back."

EIGHT

I GOT US A ROOM at this little motel called the Twilight Inn that looked off into the Pine Barrens, but it was close to the bay that separated Steepleton from the barrier islands, and you could smell the salt in the air. Mr. Spencer had given RayAnn hotel money. His stipulation for her going halfway across the country was that he didn't want us camping out in the middle of April when all the mid-Atlantic campgrounds were closed before Memorial Day. I wondered if we were any safer in this dusty old motel that reminded me of the Bates place in *Psycho*.

"I can't believe your parents let you come out here," I said, after dropping my bag, finding the chair, and taking off my muddy sneakers. "Last week, you were sixteen."

She stood and moved her laptop bag over to a table. "Parents let their kids go to Florida on spring break. Is this somehow worse? Helping to cover a story for a newspaper?"

"There's been a murder here."

"There's been a death every year in spring break havens," she countered. "And besides. Nobody's screaming 'serial killer,' not even Chief Rye, beyond his bogus warnings at the Lightning Field. It's a domestic squabble that got carried away—that's what he said once they weren't listening."

"True." I recalled our final moments by the cars. "He says he's brain weary, looking for any excuse to keep those kids out of the Lightning Field. The police really hate those kids being back there. They'd need an SUV to patrol it, and I don't think that's in Steepleton's budget."

I sat on the edge of the bed, and RayAnn plopped down in the desk chair, looking disheveled. "Four months—wow. Do dead bodies decompose that quickly?"

"She might have had some help. Carbolic acid is ringing a bell, though I'm basically clueless. If she was burned or dropped in acid, then her clothes were put in the grave with her to keep all the evidence together. Maybe. It's hard to say how a skeleton gets in a grave with fairly intact clothing, but it's among the questions we'll ask at police headquarters tomorrow."

We had made plans to meet with Chief Rye or one of his officers and pick up any news on the whereabouts of this boyfriend, Danny. I'd have a load of questions for him then.

"We're supposed to be heading out of here Sunday. So, what's up with this funeral? I know you really want to go. But it won't happen that fast. I'm out of finances if we need an extended leave, so if I'm supposed to start working on my dad, I should probably know when I call home tonight. I'll have to call my professors . . ."

"One step at a time," I said, sensing that an extended leave would be a real mess. I also had four classes next week. Claudia had me contributing one byline almost daily to the *Exponent*. "A funeral is not a great place to be asking questions. Maybe they'll all come back tomorrow."

I had saved seventy bucks for food, and beyond that, I was out of resources. I thought, as I often did, of the $6 million settlement I had pending with Randolph over the dorm scrimmage that cost me my sight. Settlements do not happen quickly, and it might be another year until I saw that money. In the meantime, I had a free ride and any counseling I would have wanted, but I had to struggle for anything extra, right down to a pair of shoelaces. Randolph kept filing extension papers, thinking I might opt for the $1.5 million they offered if I retracted the suit. They could do that until September, technically.

The story had made the local papers, which I could not prevent from happening, and I often wondered if that was the link to how my mother traced my cell number. My lawyer is the only person who knows my whole story, and the truth had worked wonders in this particular case. He also gave me advice on how to get Randolph to let me remain a student, without lying, without revealing my family name and background, and without getting parental signatures. A college student's right to privacy goes beyond your wildest dreams.

I was holding out for the bigger settlement, but I knew I could also leap and settle if I was suddenly found by my family and I wasn't ready. A million and a half isn't bad, but who wouldn't try to hold out for the whole shebang?

Yet it kept my life in a "pending" status, which I tried to ignore, but it affected all areas of my life. It was hard to see any future with RayAnn, not that anything would happen quickly anyway. I tried to remind myself of that, too. But I felt keyed up tonight, more on edge than I had ever felt in the dorm.

"Does your dad expect me to get a different room?" I asked.

"Probably." She had her laptop on a small table by the window. I took off my shades and blinked as she turned on another lamp. "Look. They let me live ninety miles from home with my great-aunt, who is seventy-five and deaf, where I could wind up pregnant anytime I wanted to make a stupid decision. I'm not stupid. They know me."

I was pretty blown away by her family's liberal ways. Even I had had this misconception about homeschooled kids before I met her, thinking they were all from families of strange religions who wanted to keep their kids under lock and key. I suppose some are like that, but by the time she was fifteen, RayAnn had spent four months in Italy, traveling from family to family on her mother's side. She'd flown alone to a sci-fi convention in L.A., did the exhibits with her older cousin in graduate school at Berkeley, and stayed with her in the dorm. She had wanted to learn conversational French, so she lived with a French Canadian family in Quebec for a summer and came back fluent. Her parents found her trustworthy enough, by age sixteen, to live in a house ninety miles away, where some distant great-aunt rented her three extra rooms to college students.

"Sorry, I can't rest until I get a grip on some things," she said, and I heard her clicking her wireless mouse, obviously trying to get online.

"Which thing are you going for?" There were a lot of issues.

After a moment, she was typing, which meant she had connected to the Internet and was surfing.

"First, that Elaine freaked me out with all that talk about five people seeing the same hallucination. But I remembered reading something once . . . back when I won a hundred bucks in this essay contest about the perils of dropping acid."

"You won a hundred bucks in an essay contest?"

She let out a blast of a giggle. "I've won, like, tons of money and prizes entering Internet essay contests."

"You're kidding."

"That's what my friends and I and my sisters did. We didn't have essays due for 'class,' so we surfed around for essay contests and entered them. Instead of an A, if we did well, we got cash or prizes."

"Sounds like a better deal," I said diplomatically, though the homeschooling idea was hard to conceive of, considering I had to implant my mother into the concept to make it work.

"I've made a thousand bucks in my pajamas. Yeah. Good deal."

I collapsed backwards on the bed and found a stain on the ceiling to stare at. While she clicked through screens, she asked with a teasing giggle, "So . . . did you use quantum thought to attract all these interviewees to a funeral?"

Her thought was rather unfunny. "Would I wish a girl dead? If Torey, Ali, and Bo were coming for a different reason, I could feel great."

"Yeah, well . . ." She sighed again. "Darla Richardson died. You couldn't help that. Now all we need is Chris Creed."

"Ha." I moved to the window to get some air, to get over the feeling that my hair was standing on end again. Jet lag, I tried to tell myself. The breeze felt good on my face, though the silence was still eerie. Not even one summer cricket had arisen from slumber yet. "I didn't want to get into it further with those kids about believing he's alive. However, this is not an occasion where we could expect Chris to show his face. He had no friendly relationship with Bo Richardson, Ali McDermott, and Torey Adams. They got friendly *because* of him, but *because* he was gone. He's got no connection to Darla Richardson whatsoever."

"I can dream, can't I? Mr. Dream Big."

"Frankly, I can write a better story without him."

"Why's that?" she asked absently.

"Because he's a myth. Once he shows up, he's just a regular guy again. I suppose I could write his memoir about the time since he left home, but then the story's over. Stories work best when they don't have all the answers."

She was distracted and didn't respond at all. I had to smile. RayAnn was a great sidebar to me. She did the work, didn't interrupt my interviews, but had plenty to say when it was just her and me. I felt the miles between her and the groups we had met tonight. I didn't sense that she had bad feelings about it.

I heard a double click after a moment, and a sigh of contentment. "Okay. Here's an answer to mystery number one," she said, "of how five kids see the same thing that isn't there. I surfed for 'mutual hallucinations' just now and came up with this article I found when I was writing that paper. It's on peyote, a type of LSD. I didn't end up using this article, but it stuck with me: 'Peyote creates a highly impressionable mind-set among users. If a user hallucinates and states what he is seeing, hearing, smelling, or feeling to other users, often those users will suddenly experience the same thing. This was noted most recently in a paper by John Phillip Marcus, M.S.W., who videotaped four users in a Honduran village. One user became agitated, seeing falling green dots in front of his eyes. As he noted this aloud, all three other users became agitated, claiming to see falling green dots.'"

Interesting, the things RayAnn picked up on her travels-without-teachers. I said, "So, one of those kids sees a hallucination of what he wants to see . . ."

"None other than Chris Creed," RayAnn followed me.

"And as he states it, suddenly all five are seeing what he's describing."

"Correct."

"Were they taking peyote?"

"Elaine didn't say what type of LSD it was. I don't think

she even knew." RayAnn scratched her head. I found her eyes, and they looked tired. "But any explanation is a start. I'm feeling slightly less like I want to forget all this and take the next plane out of these badlands."

"You're a great researcher, RayAnn," I said. "Marry me."

It was just a joke, one she only responded to with a slight nod, but it gave me a new pause to think of us here. It was like playing "married." I was alone with a girl in a hotel room. We could do whatever we pleased, so long as she was thinking the same thoughts. RayAnn was on a different thought wave, and some part of me felt relieved. I don't know why. She waited for something to download. I caught her staring into my eyes, distracted.

"You look unglued," she said. "Is it me?"

"Not at all," I lied, but she was getting better and better at reading me.

"Do you *want* me to get a separate room?"

"No."

"Thank God, because I do not want to sleep alone in this rickety motel, where the body of Christopher Creed could come climbing up through the floorboards," she said. She glanced over again at the bed I was lying on and smiled suspiciously. "I have to ask this, being that I sense your nervousness vibe whenever I also sense your romance vibe. You're not, like, also fighting some gayness vibe, right? I mean, you're going out with me for the pure reason that you're attracted to me, right?"

The glint in her eye pealed into my head, filling it with some bizarre suspicions she might have of me and . . . who? Stedman? Todd Stedman is my roommate.

"One time in high school I had a gay thought," I confessed. "Not about anyone in particular. But it was right after the last time my mother rifled my room looking for nonexistent drugs, which she thought I was doing before she found out about Sydney, my girlfriend for five days. I had been going to Sydney's house after school and not getting home until six o'clock or something like that. It was one of those thoughts, you know, 'If all women can be like this, maybe I should think of a guy.' "

"And did you?"

"For about a minute and a half. It wasn't going very well." I smiled, but she just watched me.

"I don't think that counts." Her smile froze as she watched her screen. "You *don't* think all women are like your mom, right?"

I felt myself stiffen in spite of my best efforts not to. "Not on a good day."

I crawled back on the bed until the pillows were under my head, and I found a little piece of wall to stare at. I supposed I was feeling the anxiety rush through me that I was generally able to fight at school. Chasing down this story was dredging up my own home-based demons. Coming to Steepleton meant facing real-world stuff, complete with the Mother Creed's loud and surly speeches, and kids mean enough to push me. I didn't know which jolt of reality bothered me more, but probably the Mother Creed. I was like a person with a snake phobia in a world where half the population was part snake. To me, girls look and sound normal, but if provoked, they could slither, hiss, and rattle. College caters to matraphobics: Mothers are conveniently not allowed. If I got a caustic, obnoxious female professor, I could drop the class. The coeds, the campus personnel, the female reporters on the newspaper, were often in the red zone of volume, but they weren't domineering, weren't in my space.

I didn't think that mothers like mine, like the Mother Creed, were a dime a dozen. But they were definitely a breed, a part of this world, an infusion into all of reality. One could boa-constrict around my chest, suck my air, and—

I fluffed the pillow, found RayAnn's eyes, and a haunting thought struck yet again: Was I being fair to her? She was helping me, a lot, to become more trusting, more open. But *was I being fair to her?* Runaways, I knew from my reading, find real relationships nearly impossible for years, what with that violent disconnect from their very first relationships ever looming and spreading. Hence my research on how to start over. I had double indemnity—runaway syndrome coupled with a textbook case of domineering mother syndrome—which means you find women some combination of worship-worthy and terrifying.

To say I hadn't worshiped my mom would be a lie. It was a love-driven, hate-propelled, insane relationship that had me self-sabotaging most chances of friendship at school and was driving me nuts. I'd had some therapy, compliments of the State of California, in my first few months on the road, and thanks to it, I could admit to the love part of my love-hate thing with Mom.

I sat up and pulled a set of keys out of my pocket and fingered the strip of paper that Stedman had laminated for me while I was still in the hospital freshman year. It had words on it that were important to me. Finding what I needed to be running *to*—that was an act of desperation, a need to get out from under bad frequency. By the time I lay in the hospital, blinded by a baseball, I had had so many bad things happen in my life. I started to feel certain that the next bad thing could kill me. When RayAnn was preparing to invest in this plane ticket, I told her something she had never asked about but probably wanted to hear. I just wanted to prove to her that I could write about Chris Creed, the bullied, tormented kid, with some accuracy: *The guy who hit me in the head with the baseball had done it on purpose.*

I wasn't much good at sports even when my vision was

60/40, and the guy had been on his ninth beer of the afternoon. I kept losing grounders, and he was trying to be funny. Well . . .

He left school, a deranged and guilt-ridden mess, a month later. I was back in January, with Lanz and a whole new attitude. Completely blind for the first three weeks, I had heard an audio version of Napoleon Hill's *Think and Grow Rich*. I felt the need to ask the nurse for a pen and paper, and I wrote down in tiny letters three things Hill suggested writing.

RayAnn had seen me play with these keys a number of times, had seen me reach into my pocket to feel that plastic strip dangling off it when I needed to find my center. She moved so silently, I didn't hear her until she sat down on the bed beside me.

"*New York Times* Executive," she read, as if it were brand new, her usual show of respect. It had been the answer to Hill's suggestion to "write a clear description of your major desire in life, your idea of success."

"Write great stories so that others grow with me," she read next. That second line was my best shot at a more difficult assignment: "Write a clear statement of precisely what you intend to give in exchange for that which you desire in life."

"THE ONLY ROADBLOCKS WILL BE THE ONES I ESTABLISH IN MY MIND."

That was the last thing Hill had said to write, and I had

put it all in caps. The two eye surgeries that offered little improvement in the following summers did not become roadblocks.

"I still can't believe you wrote that back when you were completely blind," she marveled, touching the lamination with her finger. She always said that. My printing had been, unbelievably, as neat as if I could see everything. So Stedman had it laminated for me on a keychain.

"Why don't you forget about Chris Creed and write about yourself?"

"Too raw," I said, "though I've thought about it for maybe ten years up the road. Twenty years might do it."

"Mike, maybe you should get some therapy."

I had refused more traditional therapy after my accident despite having been offered it for free by Randolph even before I was approached by a dozen lawyers. My reasoning was that most psychologists try to get you to keep rewinding, going over and over your bad memories until . . . *what*? *You grow numb to them?* I certainly couldn't change mine. I had somehow fallen immediately in with the gurus who encourage you to fixate on your future and let go of the past. There were so many rags-to-riches stories out there. I'd read a slew of them. Many successful people had had rotten childhoods. Mine was certainly no worse. Generally speaking, I could not have asked for better results.

But "generally speaking" did not include a stellar moment like this, when I was alone in a hotel room with a beautiful girl and my foremost thought was whether she would transform into a cobra and sink her fangs into my jugular.

I found a roundabout but very honest answer to her question.

"Writers often write to escape their personal realities. And yet there's this homing device for truth, for the concepts that define the truths you really understand, and it's your job to state those truths so that others will understand them too. I quoted Adams tonight, out in the Lightning Field, saying Chris had become somebody else. Lines Adams wrote on his website totally jumped out at me, because I've been there too. Writing about Chris Creed allows Mike Mavic to . . . to . . ."

"To become somebody else. But if the person's a lot like Mike Mavic, it allows Mike Mavic to write about himself. Sorta kinda."

"That was pretty good, RayAnn."

"What you're doing is therapeutic. You should put that in your research paper too." She squeezed my knee and stood up.

"One research paper at a time." I smiled. "You know my pace is slower than yours."

"Go for the gold. Write a great story."

I grinned, feeling the helium, blown-up feelings of being alone with a beautiful girl start to dissolve. She cracked a Diet Coke can and then stuck it in my hand. It was warm, having been in her carry-on bag, but it was my favorite fruit.

"I have nightmares, sometimes, I should warn you," I said, trying to keep my smile peaceful. "I wake up yelling."

She was back over at her terminal, I thought, to give me air.

"Does it help to play the radio?" She hit the radio feed on her laptop. Some New Age music came through. RayAnn knows New Age music relaxes me. *Thoughtful.*

"I got the feeling you weren't telling the whole truth to those kids out in the field tonight," she said.

I chuckled, sipping the warm soda. "Frankly, it was none of their business."

"I know. I thought you handled it well. But there was that part about your mother never touching you inappropriately."

"What about it?"

"You just got that click in your voice. That's all. I would notice it, but they wouldn't."

"Nah." I shook my head with all honesty. "I lie sometimes—change the details to prevent myself from appearing accurately on people's blogs if I feel endangered—but that part is true. Mostly."

"Well, *mostly* is a heavy term to throw in the middle of that. I'm not trying to pry, but . . ."

But, but, but. I squirmed. RayAnn believed in the value of traditional therapy. I figured I would replay this one tape and see if I felt any better. "There wasn't much. Toward the end, Mom had gotten to like me brushing her hair at night. She would sit in front of her bedroom mirror and expect me to brush her hair for her."

After a moment of silence, she said, "Ew."

"Yeah, it was getting very . . . borderline. She was drinking a lot. I'd been doing my own laundry since I was, like, eleven, and one night I reached in the washer to get my underwear load and toss it in the dryer, and it was like *my* underwear and *her* bras and panties. She'd thrown hers in on top of mine, saying the washer hadn't been full. It probably . . . meant nothing to her."

I watched RayAnn shove the laptop away to get her mind on this. She sank into the chair until her neck lay over the back of it and she stared at the ceiling.

"I'm trying to think . . . if I ever found my underwear in the same load with my dad's underwear. Yeah, I suppose that could have happened." She looked entranced. "I've folded my dad's underwear a hundred times."

"So, I shouldn't have been rooted to the spot when I saw that," I said. "Because I did not want to fold my mom's underwear. I did not want to *touch* my mom's underwear."

"Well . . . my dad wasn't asking me to massage his scalp

and then throwing his underwear into my personal wash load." She giggled thoughtfully. "It's very, very borderline, yes. I would call those, uh, boundary violations, if nothing grosser. Anything else?"

"There were probably twenty little things like that," I said honestly, "but nothing major until Sydney. That's when things got insane. My mother would pace around in the night. I think it was the first thing that I ever did that she couldn't . . . control. It was driving her crazy. A couple times, I woke up, like, around midnight, and she was standing right over my bed. Just staring into my face.

"I would be all, 'Mom. What the heck are you doing?'

"And she would grab me by the T-shirt and shake me, hollering, 'Give her up! She's bad! How can you do this to me after all I've done for you!'"

"Oh, wow," RayAnn groaned, as if that one really got her. "Listen, you did the right thing. Just look at your life. Where would you be if you hadn't left?"

"At home. With her," I said, and couldn't help adding, "but I would have my sight."

I didn't know what I was trying to say by that. It was a thought I had when I wasn't busy reading, writing, studying, hanging out—when nothing was popping. Could I have moved faster away from that slung ball if I hadn't been riddled with a chronic, general feeling of guilt? I had actually seen the ball coming. And I froze.

Was my sight the price I had been willing to pay for leaving home? Was it like a down payment on my freedom? If I'd been raised Catholic, would it have been like penance? *Nothing is free in this world.*

I tried to correct myself, tell myself that a *lot* was free. That breeze from the window, my good self-esteem, my confidence in tomorrow, my dreams, my visions, my writing talents—they were free and available, simply because I wanted them, wanted to enjoy them.

RayAnn is a smart person. She could have come over to the bed and tried to invade my space to help me heal from having my space invaded. A lot of girls would have been that dumb, I think. Or maybe *dumb* is a harsh word. Maybe it's gut instinct for most women to want to reach out and touch. She either wasn't there yet, maturity-wise, or she was smart. She let her attention fall back to the laptop, and she mumbled some apology that she wasn't being insensitive but she had to surf for something.

"Now what are you after?" I asked, gratefully. The tape replay hadn't done much for me except make me want to change the subject. "Can you look up those articles the Haydens first mentioned about Steepleton? The cancer rate and the car accidents?"

"Sure. But I want to get this other thing first. Or I'll never sleep tonight."

"What is it?"

She was muttering to herself, hitting keys. Eventually she must have forgotten what we'd been talking about, because she looked engrossed, then frustrated. I finally heard her say, "Lightning stations. No . . . lightning traps . . . trapped lightning . . . no . . ."

"What on earth are you doing?" I asked.

She sighed, and I heard her nails drumming the desk.

"I swear I've heard of this before . . . I just can't think of what it is called," she said. "You look fried. Why don't you go to sleep, huh? This is freaky, and you're freaked out enough right now."

I said, "Now I'm curious."

"No, you're not." She typed. "You're not this curious, trust me."

Three's a charm. I asked a third time, "What?"

She threw her hands up in an Italian gesture of frustration. "I need to know what would explain this thing that happened just as Chief Rye showed up, right after Kobe Lydee stopped that godforsaken chanting that was making me so seasick. It's some . . . thing where lightning gets trapped underground and maintains its charge until an animal or person comes along and collapses the trap. It has to do with rocks . . . some kind of rock or . . . stump. I think it can start a fire up to a year later, but I can't remember what the heck the phenomenon is called."

Okay . . . I knew what she was looking for, but I had no idea why. I waited until she finally spilled it.

"You guys were looking behind you, but I already knew Chief Rye was there. I saw him coming fifty paces off. I just happened to be looking out at the woods, right where Kobe had those field glasses pointed during his chants. A light flashed, flashed again, and then went to black. It looked like lightning, only coming *up* from the ground. You would have to think that a spirit of some sort was trying to manifest itself, if you were a believer. Which, of course, I'm not."

NINE

I OFTEN HAVE THIS RECURRING DREAM in the dark hour,
as my mother used to call it—the hour right before dawn,
when the moon is low and the world outside is black and
unmoving. In it, Mom appears to me, though the scenario
changes. Sometimes, she comes out of the closet in my dorm,
and sometimes through the window, sometimes up through
the blankets of my bed.

The Lightning Field drew me back in the dream, and I
stood by the first tree that I had touched there. I was breathing and sending confident thoughts out to the universe while

running my palm over the weathered bark and lightning crystals.

My eyes began to feel icy, and suddenly my vision opened, as if I had never been blind—always a prelude to coming attractions in this dream. I was calling Chris Creed, and I could sense a movement somewhere in front of me and to the left, and I saw a long shadow behind the nearest dead tree. The shadow had legs and arms, but its head was hidden, even in shadow.

"Come here to me," I told the shadow. It didn't move. "I need to ask you some things. Nothing awful. It's all . . . off the record."

The shadow moved, but with a step back, not a step forward. I pretended I didn't see it.

"Are you dead?" I asked. "I really need to know."

Things are distorted in shadow, and the longer I stared, the more I realized this manifestation was Chris as a younger kid. A lanky younger kid, and his legs were trembling under his jeans, sending little shudders into the shadow.

"Come out," I said, and when the shadow didn't move, I added, "Are you dead?"

The head appeared on the shadow as he pushed back a little from behind the tree, and the head nodded yes.

Yes, yes, yes. Dead, dead.

"I don't believe you," I whispered, and went on a rant that came out as a whisper also, despite my anger. "It's not a great story if you're dead! If you're dead, you're an accident. You're a pity. You're not a hero. I can't write a great story about a kid who is worms. Do you read me?"

The shadow didn't move. I supposed he didn't care about me or my writing. Why should he?

"Well, if you're not going to help me, then get the hell out," I said, louder this time. The shadow leaned in to the tree but didn't totally become part of it. He wasn't helping me at all. *Might as well be dead.*

"You're a wimp," I told him. "I've always thought that."

He didn't answer, but I realized his fingers *were* moving. He was making little sign language symbols, the ones I'd learned just this year in a sudden blast of empathy for other people with disabilities. He was making little letters of the alphabet, and I had to stare with all my ability to read them. L-O-O-K O-U-T B-E-H-I-N-D Y-O-U.

I froze, feeling her breath on my neck, too close, as always. I could feel myself shrinking, or maybe Mom was growing. I could smell her, smell laundry detergent, smell the acid breath of someone who drinks early and bends over your bed at midnight. She had a hatchet. I don't know how I knew that.

"You can't touch me. You can't hurt me. It's only a dream," I said.

"But I'm your mother. Your *mo-ther*," she said, as if mothers move in and out of dreams, in and out of real life with ease. "And you know the truth, my favorite. You always were my favorite, my precious. If I can't have you, nobody will have you."

"Leave me alone. Stop touching me."

She hadn't actually touched me yet, but I could feel it coming, and suddenly her hand cupped my neck, my cheek, where she always put her hand, where I swore if another person ever touched me I would punch them out. *Nobody* touched my cheek, my neck, my ear like she always insisted on doing—not ever. Her hand felt cold and scabby. When I turned, her eyes were her own, but the rest was the rotted flesh of a semirecent corpse. The skin on her arm dangled in tatters and only bones and corroded flesh touched the side of my face that had been her favorite stomping ground.

I ducked and threw my arm up to block her, but her bones flew into fifteen pieces in the air, then joined back together and touched my face again.

"Don't, don't," she crooned. "Come over to that flat stump. Let me do it in one clean blow. Don't fight me . . ."

I spun and looked for Chris, but he was gone, evaporated. *Little wimp. You never thought of anybody but yourself. It's good I never got a chance to write about you.*

"I'm tired, Mom. I'm so tired."

"I know, darling. Come over to the stump. Just lay your little head down, and I will sing you to sleep."

I did it. I was there suddenly, kneeling, laying my head on the stump, just to get her slithering fingers off the crook of my neck. I could see the hatchet, which she laid just in my view, and she started to sing.

> *Don't cry, my baby, don't cry this eve,*
> *The fairies are coming from make-believe.*

Her favorite song from when I was little. I'd loved that song when I was three, but she was still trying to sing it when I was ten. My head suddenly weighed a thousand pounds. I couldn't lift it, couldn't get away. But a shadow moved into view, huge like some superhero's, only more foreboding, more ominous, stronger. She stopped singing, obviously aware of it, and started weeping. Disappointed sobs fell out of her rhythmically, like kitten mews, and she beat the forest floor with her bony fist until the earth banged and bumped and started to crumble under its power.

It's me. It's *my* shadow, I told myself. *Mike Mavic will come to save himself.*

But Mike Mavic was not powerful enough. This shadow of redemption was somebody else—

• • •

I shot straight up in the bed, huffing, trying to drown out the earthquakes and cat screeches. The cat turned into RayAnn hollering, ". . . on earth is going on?"

My vision blacked out totally from sitting up so fast, and

I had to wait a few seconds to see her back and shoulders beside me. Last I remembered, she was talking to her dad on the phone, and I was lying here, trying not to spiral. She now sat up with the blanket around her waist, her sweatshirt sleeves fluttering as she stood and moved to the thundering noises.

"Don't answer the door!" I said quickly, realizing that the earthquakes were someone pounding, slowly and methodically.

Lanz kept growling and moved to sniff the door, and catching his long nose in my vision calmed me. He stuck his nostrils right up to the crack in the door, inhaling with great pulls, which he would not have done if it were someone truly dangerous. Dogs know these things.

I rubbed my hair to get the sleep out of my head and moved past RayAnn, who had dropped the blanket, causing me to stumble over it.

"Who's there?" I asked into the door.

"Let me in," a man said. "You want to talk to me or what?"

"Talk to *whom*? At . . ."

RayAnn finished. ". . . at four-fifteen in the morning."

"Who are you?" I demanded again.

"The bogeyman."

Ten seconds earlier I might have believed it, but I opened the door a crack and found the face on the other side. It was a kid, his eyes darting madly to one side. I would have pegged him at about thirteen until his eyes found mine, peering around the door. They betrayed years, sharp intelligence, a crusty need for sleep.

"You're Mike?" he asked, his voice less deep this time.

"Yeah."

"Kobe the Creep sent me."

I was already opening the door. Justin Creed lumbered past me as if it were perfectly normal to come into a motel room in the middle of the night without being asked. I remembered tales Adams wrote of Chris's not understanding "boundaries," of Adams punching Chris in the face back in sixth grade for taking his expensive guitar without asking, standing on a desk, and doing an Elvis routine. And then there were all the stories of the Mother Creed barging into the kids' bedrooms without knocking. This "boundary challenge" still seemed to run in the family, but it didn't do Justin much damage. He looked kind of impish and made you want to laugh.

He was short but stacked. He had a neck like a linebacker's, though the rest was covered in a Stockton sweatshirt. He looked all around with energy that spoke of assurance but not invasion. His eyes stopped on RayAnn as she stood by the desk illuminated by the lamp she'd clicked on. He raised and lowered his eyebrows quickly.

"Not much on romantic sleepwear, are you?"

"I call this dorm-wear," she said sleepily, glancing down at her Randolph sweatshirt and sweatpants. I thought it was a pretty good comeback . . . *considering it was four goddamn o'clock in the morning.*

Justin had Chris's alleged undying grin, but with a sharpness to it, though the rest of his framework was his own. The "mean" side of him that Katy and Chan had spoken about earlier tonight either was buried in exhaustion or only came out for cheering onlookers. I figured it was a little of both. He stared, frozen, down at Lanz, whose nose was pressed against his jeans while he sniffed and sniffed.

"If this dog were going to rip off my package, I take it you'd be pulling him away."

"He's a service dog," I said, as RayAnn giggled.

"What kind of service? Not like . . . the breakfast patrol for carnivores, right?"

"I'm visually impaired. Lanz . . ." I patted my thigh for him to come while fumbling for my glasses, and RayAnn moved for another light switch. Too much light at once could give me a knife-through-the-eyes effect.

I heard Justin plopping into the chair with a sigh. "Would you mind not putting on any more lights, please? No need to flood us out. He's some sort of blind, and I'm, well, in more need of darkness than light." He seemed a little wound up, drumming the arms of the chair and bouncing a bit. "Wish I had the Ring of Power. I could just . . . put it on and walk around town invisible, ya know?"

Lord of the Rings was my favorite trilogy, so that sucked me a step or two closer, studying him through my trusty lenses. His eyes told me he wasn't on anything in spite of his nervous drumming. He obviously had things to be nervous about. I suggested, "You're hiding from someone."

I expected him to dive into a load of grief about his mother, but he said, "Mostly from myself. Even though that's not possible. Ha. How did they put it in rehab . . . all these wonderful speeches about 'assuming responsibility for yourself.' Endless, wonderful speeches. So. What is it you want to talk to me about?"

"I was actually thinking of a different *time* . . ." I tried.

"You want to know about my brother, right?"

"Correct. I want to write about him."

"It's about time somebody else wanted to write about my brother. A couple other college dudes came around over the past couple years, but nothing was ever printed. You gonna make it?"

"I'll make it."

" 'Cuz he's different than me, but he's my brother, and I think he's awesome."

I moved my eyes to RayAnn, who raised her eyebrows at me, obviously noting how Justin just used the present tense.

"You think he's alive?" I asked.

"Of course he's alive."

"But . . . he hasn't contacted you, right?"

"Wrong," he said. "Among other things, I've had two e-mails from him."

I was speechless. "You're . . . sure they're from him?"

"It's a long story, but trust me on this one. I'll show them to you, if you want. But it'll have to be later. They're on my hard drive at home. Well hidden." He grinned broadly. "My mom still checks my e-mail every day, if I forget to cover my keypad when I change my password. She's got a video cam hidden somewhere near my terminal, so she can see me change passwords."

I shuddered, but he only cackled. He enjoyed my reaction.

"So, you . . . know where he is?" I suggested, my heart revving up like I was on the treadmill at the gym.

He was still resting his head on the back of the chair, staring straight up at the ceiling. "I can't tell you exactly where he is, but I can tell you somewhere he's coming to."

"Which is?"

"Close to here. My mom doesn't know. He's totally, beyond reasonable sanity, scared of my mom. It's ridiculous.

But you can't tell anyone what I tell you, because if he gets any idea that she may be onto him, I'll bet he won't show."

"Uh . . . we can relate to that," RayAnn said on my behalf.

I stared, a thousand questions banging through my head, starting with *When can I see those e-mails?* and ending with *In what other ways has he contacted you?*" The whole thing rattled my brain like that earthquake was still going on.

I settled on "Uh, when is he coming?"

"He might already be here. I've been kind of out of the loop," he said.

"So, he wouldn't be at your house," RayAnn guessed.

"No way. If this makes sense . . . he would be at the place you were at with Mary Ellen and Kobe tonight. The Lightning Field."

I exchanged glances with RayAnn and saw her bang her palm on her forehead, probably wondering if Chris Creed could have something to do with the light she saw out by the trees earlier, the one she said looked like lightning coming out of the ground. Could it have been a person striking a match? A flashlight beam?

Despite all this wonderful "great story" luck—or maybe because of it—my journalistic alarm was going off badly. Things were utterly wrong with this story. Justin just got out of rehab. He could be half off his gourd. It occurred to me that he might be one of those people who think UFOs are going to land next week. His friends thought he had been reading quantum thought, but maybe he was totally bats. And he had taken a seat in our sleeping quarters that he obviously was not getting up from quickly.

"Look, here's the rules," he said. "We all need rules, as they say in rehab. I have a few. I will talk about my brother all you want, as long as you want. But two things: First, I signed myself out of rehab because of Darla Richardson. I can't miss that funeral. God, Bo is gonna be a basket case. But I don't want to talk about Darla. It's too sad. I'm very at-risk right now. They couldn't stop me from signing myself out of rehab, but I was given the whole speech . . . I'm vulnerable, susceptible to relapsing, I ought to let the dead bury their own dead, whatever. I can't get myself all bummed."

"Yeah, we understand," I said. As far as I could see, we had no reason to even bring up Darla. "What's the second thing?"

He slithered out of the chair and lay on the floor, grinning at the ceiling. "Ahhhh. Give me four hours of uninterrupted sleep. And don't tell anybody I'm here. Like, nobody."

I found RayAnn's eyes, which were popping out of her head as she stared from him to me. I was pretty much convinced at that point that he had come to us for a place to lie low, not realizing how the media not only asks all the questions but watches your every move. I didn't feel victorious, like I had a real catch, though I would have if it were anybody else. But very few people in this world, I decided, would have the nerve to pull a stunt like this.

"Do you want a pillow?" I asked, and RayAnn moved with hesitation in her tread to get him the extra off the closet shelf.

His eyes rolled like he was already fighting sleep, and he said, "I've been on a bus since eleven-thirty last night. Then I had to walk seven miles from the bus stop. You guys are, um, swell. But I'm not done with the rules yet."

"I thought you said two," I said, and he ignored me, shoving the pillow RayAnn handed him under his head and closing his eyes.

"And when I wake up, you have to buy me breakfast. Wawa's good. Bagel sandwich and a Pepsi."

He must have opened one eye long enough to see RayAnn and me exchanging looks over what Claudia would say about this. He was grinning again, while reaching into his pockets. "Please don't tell me you're as broke as I am."

"No, it's an ethics question," I said, catching both his pockets turned inside out. He left them that way. "Our editor doesn't approve of us giving things to interviewees or buying them things in order to get them to talk to us."

"Hmm. Don't TV shows pay people to come on sometimes? Don't they give those people, like, forty thousand bucks sometimes?"

"If they're trashy," I said. "We're for real. Sorry."

"Just don't make me leave," he said with some fake whining thrown in, followed by some chuckles. "If I have to sleep in a tree, a squirrel might climb up my ass and make me rabid. Some people around here think I *am* rabid. I got enough problems without an up-my-ass squirrel thrown in. *Challenges.* Not *problems*. None of these guys I been reading lets you use the word *problems*."

His eyes looked so swollen with tiredness that the grin didn't fit. It was as if his body was exhausted but his brain wouldn't cool down.

"Some of your friends tonight mentioned your reading preferences," I said. "They mentioned positive thinking and quantum thought. They say it makes you happy."

"Don't get me started on quantum thought right now. If I start talking about where science meets the spiritual side, I'll be blathering and way manic in around ten minutes. And I'm actually feeling tired. You don't want to see me way manic."

"Manic," I repeated, remembering Elaine accusing Justin of actually being manic-depressive. "Are you bipolar?"

"Among other things." He grinned, rolling his tired eyes. "I've had it on and off, probably for a couple years, but

I had to get away from home to get a diagnosis. Everyone's mom wants to believe her kid 'just doesn't know how to behave,' right?"

"Well, not everyone's mom, but yours seems to fit the part."

"You don't know the half of it. Let's just say I'm from a really messed-up family, okay? Let's start with my dad's side. My dad has finally allowed himself to be diagnosed with mild autism. That's because he's finally got tenure and the faculty will be forced to give him perks instead of a pink slip. Dad doesn't care for affection, but somehow managed to produce three sons and marry two women. Weird? It gets better. My mom is bipolar, in denial, and tries to self-medicate with alcohol. Some say Chris is mildly autistic. I'm bipolar, and my brother Matt? We don't know about him yet. He's a straight-A student and a superjock who lives with my dad and his new wife. He's the one people say is perfectly normal. But this one time when I barged into his room last year? I caught him with a Barbie doll hanging up naked to the bedpost, from a shoelace tied around her neck. He was whipping it with the other shoelace."

I cringed, horrified, though somehow he was making me laugh. I'd never tried laughing at my family problems. I don't have much sense of humor, I guessed. But my reaction propped his eyelids open a little. He pointed at me.

"I cracked you up, see? Well, if you don't laugh you'll cry. Yah, I'm bipolar with a drug history. A very recent drug history, actually. I never even touched a beer before this December. I always thought I didn't want to end up like Mom. I ended up being *exactly* like Mom."

Sounded like a rehab realization. I almost admired how he seemed able to look stark reality in the face and not get all upset about it.

"*I'm* the most normal one in my family, if there is such a thing as normal," he continued with a strikingly easy smile. "I've got a bipolar mom who drinks, an autistic dad who's gotten laid at least three times that we know of, though it's likely my stepmother is something that people call a 'eunuch.' That's biblical for 'no interest in romance whatsoever.'"

RayAnn found that one amusing enough to crack up. He was making it sound funny and fed off our interest.

"They're a perfect match! I've got an older brother who is famous for being a *nothing, a vapor,* another brother who will probably run for governor someday and get arrested for pounding off under his desk while surfing eBay for 'naked Gymnastics Barbies, slightly used.' It's a real treat, being a Creed."

"Um . . . no family is perfect," I said stoically, but my heart went out more than I would have liked it to. To keep it professional I said softly, "Justin, I should probably remind you that we are journalists. Anything you say . . ."

". . . can and will be used against me? Damn. I *am* stupid, aren't I?" He threw his forearm over his face, still laughing a little. His eyes looked weary above his ever-running mouth, and it took all my self-discipline not to add, *You can talk off the record.*

"Why don't you just crash now," I suggested instead.

"I'd love to. Can't say how that will work out . . . I only just got on my medication last week, and it takes three weeks to be fully functional. Hence they would say you're actually looking at a manic episode." He pulled his arm back and watched my eyes to see if I was impressed. "What do you think? Would I be voted most likely to talk somebody's ear off?"

At four in the morning? Yes.

"That's *my* manic MO. I talk too much, think too hard. I don't think I'm, like, Jesus Christ going to feed the multitudes and raise the dead. Though one manic chick in rehab thought she was the reincarnated Indira Gandhi for about three days . . ."

His eyes rolled, and I figured he was out of juice. But he went on. "Tomorrow I'll tell you about quantum thought. Counselors at school told me I should be a teacher. They say the craziest students make the best teachers. You gotta believe in some weird shit to keep a student's attention . . . I believe in quantum thought. I believe in weird energy. I believe you can bring yourself great things in the Lightning Field. And . . . I *don't* believe in ghosts . . ."

And he was sleep-breathing deeply that fast. I even suspected he'd knocked off before that last sentence.

RayAnn backed onto the bed, trying not to creak the mattress. I sensed she was slightly more unnerved than I was.

"Mind if I leave the light on?" she whispered.

I pulled off my glasses, slowly, saying, "Why would *I* mind?"

She let out a tired chuckle. "I love you, Mike."

I just sat at the edge of the bed, staring down at this kid. I didn't answer.

TEN

I LET JUSTIN SLEEP UNTIL EIGHT THIRTY. But when neither RayAnn's nor my shower noises had roused him, I kicked him lightly in the shoulder a couple times until he opened his eyes.

"RayAnn and I have to be at police headquarters in a while," I said.

He sat up, surveying the room sleepily. Finally he said, "Oh my God. I was having a nightmare that my brother was lost in the Lightning Field. He was swinging a lantern and calling my name."

RayAnn had been brushing her hair upside down, but she flipped it over with a *Bride of Frankenstein* hairdo. We exchanged glances. She hadn't mentioned to him that she'd seen a light out there.

"You want to go down to the Lightning Field?" I asked. "We've got an hour or so."

"No," he finally said, standing up. "It's where I did most of my partying. I should prob'ly be a good boy and eat and drink. Take care of myself for the days ahead . . ."

We hit the Wawa. He put a dent in our dining expenses, insisting on cigarettes, too, in spite of his blather about taking care of himself.

"Turn right onto Route 9 and take the first left," he said. "You wanna see where Torey Adams lived?"

There was no shoulder on this narrow spit of road, so we had to pull over into some trees to look through the break in the woods.

"There," he said, pointing between us with the cigarette in his fingers, stinking us out. It was easy to ignore the smell, what with the overwhelming feeling of déjà vu. The Adams house was old, with major chimneys coming up on both ends, but there was nothing showoffish about it. It looked like some Civil War farmhouse that had been well taken care of. It was set back far off the road and had a huge lawn that obviously turned as green as Ireland in the summers.

"It's funny," I said. "You see music stars on TV or at a concert, and you don't think about the house they were raised in. Most of the time it's something normal like this. I guess . . ." It was actually a lot more stunning than some of the row homes and shacks I'd seen in musicians' bios.

"They're probably in there, since it's Saturday." Justin swallowed, then took a drag. He held his cigarette smoke in as if it were joint smoke. "Mrs. Adams refuses to avoid my mom, being all Miss I'm Fair and Just, even though the gossip around here went crazy that Torey was involved when my brother went missing. She knows my mom didn't start any of that. She might actually call Mom if she saw me. Let's take off."

In Torey's web tale, his mother never held much against Mrs. Creed, though the rest of the town seemed to feel she drove her son out of the house, out of town. I couldn't tell if Mrs. Adams simply didn't believe that, or if she was just good enough not to throw more dirt onto the gossip mound. She was a great mom, the type any kid would want to have.

"You have their phone number?" RayAnn asked as I gave her the sign to take off. Jason stuck his head out the window and let go of a huge blast of smoke.

"I got Torey's cell number, that's all," he said, and my eyes almost bugged out of my head. "But it's in my cell. My cell's been dead for about ten days."

I rolled my eyes. Leave it to a kid to take off and forget his charger. "You have Torey Adams's cell number?" I repeated in awe.

"I haven't used it in about a year. We used to talk every once in a while, though I've never been as friendly with him as I've been with Bo. For one thing, Adams never came back to Steepleton after Chris disappeared and all that gossip came down on his head. He's basically been polite whenever I've called him. Honest. Big heart. But I can sense he doesn't really like hearing from me anymore. I'm part of his past. Bo stayed around for a couple years, working at Sunny Sunoco. We got thick before he left."

"You have his cell number, too?" I asked. Inexperience. I should have asked him this ten minutes after he was awake.

"Of course."

"What about Ali McDermott?"

"Yeah. If it's still her cell number. She was my babe, my secret 'older woman crush' for a lot of years. She used to call me a couple times a month from Boston, but that was a couple years back. I don't know what's up. She's a senior, supposedly, and that's all I know, 'cuz I haven't heard from her. I got my own problems, so I haven't called."

A gold mine, I thought, but nodded in sympathy.

"My charger works on Mary Ellen's phone, too. But you can't drop me off there right now. Her dad doesn't go to work until eleven. You want to see where Alex Arrington lived?"

Alex had been Torey's best friend until Bo and Ali became his better friends. Torey had dropped Alex to latch on to friends with some depth. Alex held the distinction of being the first to accuse Torey of participating in Chris Creed's murder.

"Absolutely."

"Then step on the break. Fast."

RayAnn did, and we all flew forward and snapped back. Justin cracked up.

"I almost set your bloody car on fire." He flicked his butt out the window. "The big modern house on your right. Dr. Arrington, illustrious head shrink, and his wife still live there."

"Where's Alex now?" I asked.

"Senior at Middlebury. Most expensive school in the country. Some guys have all the luck. He just whizzed through the LSAT and will probably waltz on over to Harvard Law."

"Yeah," I agreed dreamily, the now famed Creed letter on the front page of Adams's website dancing through my head. *I wish I had been born somebody else . . . Torey Adams, Alex Arrington . . .*

"Don't take it too hard," Justin chuckled sleepily, probably sensing the angst in my tone. "Arrington is a buttwipe.

Nothing's ever happened to him, and nothing ever will. His Facebook survey probably would say, 'I was forced to grow up after Sally Jane Shimmer-Hair broke up with me.'"

I cracked up. Probably accurate.

The house was huge, probably eighty percent glass, looking over the marshes, but it didn't have the character of the Adams's house.

"He still play music?" I asked.

"Not that I know of. Not that he was ever any good in the first place. Adams was desperate for backup in high school."

RayAnn pulled ahead but slowed down again as we arrived at what looked like a wooden bulkhead with only marshes and little salt rivers flowing out to the bay, a blue line running parallel to the horizon. I took out my recorder.

"You heard Adams play music?"

"Sure. He used to take his guitar down to the ball field all the time. I hung out with my friends at the playground next to it. That guitar was like his third arm. He could do the runs from some Eric Clapton tune while having an intense conversation about something else. Some guy would be talking to him, half listening, and all of a sudden he'd be going, 'Oh my God. He's playing "Layla" while giving me a lowdown of the last Steelers game.'"

"So, your mom never thought Torey helped kill your brother, as the gossip went?"

"No, my mother never thought that." He rubbed the bridge of his nose with two fingers. I sensed impatience. "She thought *Bo* may have killed my brother, like, by accidentally getting too violent with him. Bo sent my brother to the hospital one time about a year before he disappeared . . . playing too rough with him, punishing him for being weird. She thought maybe some boons, maybe Bo himself, lured him into the woods to mess with him, swung a pointy stick, and accidentally impaled him with it, something like that. Then they buried him in the Pine Barrens so they wouldn't go to jail. I never felt like my brother was dead, so I surely never blamed Bo or Ali for anything. Those two were . . . sincerely real." He grinned, and finally his hand dropped from the bridge of his nose.

He continued with chuckles, "As for Adams, it was one of the few times my mom actually enjoyed keeping her big mouth shut. She was really enjoying how all this gossip was coming down on his head after he befriended the 'wrong people.' She had started calling Ali a 'fast filly' the summer before. You should have heard her smirking around the house. You don't *see* my mom smirking. That's beneath her. You *hear* her smirking, all, 'Mmm, mmm. Maybe he'll stick to the right people now.'"

"Pretty out here," RayAnn breathed. Not having the panorama available to me, I was hooked into this interview.

Justin said, "Me and my brothers, we never came back here as kids. It was a miracle when we were allowed off our street. If you look at my childhood you'd say I'm licensed to be crazy."

I wondered how everything had changed, what the chronology of things had been, such that he could take off for two weeks at a time with a mother who had once been beyond strict. I wondered if, as in many dysfunctional families, the rules had gone from a ten to a zero with few if any of the much-needed fives.

"So . . . you stayed friendly with Bo and Ali, in spite of your mom."

"I didn't exactly wave any flag in my mom's face about it, but yeah, they were very cool," he said. "Bo gave me back Chris's diary as soon as he got out of juvenile detention, like, nine days after they sent him up. There was an informal hearing, and Principal Ames came, said he didn't think Bo was capable of it, and Mrs. Adams was there, representing him. My mom was there, too, but the only thing she had to offer was that none of the three thousand bucks my brother had saved in his bank account had moved, so obviously he had not run away. No charges were ever filed . . . mostly because there was no evidence of a crime. Bo and Ali and me, we've been friends ever since."

"Can you let us look at Chris's diary?" RayAnn asked.

"Can't. Sorry. My mom found it maybe six days after I got it. I kept switching hiding places, but she was just too meddlesome. She keeps it in a safe-deposit box at the bank. You can ask her if you want to see it that badly. She disappears for a couple hours at a time some days, and I imagine her down there in the bank vault, reading it all by herself."

I thought of her keeping the diary in a locked vault because she hadn't managed to keep her oldest son in something similar.

"What do *you* think happened to your brother?"

Justin was rubbing his eyes again, swollen with strain but sparking with alertness. He chortled some and delivered what I viewed as a million-dollar speech. "I think my aunt Dee Dee had something to do with it. They're two of a kind, her and my mom. Both are stubborn and idiotic, with a streak against each other that can get downright evil. Too much alike. My aunt Dee Dee was the oldest, my mom, the youngest. There's a middle sister, my aunt Loraine, but she's a mealy-mouth. They were all raised out in the boondocks, ya know. In a shack with two bedrooms, one bath that only worked half the time. Mom's dad had tied her up with ropes in a few drunken episodes. He used to hang her upside down."

"Yeah," I said, remembering this part of Adams's tale being particularly intriguing to me. Mrs. Creed came to the principal's office the day she accused Bo, reminding Principal Ames and Torey and Ali that she'd been raised in the boondocks and her dad used to hang her upside down from a tree. Her point was that boons should not get any sympathy vote simply because they were poor.

"Before we were born, my aunt Dee Dee married my uncle Lance, who was in the military. They got stationed in Texas after a few other places, and they just always stayed there. Aunt Dee Dee took in my grandmother once Grammy decided to leave my drunken grandfather. Grammy remarried a really nice Texan who was more like a dad than a stepdad, even though the kids were grown. Aunt Dee Dee and Uncle Lance also took in my aunt Loraine, who went to college out there. But Aunt Dee Dee and my mom? Fire and fire, man. Too much alike, though that is the last thing either of them would admit. They each think the other one is evil.

"I can remember my aunt Dee Dee calling me aside a few times when I was a kid and we were out there trying to, uh, *make lovely*. It never worked. She'd be fighting with my mom within two hours, and she would pull me aside and say, 'If she ever gets too domineering, you just call me. I won't have my nephews destroyed.' I was all, 'Whatever, Aunt Dee Dee. I can handle Mom.' My brother, on the other hand? He was like . . . How does the saying go? A lamb led to slaughter? You gotta be a bull, not a sheep, to get by in my family. Why was I telling you this?"

If his overtalking was genetic, I wondered if I'd have as much luck with Matt. "Any chance I can talk to your brother today?"

"If he's home," Justin said. "He's looking to be all-star baseball, so his coach has him and these two other guys at extra practices. We don't talk much since the dreaded Barbie incident. Dang, I should not have told you that one. I was, um, overstimulated last night." He laughed anyway.

"Personally, I don't think it's that big a deal," I said, concerning Barbie. "Bedrooms are private places, ya know? They're where you try thoughts out. It doesn't necessarily mean you're adopting a policy."

"Oh, I didn't think it was that big a deal either," Justin said. "But *Matt* didn't speak to me for a month. Honest to God, he tries to be Mr. Perfect, probably to make up for the rest of us. It's like his job. You want a really sucky interview? Like, the opposite of me? Call him sometime."

"So, you think Aunt Dee Dee brought your brother to Texas, financed him."

"Not Texas. You gotta be kidding. My mother is not stupid. While Torey Adams was still in the hospital, she bought herself a plane ticket and paid a surprise visit to Aunt Dee Dee, hoping she would find him there, despite her feelings about Richardson. Not a trace. Aunt Dee Dee sent him somewhere, that's what I think. Alaska, California, who knows? They moved around for a bit when Uncle Lance was still in the military, had friends all over. My brother could have been living in Saigon for all we know. They were stationed there for a while."

I kept staring at him, in awe of one thing.

"Justin, you don't sound too scared of your mother."

He looked at me and chuckled softly again. "Mary Ellen and Kobe spewed all their gossip last night when Mary Ellen called my clinic. She said there was this blind guy who was a reporter. She says you're as scared of your mother as my brother was of my mom. Whatever you told her and Kobe last night must have been off the charts."

"I mostly remember telling them things so they would agree to find you," I said. "My personal woes were a tradeoff."

"I'm flattered," he said. "Though I was not extremely close to my brother, and I'm not exactly close to my mom. Maybe I can't help you much in the great-story front. But maybe I can help you get over your mother garbage. I just came from rehab, where everybody is getting over something—believe me. I'll probably go home, sometime tonight, tomorrow, whenever I get my act together . . . I just need a chance to brace up for it. I can take you with me. You can break yourself in for your own bullring by meeting my mom. She doesn't bite. Usually."

No thanks. I had planned on sending RayAnn to do that interview, but I didn't like how he was chuckling and watching me. He just didn't get it.

"What's so good about your mom?" I asked. "Yeah, truthfully, I thought she sounded very self-absorbed and loud and . . . terrifying."

"She's loud. And self-absorbed, I like that word. She's never laid a hand on me, if that's what you're after."

"No . . ." I wasn't sure what I was after. I'd always felt under my mother's power somehow. She was huge to me. How the Mother Creed would not be huge to Justin was beyond me. "I just don't picture her as the goodhearted type, I guess."

He sat up and lit another cigarette. Then he lay back, dangling it out his window and trying to blow smoke upside down over his head.

"Remember that part in Adams's story where my mom told him, Ali, and Principal Ames that her dad used to hang her upside down with ropes and chains outside their shack in the boondocks?"

"Yeah."

"Scary guy, huh? I was never allowed to meet my grandfather when I was a kid. I didn't even know he was out there until a couple years ago. Then one day, Mom decided we were old enough and she took us out there to meet her dad."

"What was he like?" I asked.

"Drunk. Pushing seventy, but looks ninety. Basically harmless by that point in his demented existence. I couldn't put this old man with the Santa Claus beard, gumming his food, with the morning-after tremors, in with the picture of little girls all tied up and hanging upside down from trees."

"The place was a pit?" I asked.

"No, actually, it was spotless. My mom had been going out there for years to take care of him."

I felt pushed back, as if he'd said it with the intent to amaze me, to prove something. He just kept blinking at me in a satisfied way.

"She took care of the guy who abused her so badly?" I asked increduously.

"Yeah. She wouldn't let him live in our house . . . not with a whiskey habit that supposedly could turn him into a maniac without notice. Mom's been going out there at least once a week since Chris was born to clean up. Lately she has to bathe him, shave him, and change his Depends. Now she goes every day."

"How does he still get booze if he's gumming his food and, uh, using diapers as a toilet?" RayAnn asked.

"I got a handful of McIntyre cousins out there, descendants from a first marriage of my grandfather's. They're in their thirties. Mack and Ozone are my favorites. And while they don't help clean up after Grandpa, I suspect they keep him in Ol' Sweat Sock, figuring he's got nothing else to live for, so let him gum a bottle neck if he wants to."

"She still goes?" I asked. I wanted to ask about *her*

drinking habit. Drinking would seem like the last thing she would want to do, though I understood parental drinking from watching it develop for years. I don't think *wanting* to drink is a prerequisite. It happens so slowly, and the drinker is the last to notice anything amiss. Justin was on a roll, so I let it lie.

"So, she's not this evil witch. Mom doesn't know I've done anything more than shake hands with Mack and Ozone. They make me think of what Bo would be like without the army. They're burly biker types, but they take me on dirt bike rides all over the place. I've gone out there to shoot pool. There's this bar out that way, Brownie's. They call themselves the Brownie's Mafia, and other boons treat them with respect. I know, 'cuz they take me in the back entrance. Big hearts, the McIntyre clan. They just . . . a lot of them always want their own way and it gets them into trouble."

"Last night at the crime scene, some people told me you hit your mother once." I wondered if I should have gone after her less controversial drinking habit. I didn't want to upset him, and suddenly his energy went to black. He hardly moved, but his eyes cleared of humor and his cheeks flamed up.

"I'm part McIntyre too. Maybe that's an excuse. I guess you could say . . . my mom and I were at a crossroads that night. If I didn't stand up to her, I'd have ended up like my brother, doing everything she said and hating every minute of my life. I did *not* want to be my brother. I love my brother, but there's one thing about him I don't respect, okay? He's a runner. I gotta face down my devils, or I lose, okay? Which doesn't mean to say that it's easy to hit your mother. Oh my God. She got me in some military ju jitzu hold right afterward that I could have easily gotten out of, but I just let her win. Because once you've beat your mother, what does that say about this world? What kind of a place is this? You know?"

"Yes, mothers are sacred," I said, despite that I saw it from a different angle.

"She let go of me to call the cops, and her face was all bleeding, and I just peeled out of the house. Had somewhere important to go that I couldn't tell her about."

Drug deal? I could sense his honesty shutting down. Fistfighting your mother could stress anybody. Time to close it up.

"I could listen to you forever, I think. You're smart for high school."

"Tell that to my teachers," he said, with no joking smile to cut his tension.

"RayAnn and I have to go to the police station now. But I don't want to lose you. How can I get ahold of you later, or where can I find you?"

"Gimme your cell."

I handed it to him, and I heard him punching his number in. I could also hear him sniffing up tears suddenly.

"Shit. I can't see." He swiped at his eyes, tossed the cell into my lap, and opened the car door. "I won't go home until I get myself together and the hour is right, probably late tonight. Until then, I'll be at the Lightning Field."

"I thought you said the Lightning Field was—"

"Yeah, my party haven," he admitted quickly. "It's where I also get my peace."

He got out, slammed the door, and started walking away.

Between my guilt and my curiosity, I was tempted to bag on the cops and go with him.

RayAnn stopped me with valuable wisdom: "Mike, he's not Charlie. Don't get emotionally involved."

Charlie . . . *my brother.* RayAnn knew a lot of things about Charlie because she'd dug it out of me a few times. I knew she was right.

My mind was good enough to remind me of RayAnn's age and her lack of school experiences. "You're not going with him," I said. "We'll find him together later."

RayAnn spun the car around, we came up beside him, and I spoke out the window.

"Do you want us to drop you off? We have time for that—"

"No, I just want to chill by myself for a while."

"No drugs. Okay?"

"No coke, no 'ludes, no 'shrooms, no Vals, gotcha," he said, but almost in a trance.

"You mentioned medication last night," I said, not very professionally. "Do you have it with you?"

I felt mortified at my breeches, especially when Ray-Ann said under her breath, "Not Charlie! Be careful." Yet I couldn't help feeling relieved as Justin reached in his jacket pocket, pulled out a prescription bottle, and muttered, "Thanks," as if he'd forgotten about it.

He went on, "Things don't get popping at the Lightning Field until dark. You can meet up with me by then, if you want. It will probably be a temptation station after the sun sets. The only person to care about it before sunset is me."

"We'll be back by four," RayAnn said. She had our list of perspective interviewees and had probably thought out a schedule last night after I fell asleep.

"Have fun with the cops. They're going to try to blame Darla on Danny Burden, I guess."

Chief Rye had mentioned Danny Burden as the boyfriend. "I think that's what makes sense. You know where he is?" I asked.

"Not a clue. But they're barking up the wrong tree."

It was a blurting moment. And it was the first clue I

had that maybe Justin wasn't crying about fighting with his mother. He had told us not to bring up Darla, I recalled. These stories he told about the boondocks, the people he knew from back there . . . I had read somewhere in the farthest corner of Torey Adams's site that Bo had asked Justin to look after Darla when he went into the service. It was just a line in a gossip post that I hadn't given much thought to until this moment. I wondered if maybe Justin had taken it seriously. The hell. He was only sixteen years old. He wasn't the angel Gabriel.

"What do you know about it?" I asked.

"Nothing," he said. "But I'd like to hear later what the cops tell you. Let's see how smart they are this time. Darla committed suicide."

I wanted to ask what gossip network he'd spun into to hear that . . . and how she got into an amateur-dug grave if that was the case. But he darted off into the woods, obviously some shortcut to the Lightning Field, with his hands at his face, probably pushing tears away.

ELEVEN

AT THE POLICE STATION, RAYANN AND I were asked to wait for Chief Rye in the lobby. We sat in what I imagined were the two chairs that Torey and Ali had sat in on that night long ago: the night Bo Richardson had been busted for trying to break in to the Creeds' to get Chris's diary. Ali and Torey had also been brought in for questioning. For RayAnn and me, it was like walking into the pages of a novel. I had to force the peaceful grin off my face.

The chief was pacing and talking and pacing and talking with the officer I'd met last night, "Tiny" Hughes, behind a big picture window. There was an elderly secretary named Millie at a desk. I could hear seemingly meaningless words floating out from him and Officer Hughes: "Fax us the . . ." and "Why would Danny have . . ."

I figured we might wait quite a while. RayAnn had her laptop with her.

"Look up bipolar disorder," I said.

She rolled her eyes, keeping me in check by saying, "He's *not Charlie*."

I said nothing, which probably got her feeling some level of sympathy. RayAnn had had Abnormal Psych last semester too, but in a different section.

"As I never was forced to study-for-the-test/forget-after-the-test, I don't forget things after the test," she said, alluding to the three weeks we'd spent on this fairly common disorder. "What did you forget that you'd like me to remind you of?"

"How bad a case Justin has?" I suggested.

"Well. We know that manic doesn't mean happy. It means hyperalert to certain situations and sensations. It can mean that people's minds race, which his does. It can mean that people will believe they'll be millionaires next week, or that they're vital to the operations of the universe. He doesn't have that last thing, thank God. Believing you're the God of the Underworld is where it gets serious."

"And he didn't claim to have heard voices," I said. "That's *really* serious."

"Yeah, let's hope he didn't hallucinate," she said, obviously thinking, as I was, of his mystery statement before dropping off to sleep last night: "Quantum thought works . . . and *I don't* believe in ghosts . . ."

She dropped her fist onto my leg, punching lightly with affection.

"I'd say he's not too bad. He's probably like millions of people out there: if he stays on his medication and away from controlled substances, you'll never know he has it," she said, then added with more concern, "unless it's his mania that's making him interested in quantum thought. There's a thin line between believing your good energy is powerful enough to bring you good things, and having a mental illness that has you convinced you're drawing your brother back."

"I know," I said.

"Aren't you anxious to see those e-mails? See if there's anything to them?"

"I . . . have a horrible feeling that they're a scam," I said. "Though the timing—a couple weeks after he'd been trying quantum thought—is very strange."

Chief Rye's voice carried out of the office, saying, "Sorry, I don't have anything for you yet. Call back at . . ." It became inaudible, but he soon walked into the lobby.

We stood up. Chief Rye did a double take.

"Oh. My college students. I forgot about you. Um . . ." He beckoned to us, and we followed him into a detention room, where Lanz had to sniff the chairs loudly. Probably twenty years of sweat residue was on them. "I just told the *Press of Atlantic City* I have nothing, but they have a daily deadline. There's nothing I have that they can print for tomorrow, but I can tell you the half of what I've got."

We sat down at this long table, and he sat beside us, fingering some papers.

"Did you find Danny Burden?" I asked, flipping on my tape recorder, and I could hear RayAnn click a pen.

"I hope not," he said. "His mother, honest to gosh, thought those kids were in Las Vegas, same as Darla's mother. Mrs. Burden *knows* Danny was in Las Vegas, because he called her from there twice, and she still has the number in the caller ID. It belongs to a small hotel, not on the Strip, and the owner has no record of a Danny Burden. So we traced the call time and location from the hotel—he apparently didn't own a cell phone—and he'd been registered under the name Danny Richardson."

"But . . . you're saying Darla wasn't with him?" I asked.

"We think not. The desk clerk at the hotel said he never saw any sign of a girl. It was only Danny."

Interesting. "What do you think happened?"

Rye's jaw bobbed up and down. "Actually, the Pinelands

is not our jurisdiction. We're only investigating this because the body was found in our parts. I don't know these Conovertown folks well. But I was cruising around out there, knocking on doors this morning, and if you could have heard the neighbors . . . you would think I was asking questions for the whereabouts of the Apostle Paul. Danny Burden never did anything in his life, never even had a speeding ticket. People always told him not to get too close to Darla, she was poison; she was too off-the-wall wild and could ruin him. He, according to everyone, is a godsend. He's got a handicapped older brother, a guy named Wiley, and Danny worked two jobs while going to school last year to afford his brother's therapy. Wiley was born with cerebral palsy. He's never had much therapy, much chance to improve, because anything new was experimental and the state wouldn't pay."

I agreed that Danny Burden didn't sound like a killer. RayAnn jumped in.

"So, what was Danny doing in Las Vegas without Darla?"

"One obvious theory is running from the law."

"But you don't think he did it," I said.

"I'm not a court of law." He held his hands up defensively. "All I'm saying is that nobody in those parts can believe it. They say Darla was wild and out of control even before she was depressed; Darla could have killed herself . . . except that, obviously, she didn't dig her own grave and jump into it."

I remembered Justin saying she'd committed suicide. I couldn't begin to guess what would have made him say that, and I wasn't about to bring up his name now.

"Did the Las Vegas hotel have any clue where Danny went after he left? Forwarding number? Anything like that?" I asked.

"No. In fact, he never checked out, so they still have a backpack and a gym bag that were his. Or, at least, the maids turned them in after the third morning it looked like he hadn't slept in the bed. They're looking to see if they threw them out."

"He took off without his bags?" I asked, confused.

"Or something may have happened to him. I called the city morgue out there, and they've got a fairly young John Doe who either fell or was pushed off a balcony of one of the bigger casinos. It's an unsolved, but it could be him. I'm waiting to hear from them, too."

I could see why the *Press* would only be frustrated with this much. There was nothing reportable in it. Everything was pending.

"Do you have a cause of death on Darla yet?" RayAnn asked.

"There are two holes, one in either side of her skull—the small one being the point of entry, and the larger one, on the other side, the exit wound. Blowing out your brains takes on meaning with certain firearms. The Burdens owned one. Danny's mother wanted to hand it right over to the police. It hadn't been touched in years, she said. But when she went to get it, it was missing."

"What kind was it?" I asked. "Would the bullets be a match?"

"All we know until we have a ballistics tester down here is that it *could* have been the gun. The Burden gun is size-appropriate for both the entry and exit wounds. Excuse me."

He left the room, and RayAnn muttered that Tiny was holding the telephone up from behind the glass window.

"What do you think?" she asked.

From my dealings with the campus and city police, I was comfortable here, plugging Chief Rye. Crimes are public knowledge, falling under the public's right to know. Cops are not in the business of keeping too many things from the media. Generally, the relationship is friendly, unless a reporter oversteps. It's hard to overstep if you're too confused to put the facts together.

I just laughed.

"We're so out of our league," she said. "I feel lost."

"I have to call Claudia today. Maybe I should do it right now. Maybe she'd have input."

RayAnn got out some notes from last night, helping me remember that I was supposed to ask if the body had been burned or dropped in an acid to help the decomposition process. I called Claudia and had to listen to her whistle Dixie for a couple minutes about having to cover the spring formal.

"So, it wasn't the missing kid," she finally said.

"No. It's a local girl."

"Damn. You don't have a story."

She could be shortsighted at times. "Claud, I got more story than I know what to do with. Trust me."

"You're always saying to trust you," she groaned.

"Have I generally been right?"

"Look. If you're going to write a think piece on what happens when a weird kid disappears from a small town, then go interview the town. Don't waste too much time on the forensics of the dead girl. That's not in your cookie jar."

"Right," I agreed.

"And you need to think of a hook for our readership. We're a college five hundred miles away. How does he relate to our student body?"

Because there's somebody like him on every floor of every dorm.

I said, "I would call your contact at the AP wire service, tell him it will be in Thursday's paper at the latest. Give him a heads-up."

"You really think you can write this so well that the wire service will buy it?"

It was a leap, but as usual, I said, "Don't worry about it."

"Yeah, trust me, he says." She sounded annoyed.

"Justin Creed showed up at our door at four a.m."

"The brother of your one and only?"

"You got it. He'd been missing for two weeks. But when we showed up, he decided to come back."

I almost had her, but Claudia is hard to impress.

"And what do you mean, *our* door? Jesus, Mike."

Claudia thought RayAnn and I were bosom buddies. No one knew about *us* at school, save Stedman. Technically we *were* only bosom buddies, if you discounted the fact that I'd kissed her a hundred times.

"We're saving money," I chided. "She sleeps in Randolph sweat apparel."

"You keep your hands off her. Isn't she a minor, something like that? Some homeschooled brainiac . . . I haven't talked to her much yet. I don't warm up to children well."

I sighed. "I know what I'm doing—"

"You'd better hope so. If you get locked up on a statutory rape charge, I'm not bailing you out."

"So send me some money for an extra room. I could use it. I'm paying for this myself, you know."

"Like you'll ever let me forget it. How much?"

I told her the amount for an extra room, figuring I could use the money for something else. So long as I didn't "statutorily rape" RayAnn, we were in no trouble at all.

"I'll do a PayPal." She sighed. "I'll create a travel budget and look ever so important. And be back here by tomorrow night, right? I need you. We've got a case of plagiarism in the EE Department involving twelve students. One of them hacked into the professor's files and the others were silent takers."

My neck snapped. EE is electrical engineering. That was a huge story for a campus. But I'm used to remaining calm in the face of some fierce energy.

"I'll be there," I said, though if I couldn't meet Torey Adams and Bo Richardson before this funeral, I was staying. Somehow.

"So, where's Chris Creed?" she asked, finally. "According to his brother?"

"Justin says he's coming here, might already be here," I said.

"But you don't believe that."

"Why shouldn't I?" I asked, but my sarcasm bled through.

"It's too convenient. You're not that lucky."

Chief Rye was motioning to us through the picture window, according to RayAnn.

"I am beyond lucky in all ways, and you know it," I said, standing up.

"And that's why I love you and need you." She blew a kiss through the phone.

I blew one back before clicking us off. Maybe that's why Claudia could imagine me in the same sentence with statutory rape. She was a sexual harassment charge waiting to happen if she ever got around some disgruntled prude. Claudia was beautiful, if you're into tall, lanky, and full of oneself. But she told vulgar jokes like a guy, liked to stun starting reporters with her unflowery speech, and blew kisses to those of us she was grateful for and admired. She liked ruffling people, but she hadn't managed to ruffle me. I was experienced with women so domineering that she only made me laugh.

Lanz stopped me before I walked straight into Chief Rye, who was coming out of the window room with papers in his hand.

"Well, apparently the motel where Danny was staying did not destroy his belongings. The manager found the bags, searched them, and found what sounds like a suicide note. While I was getting the fax, the morgue called with a list of distinguishable body markings on the DOA. There's a birthmark on the ankle shaped like a missile and a tattoo on the left arm of a sinking schooner. When we talked to Mrs. Burden this morning, she mentioned a birthmark on his ankle and a tattoo of a sinking ship."

"So, it's him."

"We'll know for sure by around four o'clock, but I'd say it's all formality."

I felt RayAnn reach past me, and papers rumpled. I assumed she had the fax in her hand. Or maybe he refused to give it to her, because suddenly Chief Rye began to read.

"*Dear Mom, Dad, and Wiley:*

"*I've rewritten this letter thirty times. I'm trying to figure out how to say everything. I can't, so I'll just throw down thoughts and leave you to believe that everything I am saying is true.*

"*Something is going to come up if it hasn't already. It will look like I committed a murder, Darla's, and you all know how I loved her and wanted to make our baby a decent life. I was prepared to, and when Darla lost the baby, I was sad that I would not have a baby. I knew it would be hard, but I was looking forward to the baby.*

"*I guess Darla was too, because while she never said that, she was very upset when the miscarriage happened. She cried for a month, and it was because I kept saying I would not marry her without the baby. I wanted to go to community college and get my degree first.*"

RayAnn and I had turned to look at the fax, too, and Chief Rye just dropped it into our hands. "I've read it twice. There are too many flaws in what he's saying. Something's wrong with the big picture, even if he's telling the truth, but have at it."

He went back into the office. We read silently and slowly, as Danny Burden's penmanship was a mess and I wasn't as good as the chief was at interpreting it.

"So here is the hard part. She threatened to off herself and even though I promised to help her get in rehab or to go see a doctor for some depressed pills she would not listen. On Sunday night, December 29, you guys were at church and she was over and I couldn't stand to listen to her complain and feel sorry for herself anymore so I shouted GO AHEAD THEN! GET IT OVER WITH!

"It was the worst mistake of my life because she knew where Dad's gun was. I had told her once and now she took it and ran and I ran after her and she fired it into her own head in the shed at the back of the property. The one with Dad's motorbike in it, so she is in there and I am so sorry to have to tell you that. Just call the cops and don't go in there, it is a bloody mess and I am a crazy person.

"I could not have called the cops, however. I had just screamed at her and I know the Baldwins were home and probably heard that and she had Dad's gun and I have touched it so many times and they would think that I killed her because I didn't want to marry her or something. Remember when Chris Creed disappeared and everyone automatically assumed that someone down here did him? Well I didn't think I should end up in jail just because Darla made a bad mistake on our property and with Dad's gun.

"I came out here just to run run run. I didn't get to Darla in time. I could have stopped her if I had been faster or smarter or something. I could not hug or kiss her goodbye because if I touched one thing in that shed it would have looked even more like I did it and I didn't want you guys to ever deal with any suspicion that I did something bad. I am sorry about the mess, totally sorry, I should have called the cops and not run.

"I did love her. I know most people don't understand that because they think she was a loadie and any one of them could have thought she made me so crazy just from her constant yelling to get out Dad's gun. But I did love her and I could never kill her and now I can't stop seeing her head blow open and that stream of blood running down the side of the wall back behind Dad's bike. I want to be with her even if it sounds crazy. It will be better than being in jail. She didn't want me to get blamed, she's not that evil. She just didn't think. But who will believe me? Nobody, so I'm going *on to Darla. She knows the truth. I love you all and*

especially you Wiley."

I almost had a charley horse from shifting my head every half line to read it. Sad, sad, sad. Bad, bad frequency. Like most people who are well liked, Danny Burden was unaware of it, unaware of the gifts it can hold. Between the neighborhood's word and the evidence, the police would probably have believed him.

"So, Danny Burden is saying he committed suicide because he missed Darla and he was afraid he'd get blamed for it," I summarized tentatively. The kid was a massive run-on sentence.

"Essentially, yes." Chief Rye had emerged from his office and took back the fax. "You need a copy?"

"Yes, please," I said, sensing his anxiety. "You're obviously not taken in by this. Any specifics?"

"At first glance, only that the body was dropped in acid to speed up the decomposition. The clothes were thrown in with a semi-decomposed body to keep all potential evidence together."

The answer to my number one question.

"And if she committed suicide, why burn the body?" Rye asked. "And how did she get into that grave?"

TWELVE

WE LEFT THE POLICE STATION with plans to come back in a couple hours for some confirmations, including the formal ID of the body. Authorities were at the Burdens', looking to see what evidence they could still find in the shed. Rye had said the property was irregular, narrow enough to have close neighbors in the front but proceeding backwards and out for four acres. The shed was at the back, which might help explain why the neighbors never heard a shot fired. I was especially interested in the results of that search.

But not enough to ask RayAnn to head over there. I

was thinking of Claudia's stance, which was correct: The town was my business; the body was not, except in how the town was responding to it. Having visited the Adams homestead today, I was ripe to speak to Mrs. Adams.

But as we got into the car, I spouted, "I'm worried about Justin."

"He didn't look good when we left him," RayAnn agreed. "Do you want to stop by the Lightning Field?"

Walking for ten minutes at least into the Lightning Field and back out seemed like a waste of precious time, but my heart had hooked in to Justin more than I cared to admit. I wanted to make sure no druglords had found him, and I also wanted to frame out this place in the daylight. It had been nothing less than crazy at night.

We parked as close as we could, and RayAnn led the way, with me encouraging Lanz to keep up with her. Only twice did he turn his nose to stop me, both times from puddles of rainwater from yesterday's deluge.

The field was just as eerie in daylight, but in a different way. The trees still glistened, a pasty color at the tops of the burned-out trunks, some ending thirty feet up, mixed with black trunk nearing the bottom. Whatever fire ripped through here probably left the ground bald, but now there was a nice bed of soft foliage resembling the wintergreen that grew around tree trunks near my childhood house. Except the flowers were white instead of purple. It was a very white place, between the endless tiny blooms and the weird dead trees. The eeriness, I suppose, came from the silence. The trees in the distance, when I focused long enough, bore a slight shade of green, implying that the summer leaves indeed were in bud stage. But there were no leaves yet to rustle in the breeze.

"Justin!" RayAnn shouted it over and over, and I did, too.

No answer.

"He wouldn't do anything stupid like jump in the freezing bay," I said. "Right?"

"I don't know him," RayAnn replied. "But crying over your life and taking your life are a mile apart. Let's hope."

RayAnn searched over by a pile of large jetty rocks down near the water, as it was the only place big enough to conceal a person. She came back alone but with something in her hands. She held up Justin's prescription bottle and shook it.

"Leaves his charger at home, leaves his medication in the field," she said. "I don't think he's very organized."

"He's got a lot on his plate," I said, holding my hand out and taking the bottle.

"Yeah. Maybe we should just put it back where I found it. He'll probably think of where he left it and come back.

I'm guessing he sat down there for a while, then decided to charge his phone at Mary Ellen's. The rocks are kind of shaped like a giant seat, like a throne."

We could try to give it to him, but I had no idea where Mary Ellen lived, or even if he'd actually been there.

"What are you doing?" RayAnn asked.

"Just . . ." I pushed hard on the cap, turned it, and popped it off. ". . . making sure he isn't supplementing."

"Nosy, aren't you?" she asked.

"I'm a little too emotionally involved," I confessed. "You're supposed to stop me from feeling like . . ."

I stared into the container, and instead of fussing at me, she looked, too. I think she heaved a sigh along with me. But there was only one type of pill in it. I put the lid back on top.

I suddenly sensed bad energy wafting around the back of my neck, what with energy so mysteriously easy to sense in the Lightning Field. Like a psychic, I flashed to my dream last night of Chris Creed and sign language: L-O-O-K O-U-T B-E-H-I-N-D Y-O-U. Lanz whined.

"Tell me it's not Miss Gulch," I said. But I just knew, as if any meager ESP talents I possessed had gotten super-charged with lightning-tree energy. *What in God's Almighty name is she doing here?*

RayAnn's smile crept back, as she watched with intrigue

over my shoulder. "There's no picture of her on Adams's site. And you said last night in the rain she looked like the Grim Reaper."

"Guess I should pick one film character and stick to it," I muttered, but refused to turn around. The Mother Creed came slowly around in front of us. There actually *had* been a photo of her on Adams's website early on, but it was taken down almost as quickly as it was posted, leading me to think she'd managed to harass Torey and threaten him with libel or something. She'd aged ten years instead of four. My heart melted maybe one ounce before hardening up again when she spoke.

"What are you doing here?"

I almost choked on her lack of boundaries, but RayAnn was pretty solid.

"Ma'am, this is public property," she said. "We're within our rights to be here."

The woman chuckled down at her shoes and said softly but haughtily, "Okay, let's try this again. I *asked* you a *question*. *What* are you *doing* here?"

Jeezus, I thought. *My nightmares are materializing.*

RayAnn sensed my phobia exploding out of its shell, I suppose, because she went into attack.

"Ma'am. This property belongs to the state."

"You. Didn't. Answer. The question." The Mother Creed

stepped within two feet of RayAnn, and I put my hand out, saying, "Whoa. Ladies . . ."

But they locked eyes, and RayAnn took it so easily, I was amazed. "I'm not answering your question, lady, until you give *me* some answers. What were you doing back there? Spying on us? That's a little creepy."

"I'm waiting for someone." Mrs. Creed broke down first, which made me want to 'five RayAnn.

"Well, obviously there's nobody here but us," she said evenly.

"Whom are *you* waiting for?" The woman wasn't barking or yelling, so her voice alone was not galling. It was her sense of entitlement, as if she had a perfect right to information. "Did I not just hear you calling for someone? Might that person have been my *Justin?*"

She hissed and spit a little on the *st* in Justin. RayAnn blinked as it hit her eyelashes, but she held her ground.

"Ma'am, we're reporters, not that it's any of your concern." That we were professionals and not high school kids seemed to take her aback a little, and she looked at me, probably to confirm. RayAnn went on, "We'll be here, there, and all over town. If we need to speak to you, *we* will approach *you,* though it's not on our schedule for today."

"And what are you reporting on?" the woman continued to press.

"You ready to go, Mike?" RayAnn ignored her and turned to me. I wished she hadn't. It turned the woman's attention on me full force.

"You're blind," she noted.

You're fucked up. I tried to walk around her, but she stopped me, pointing to the prescription bottle in my hand.

"I'll take that."

I could have kicked myself seconds later, but I simply went into domineering-mother-syndrome autopilot. I handed it to her. That caused RayAnn to nudge me hard, and the woman shot her a victorious glance. *One pushover out of two would satisfy her.*

"Um . . . that's not yours," RayAnn said.

"It's my *son's.* I *think* I can *have* what belongs to my *son,*" she said.

RayAnn was in a quandary. If she insisted that the woman leave it where we intended to for Justin, it would also confirm that Justin would be coming back. Instead she made a suggestion, not that the woman seemed open to them. "Fine, take it. I suggest you go home now."

"Oh, you do, do you? What do you know about my son? Where *is* he?"

RayAnn unleashed, leaving me half amused and half petrified. "Mrs. Creed. I know what most people have enough sense to know: Spying is not very endearing. If you spy on your son, he's not going to like you. If he doesn't like you, he's not going to stay around very long. How many sons do you plan on losing?"

Whoa! The comment would have driven through most any parent like a sword—especially if that parent already had one missing child and one that moved out. The Mother Creed's eyes did flicker, but beyond that, her expression never changed. This time as we stepped around her, she didn't try to stop us. I could feel her eyes all over us as we departed down the trail. I prayed to God she wouldn't follow us.

"I think her behavior's gotten worse over the years," RayAnn said with a shudder. "Remember in Adams's story the plea she gave in church when Chris first disappeared? She could sound half normal in public. If you weren't listening too closely."

"She drinks. That would eat brain cells . . ."

RayAnn sighed. "You may have seen the last of Justin. If she catches him? How's he supposed to get out of the house?"

"I don't know. What's worse is that Justin implied last night that she's in denial about his illness," I reminded RayAnn. "What if she keeps his medication from him? I can't believe I just gave his pills to her."

THIRTEEN

WE PAID A VISIT to the Adamses' quaint Civil War farm-house. I wasn't hopeful, figuring it was now noon and that on Saturdays comfy women like Mrs. Adams play tennis, go to the gym, go to club meetings for charities. After knocking twice on the door and not seeing any cars, I was ready to leave.

Then suddenly there were sounds from inside. It was a light, womanly step, and suddenly the door was open and she was staring at us. Her eyes were dark brown and round, whereas her son's were blue and that sort of a triangular shape, wide on the inside and coming to points on the outside. Even before the door opened I was anticipating this would be quite a switch from the mother we'd just met.

"Hi. May I help you?" She opened the door wide.

We gave her our creds, and she remained calm and polite to tell us that her son avoided media, didn't grant interviews without being told to by his agent, and in fact was not here in Steepleton.

"I know your son's music well, but actually I'm writing a feature on Chris Creed's disappearance. It's you we'd really like to talk to."

She was an attorney. She could handle it, I wagered, motionless with my polite smile as she checked her watch. She didn't look thrilled.

"I only have a few minutes. I have to go to Philadelphia," she said.

Airport? Picking somebody up? I let it go. "That's all we want for the time being."

She moved aside. "Come in. For a few minutes."

She sat at the edge of a couch in the living room. Very reserved, this woman, but there was a niceness about her voice. I could not read her energy to save me, except that it didn't want to be read. The inside of the house was stunning, a combination of expensive antiques and modern stuff. The most modern thing was a huge picture on the wall of Adams rifting out some run on a double-necked guitar at some huge concert. A spotlight covered him, but in the background were heads of thousands of people. From up close, I could see traces of a sizable balcony in the background lights. Must have been a good-size concert hall.

"He still has that ponytail," I couldn't help mentioning. It wasn't long and straggly. Adams had really straight, thick blond hair, and the ponytail was only about six inches long, but he'd had it since he left Steepleton.

"Yes," Mrs. Adams said with a tight smile. She already said she wouldn't talk about her son.

"You're an icon of Steepleton," I said, pulling out my recorder and finding a seat across from her. RayAnn sat beside me.

I heard a warm, appreciative chuckle. "I suppose that depends on whom you speak to. I don't have much involvement with the town. Don't have time."

I sensed it was a pat answer, one she'd designed for writers who came before me. This might not be easy.

"But you've lived here your whole life. You were here when Digger Hanes disappeared, your generation's Christopher Creed."

"Yes, I was." The silence was long, but I could sense that she wasn't looking to stonewall us. She wanted to help, if we could provide the right questions.

"Your son found the body of Digger's father, Bob Hanes," I started. "For a few weeks, Torey said on his website, he thought it was the body of Chris Creed."

"I don't know how long it was, but yes, he thought that."

"Did you ever think it was Chris's body?"

"No," she said. "The decomposition in that case raised a lot of questions, but I was pretty certain the corpse had been there quite some time. And there were other things."

"Such as?"

Her answer pleased me. "Well . . . my intuition? I have to work with intuition a lot as a trial attorney, and as a defense attorney for juveniles. Kids and teenagers are not always articulate, so you have to watch faces, watch words, watch actions. I simply had never pegged Chris as the angry type, the violent type. He could get depressed, I'm sure, as he was picked on since I could remember. But it takes a certain degree of fear or violence—my humble opinion—to take a life, even one's own."

"Do you think Steepleton has changed since all of this came down?" I asked.

She studied her fingers laid on top of her knees, and finally laughed uneasily. "Well, we're hearing a lot more spooky stories about these woods. And finding another body obviously won't help that. I'm a little concerned for the kids, truthfully. Imagination is great. But if they fixate on all these dark tales, it can make them morbid. I think . . . these woods allow people to see what they *want* to see, what they *need* to see."

I smiled, thinking of my chance meeting last night with the ghost chaser et al. "Right now, some of them want to see a certain ghost."

"Yes, they do." She laughed, even mentioned Kobe Lydee by name, but with affection, not disdain. "If that poor boy doesn't see the ghost of Chris soon, he'll have to succumb like the rest of the student body and actually start studying, preparing for a career. That would be a good thing!"

The woman exuded peace—with herself, her neighbors, these woods.

"Do you think he's alive somewhere?"

"I do," she said, "which sounds pretty naïve for an attorney. For this one, I've always relied on my son's intuition, his instincts. They're pretty good. I support him."

That was obvious. I was at a loss for words, jealous as I was for Torey Adams's good luck. I reminded myself quickly that we create our own luck, but any real questions were in the black hole. I settled on "Do you think Chris will ever show up here?"

It provided fodder for some great lines.

"I would imagine so. Sylvia takes care of her father over in Conovertown. At some point, someone will need to take care of her, and I would imagine all three boys will kick in. I don't see Chris's disappearance as the scandal that other people see it as. I think of it as a reckoning—a healing—and I really think Sylvia will come to terms with it, though she's in a rough passage right now."

She didn't elaborate on that, and we didn't confirm what we'd just encountered. She simply went on, "I think, someday, we'll simply realize that she's been talking to him by phone, and if and when he shows up, it won't be with any big shebang. No parade. People will have forgotten; people won't recognize him . . ." She laughed. "He'll probably do like we all do—develop some wrinkles, put on a few pounds, lose some hair, gain some vocal cords. Torey used to have one adorable imitation of him, if it's okay to say this . . . of when Chris was picked on and would start whining. His voice was just changing. He would go, 'I DID-n't DO anY-thing. It's no-O-t my fau-AU-lt.'"

I could use that quote. It was the human side of myth. She'd described your average kid, a late bloomer in ways, with the rickety, changing vocal cords.

"I'd like to think that someday Torey's dad and I will just be going about our business, hopefully before a need for canes and walkers, and someone will say, 'Boy, that Chris is such a great help to his silver-haired mother.' And that's how we'll know he's been back awhile."

She sure was levelheaded. I could see even more of how she'd have been such a stronghold to Torey in his childhood. Nothing could get too out of hand in a home like this.

"Was it hard to send your son away? I take it you wanted to protect Torey from some of the gossip flying around town . . ."

". . . that he was involved in Chris's death." She nodded easily, as if she'd become used to saying it either to press or to close friends. "We didn't send Torey away to . . . to avoid Steepleton, as much as to put him on the track he's on. He just needed more scenery, more variations of people, more input to fulfill his dreams. He had a horizon view of the world, as he puts it, and he needed a bird's-eye view. That's all."

She was a nice person, and given a couple hours, I could probably walk away with enough counter-fodder to write a *nice* book on Steepleton. She definitely hadn't fallen prey to bad frequency.

"All I can say about that is that Torey is not the type to find a dead body. He's . . . all poet, all insight, all sensitivity. I didn't think he could heal around here, but more than the people, it's the woods." She jerked her head with a polite smile toward another room. When I found it, I could see a kitchen table, the place she probably told Torey and Ali about Digger Hanes disappearing and the possibility of Bob Hanes being dead out in the woods.

"The woods are dark out those windows at night," I guessed.

"Yes."

"And the Indian burial ground, where he found the body, is a stone's throw from back here."

"Yes."

"And . . . he inherited from somebody feelings of being watched in the dark . . . in the basement, but especially from out that window."

She laughed heartily. "I admit it. I do let my imagination get carried away when I'm alone in this house. Ms. Attorney, who visits jail and juvenile detention twice a week without a flinch. My imagination is nothing compared to my son's, but I was thinking I ought to pass him on to others for the time being, others who might not radiate those phobias."

"You're a little phobic of the woods," I clarified.

"A lot of people are." She nodded. "Though it's debatable whether there's anything out there except a lot of imagination run wild. Like I said, these woods allow people to see what they want to see."

I thought of Elaine and her band of acid droppers. Mrs. Adams looked at her watch and stood up. "I'm really sorry. I have to go now."

"You going to the airport?" I stood with RayAnn.

"Yes."

"Can we come back later?"

"I'm sorry," she said, politely stonewalling me. "My son

doesn't do interviews, as I said. And of course, this is a sad occasion."

We hadn't talked about Darla Richardson, but she seemed to understand that I knew why Torey would come back here. "Are you involved as an attorney with this crime in some way?"

She walked us toward the door. "I got a call from Chief Rye last night, saying I might hear from the Burden family about representation for Danny. Then just before you came in . . . I heard it wouldn't be necessary."

"Yeah, we just came from police headquarters," I said. "I know the scoop. Any insight into what's going on?"

"If you mean how does an alleged suicide get into a grave? Starting with the fact that I wouldn't commit to the Burden boy being a liar, I haven't any idea. That's police business. I'm sure they'll figure it out."

We shook hands, me trying to look grateful and not totally disappointed that she wouldn't let us back to talk to Torey. Well, she probably wouldn't keep him under lock and key. Maybe he'd go to the local tap for a beer or something with Bo. I'd work on getting to Torey after we went back to look for Justin one more time.

FOURTEEN

WE STOPPED AT POLICE HEADQUARTERS and I went in to
find out if the confirmation of the body was complete
yet and what the search of the shed had turned up. Officer
Hughes was at his desk, eating a turkey sandwich, but Chief
Rye was still out investigating, he told us.

"Are they calling it a suicide?" I asked.

"They're calling it *weird* right now," he said. "They don't
want to call it a homicide."

That implied they'd have no choice if they couldn't figure out how the body got into the grave—the skull having

two massive bullet holes in it. Calling it a homicide meant finding someone to prosecute. I hoped Mrs. Adams was right in all her optimism that they'd figure it out.

"You might want to know . . ." I said before clearing my throat. "Mrs. Creed was out at the Lightning Field today, acting strange and defiant."

"To you two?"

"Yes," I confirmed.

"I'm sorry."

We laughed uneasily. I knew better than to think that gave him grounds to take a run down there to clear her out. I don't know why exactly I wanted to share that, except my instincts told me to go there.

Officer Hughes laughed. "She's down there once a day, spying to see if someone will give away Justin's whereabouts. She usually only finds a few of the vo-tech kids. They only do school until twelve-thirty, then smoke cigarettes out there before going to jobs." His chuckles indicated the absurdity.

"My wife, Maggie, and I bought a house on her street two years ago." He held up a brown lunch bag, which dangled heavily, as if another sandwich was in it. "I've been brown bagging my lunch lately, because if Sylvia sees my squad car out front, she'll come over and tell me what all those kids said. I've told her five or six times now, 'Sylvia, I can't arrest them for discussing the sex lives of their classmates or smoking cigarettes.' She's somehow convinced that if she keeps this up, she'll find Justin out there."

"She came pretty close today," I said with a shudder.

"Yeah? Is he back?" Hughes looked interested but not overly so. "Rye told us not to list him as a runaway, which means the guidance office at school knew where he was all along. You think *I've* got trouble. She's been visiting the guidance office every day, trying to get them to spill, which, technically, they don't have to do. A minor is allowed to get psychiatric care without parental permission. All they have to say is that they know where he is and they helped him get there. Why she checks the Lightning Field, I can't fathom, but her actions are regulated, like a drill sergeant's."

I could see clearly the scene from Adams's tale when they were watching her systematically taking apart her missing son's room looking for clues. She did a half hour every night, starting with one wall and proceeding around.

I wanted to head back to the Lightning Field but had misgivings. "So, um, what time does she usually leave?"

"As I'm also trying to steer clear of the woman, I don't know her every move. But . . ." He pulled out his cell and speed dialed, giving me a wink. "Maggie? Look out the window. See if Sylvia's car is in her garage."

He held the phone patiently for half a minute, then said, "Thanks," and hung up. "She's back home."

"And . . . there's no chance she'll go back."

He watched me, chuckling at my concern and shaking his head. "One thing all the neighbors know: Sylvia does all her errands in the morning and early afternoon. She's in for the night by three o'clock. You won't see her—unless a body turns up or something highly unusual like that. Hopefully, we're done with bodies for another year or two."

He seemed so emphatic about the woman staying home that I believed him. I returned to RayAnn and Lanz, who were waiting in the car.

"She's home to stay is the good news," I told her. "Bad news is . . . they may have to list Darla's death as a homicide."

RayAnn turned on the engine. "That's not bad news, because that's not part of your story."

"Right," I said. "I'm not emotionally involved. I'm not, I'm not."

Nonetheless, we hurried back to the Lighting Field. When we got there I left Lanz standing on the floor in the back, eating dog food out of his dish. No sense dragging him where he didn't want to be.

RayAnn spotted Justin on the other side of the rock formation where she had found his pills. A flat rock was backed by three higher rocks, and he was using the middle as a back rest. The whole thing, once I zeroed in on it, looked like a primeval lawn chair.

"My throne," he said, motioning to his feet. "Kneel and pay homage."

I wanted to share his upbeat mood but broke the news to him: "Dude, your mother was here earlier."

I thought he would gasp or maybe yell. His smile didn't even waver. "Yeah, I heard she's been doing that. Have fun on your interview escapades?"

"We did," I said. "But listen. Your mom took your prescription. You had left it on the rock."

He just kept smiling, leaving us in awe. "I'll get it tonight. Don't sweat it. My God, you *are* a stress puppy. I've been living with my mom for sixteen years, and I'm not dead yet. I have a recent *chemical imbalance in my brain,* but that's probably more her genetics than her ability to upset me."

Again, I just smiled. The kid amazed me.

"There, see? A smiling face is a good face. You should know that you can't give certain people power over you." He looked up at the sky, gazing at puffy clouds, gray on the bottoms. It had turned the Lightning Field from a diamond-twinkling dance of tree trunks and white blossoms to something almost like a black-and-white film clip.

We stepped close enough to get a whiff of his clothes. He stank worse than Woodstock.

"We're paying homage to the party Gods, I detect." I inhaled and faked a cough I almost didn't have to fake.

He kept his ornery grin and offered nothing.

"We don't honor our promises," I said.

"I promised you 'no coke, no ludes, no 'shrooms, no Vals.' I'm good to my word." When neither of us spoke, he spread his arms wide and laughed in amazement. "Pot is like smoking cigarettes—once you've done the chronic stuff! We don't count marijuana."

"Oh, *we* don't." I turned until I found RayAnn's eyes, which spoke volumes of *no interviewing of loadies.* I shuffled around, letting my determination build to abandon him. It wasn't all so easy to leave, even with the cloud cover taking the shimmer off the place and making it more than creepy.

RayAnn sort of read my thoughts, muttering, *"On peut se demander si Charlie est comme celui-ci."* That's French for "You wonder if Charlie has become like this."

"Ah, non, non," I argued, but without any conviction.

"Ne pas obtenir impliqué émotionnellement. Il ne peut arriver à tout bon." Don't get emotionally involved. It can't do you any good.

"Frère Jacques, frère Jacques, dormez vous?" Justin sang out of key, with a giggle. It was the extent of his French, I took it.

I had learned a lot of French from RayAnn, but she was reciting truths that she had learned from me. Just because I'd left an alcoholic home didn't mean I was automatically free of the awkward dance I had learned to do with addictive personalities. I still went to Al-Anon meetings at school, at least once a week, to prevent myself from getting swept up with the guilt over leaving—or getting swept into new, deeply manipulative relationships.

RayAnn didn't have to remind me that the beginning of sanity in any Twelve-Step program is to look after yourself first. And she was accurate on the Charlie/Justin angle. She was reminding me that looking after Justin should not be some sort of penance for my leaving home.

"Okay . . . we're not staying," I said. "It's really bad journalism ethics to interview a person who is not sober."

"So? Don't interview me. Just kick back! Take a load off. God, you guys are high-strung. Coupla nervous creatures . . ."

We were no more high-strung than your average sober person. It was meant to wear us down.

"Look, marijuana does nothing to me, in the sense that it does not impair my . . . whatever. My judgment. I am the same as when you left me. Only now I feel slightly more relaxed. And my mouth isn't running so fast."

He did sound calmer, but it seemed as if he were throwing two weeks' worth of rehab down the toilet.

"Why don't we work on getting you this missing dose your mom just took off with an hour ago, and quit adding to the problem?" I asked.

"Relax!" he tried again. "Let's just say . . . I know what I want. Right now, I need to feel *alive*. I need my energy. I need to feel more and talk less, so . . . maybe it's good my mom showed up. She took away the drug that makes me numb. It's all good."

Nice try.

"We'll see you later, maybe," I said, and we headed back toward the trail. He shimmied over the rocks and followed us.

"Come on, you guys. Don't leave me alone."

I paused, hearing a pleading behind all the joking. Justin was vulnerable, and it probably was not wise for him to be alone. But he had already crossed over into Stonersville, and I ought to let him reap the consequences of his actions.

RayAnn dug her fingers into my side with *"Ne pas succomber."* Don't succumb.

I could think of only a couple reasons to stay, which had more to do with our profession than his condition. I had promised him we would not bring up the subject of Darla—at least not directly.

"They're telling tall tales down at the police station. Suicide . . . murder . . . it's all up in the air." I was walking away backwards, which I wasn't very good at.

We exchanged silent grins for at least three steps. I won, in that he spoke first.

"Couple years back, when Bo left for boot camp, he

told me to look after Darla. Guess I didn't do a great job." He toed the ground, and when I found his face again, the grin was gone. He turned and moseyed back over to this throne, which was facing the water, away from us.

"Round one, Justin," RayAnn groaned.

We moved slowly back toward him, this new bit of intrigue all but irresistible. But I knew how deeply manipulative people in addictive families can be, and how they always seem to get their way, even though it appears you're making all your own choices.

I eased down on the flat rock by his feet and heard him light a cigarette. His arm waved to get the smoke going in the opposite direction, but the wind was not our friend. I ignored the blast of staleness.

"So, you think you failed Bo," I proceeded cautiously.

"I *know* I failed Bo."

"What made you say it was a suicide?"

"Gossip runs thick in these parts." The line sounded terse and rehearsed, but I couldn't argue with it.

I was looking for something not obvious to reply with, but RayAnn shot off in a simple direction, and sometimes keeping things simple is the answer. "Justin, you're sixteen years old. If Danny Burden couldn't handle Darla, how are you supposed to? She didn't even go to your school anymore, right?"

"Right," he muttered quickly. "I only saw her a couple times a month. She returned my calls when she felt like it. Sometimes a week later, sometimes not at all."

"Have you . . . seen Danny Burden lately?" she asked. I didn't think she planned to tell him that Danny Burden was dead if he didn't know, but I cleared my throat to warn her, just in case.

"No, no. I haven't seen him since . . ."—he waved his hand in a motion I took as "way back"—"since before Christmas. Bo didn't tell me to look after Danny. In fact, after Danny came along last fall, Bo said he thought she was in good hands . . . maybe Danny would finally be the person to calm her down. But one of my disorder symptoms is a slight obsession with things. I thought of her five times a day. Not that I was ever stupid enough to call her five times a week, even. I just . . . I knew I was supposed to look after her. *Ha.*"

I wanted to know in the worst way how he fell into that suicide gossip. When something weird like that turns out to be true, you want to jump on it. But my instincts were telling me not to upset him.

I bided my time. "Justin, you need to look out for Justin. Everybody's responsible for themselves in this world. Including Darla."

"Including Darla . . ." He smoked the cigarette until it was halfway gone, then dropped it absently into a crack between the rocks. My heart went out in a way I wished I could control better. I resisted the urge to rub the back of his head, and said nothing.

"Don't look back . . . don't look back . . . don't look back," he said, as if trying to drum in something he'd heard. "Look ahead . . . look ahead . . . look ahead."

"They teach you that in rehab?" I asked.

"They were heading in that direction. Place has cool counselors."

My one challenge with the support group that I'd become involved with on campus is that the people seem to spend as much time talking about their ill-begotten pasts as their promising futures. It's as if people are drawn to looking back. They can't move on until it all makes sense. Humbly submitted: It never does.

"At least, I *think* they were heading in that direction. I get most of my meat from in here." He pulled a paperback out of his jacket pocket—the inner pocket that can hold bigger things. He dropped it on the rock in front of me. I did my bobble-head routine to take in the wide title: *Quantum Thought: Science and the Power of Your Mind.*

I'd actually seen the jacket on Amazon. It featured three geometric cubes—a red, a yellow, a purple—sort of spilling into one another and creating a shimmering effect of every color in the rainbow. Seeing so little color in my days, I was always hungry for it.

"Don't judge me," he said defensively.

I hadn't been—not exactly. But I imagined he'd suffered through comments from friends around here.

His face was red and strained, but his eyes were dry. "If it weren't for quantum thought, I would be so depressed right now that I might have thrown myself into the bay. Did you know your thoughts have energy?"

"I . . . yes." I shook my head a little, trying to get on his track. "Being blind makes you very aware of that. I don't have to see people to know what they're thinking. I don't often have to hear them either."

"Ta! I'm not *that* good. But I believe it in theory. When Henry Ford developed the eight-cylinder engine, he was using quantum thought, though he probably wasn't aware of it. Your desires leave your head. They have energy. What happens to the energy?"

I shrugged. "It dissolves?"

"Uh-uh. My dad says energy can't dissolve. It goes somewhere. It does something. Where, and what? You think of something you really, really want. You imagine yourself getting it over and over. You fill your mind with what could happen, over and over, until it gets to be a habit, until it replaces all the reasons something couldn't happen. You keep releasing that energy. It's scientific how belief energy eventually replaces doubt. You get what you want."

I couldn't help but smile. "I don't think a legitimate scientist would love this."

"Probably not, but they're all screwed up with their paperwork and politics. You should hear my dad talk about the fights at the college over research money. Trust me, there's no money for quantum thought. It falls between the science and soc departments, and they're too busy fighting for money to trust each other."

"Touché," I said. One of my biggest stories in the fall had been about faculty scrapping over research funding.

He leaned back on his throne in exhaustion. "Why'd you let me smoke that blunt?"

"Sorry."

That made him laugh. "I'm not a scientist. I can't always explain what works or why or how come. But I know quantum thought has worked in my house."

"Really?"

"How do you think I manage to get along with my mother? My brothers couldn't do it. Chris, man. He could not get a handle on her to save himself, and all I did was shift my vision. I *see* myself as bigger than her. I *know* the responses I want from her. After I started seeing my energy as being bigger than her energy, she started to react like it was real. It had *become* real."

"So . . . how does she act now?"

He leaned forward and grabbed my arm for emphasis while laughing victoriously. "You've read Torey Adams's whole website and you met her in the flesh this afternoon. You'd think she was a bull rhino. News flash: My mother is a small child. It's just covered up in all this bluster. She drinks from the part of herself that is a small child. She cleans and scrubs and takes care of the house, me, her dad, all day, but at night she's a scared kid. And the nights are starting earlier all the time, if you get my drift. I almost wish she *weren't* such a small child."

I thought of Officer Hughes's emphatic statement that she never left the house after three. Was cocktail hour starting at three? Alcoholism is a progressive illness, and she could easily be . . . *His mother my mother his mother my mother* . . . Images started diving through each other frantically.

"You're inspiring me," I had to confess.

Obviously, contacting my mother was not something that would happen tomorrow or even this year. I had never been a fast mover. But if he were onto something that magical, there were some *maybe*s in my future.

Maybe shifting my energy could keep my mom in boundaries. *Maybe* I could march back into my own home, using this type of energy I had never really thought about. *Maybe* my mother would respond differently.

It was an epiphany moment. RayAnn had gone off

toward the water and I hadn't heard her return. I just felt her hand on my shoulder, and I laced my fingers absently through hers.

"Are you thinking about going home?" she whispered. We had just talked the night before about how maybe I could *write* about myself and my own life in twenty years.

"Uh . . . no. Capital *N*," I said dizzily. "For the moment, I'm just enjoying Justin's lessons in quantum thought. It's, well, kind of interesting."

Justin jumped up excitedly, climbed over the rocks, and moved to a lightning tree, my eyes following his one shoulder. I was suddenly feeling cautious. He hadn't said anything so far that I didn't believe myself. I'd forgotten for a moment that he was stoned and might be prone to lapses in judgment.

He was touching one of the lightning trees—very much the way I had touched one the night before. It was a freaky coincidence watching him do exactly what I had done on instinct, taking in the same deep breaths.

"I know I can find my brother this way. I can use quantum thought to bring Chris back."

Hearing that made me draw a line in the sand. I believed in the power of my own thoughts to bring me good results. He believed—

"I touch this tree, and I focus, and a lot of the time I

can get an image in my head of where my brother is. I have gotten his attention. I have made him think of me. I'm drawing him back to me."

"What is he doing?" whispered RayAnn, close to me.

I scowled at the sky, which was now dark with cloud cover, making it seem more like sundown than three-something. It didn't feel like rain, but I suddenly felt nervous and a little foolish. I settled on sarcasm. "I think he's being a loadie."

FIFTEEN

THE ONE THING I DIDN'T DOUBT, due to personal experience, was that if I got too close to Justin, he would sense my skepticism. A part of me related—this place could make you believe weird things were true—but he was carried away, and I was afraid the results could be devastating to him.

But he didn't sense my negative energy. In fact, he beckoned me closer. I didn't move, and he didn't seem to notice that either.

"I'm not always good at this," he confessed, shutting his eyes tighter while clutching the trunk. "You've had your personality tests, and I've had mine. Getting diagnosed as bipolar started with a symptom that kept getting me in trouble in school. When my mind races, I can't slow down and observe things like other people do. I can't tell when I'm hurting people's feelings and when I'm being inappropriate. They say most people learn that just from watching others' responses to them. I . . . don't watch. So, the fact that this has even worked for me a few times—that I can see details of a person I'm not even looking at—is utterly amazing."

"Okay . . ." I said, though "utterly fictional" seemed more reasonable. "What exactly have you done?"

"I *saw* him. It was *not* my imagination. I had never seen this place before, had no reason to throw it into my own head. It was just a big, dark room filled with guys. Looked like an army barracks. Lots of guys' voices . . ."

"Looked like an army barracks," I parroted. It kind of reminded me of psychics always saying things like "You'll find the missing person in a watery grave." Pacific, Atlantic, Lake Superior always seemed to be missing among the details.

"What did he look like?" I settled on.

"I don't know. It's more like . . . I was *in him*. I was seeing the place through his wet eyes. He was crying about something. I think his soul reaches out when he's upset. Because this other time I saw him, he was also crying. This is why I don't tell my friends much. They'd think he was some sort of a ghost if they heard this one. But one time I felt like

I was seeing though his eyes, he was passing through a cemetery. He was reading all the names on the tombstones."

I felt a little weird. Memories charged through me—of seeing the trees under the glow of a white moon last night, of Kobe Lydee calling upon the dead, of RayAnn seeing lightning come from the ground, of my mother manifesting in a terribly abusive dream . . .

I found myself framing out the edges of the field, far off, and into the darkened woods, looking for—

Stop, my generally stable mind shouted to me. *Stop and find common sense here.*

"Justin. Stop obsessing and talk to me."

"About what?" He opened his red eyes and watched me. Skepticism must have been written all over my face, because he said, "What? You think I'm being a loadie, right? You can think what you want. But two weeks after I did this last time, I got two e-mails from my brother, and I hadn't heard from him in five years."

I so wanted to get a look at them, but that was for later. "I'm not trying to put a damper on this, Justin. But let's stop ignoring the elephant in the living room. What drugs were you on?"

"Listen," he said defensively, "the laws of quantum thought will work for anyone. It's like falling out of an airplane. Whether you're a good person or a bad person, drunk, sober, or anything else, you will hit the ground. When you have a strong wish—"

"Were you all drugged out?" I repeated.

"No . . ." he countered with a halfhearted stab at patience, and he surprised me: "I'm a little drugged out *now*. That night was before my rampage started. In fact, that night *brought on* my drug rampage, because I was desperate to get it back . . . get those visions back. Get more e-mails . . ."

Okay . . . I rolled my eyes, which he couldn't see due to my glasses, but he couldn't have missed the sigh. I figured a little disappointment now might help prevent a deluge of it in the future. I tried to keep my voice even. "Here's my *biggest* problem with what you're saying. I believe I can manage *myself* better with positive thinking, which is natural and normal. What you're saying is that you can manage *others*. The problem is that others have desires, too."

"You think . . . I imagined this because I was getting manic," he suggested, which also was a possibility, but it hadn't been my thought. He just didn't get it.

"No, I think you're being a Creed. Whether it was your mom out here today, or your brother disappearing, or you feeling like you're going to get your brother back no matter what . . . It's always about *that person's* needs. To hell with everyone else. Your brother *needed* to disappear. Didn't you get that from Adams's story? From your own life? It might serve *your* needs to get him to come out of hiding, but what about *his* needs? Your mom feels one thing, that she's going to find out where you are and seize control of the situation, Justin. The fact that you're probably better off without her while you're trying to get a grip is utterly lost on her. What about *your* needs? Honest to God, I've never seen a family more likely to self-destruct."

"We're selfish," he breathed, his eyes darting from side to side.

"You just don't think, that's all. I highly doubt Chris was thinking about the reverb his disappearance would cause all over this town. As for you, look at yourself, knocking on our motel room door in the middle of the night."

"What about it?" His eyes burned through me defensively. "Would you have preferred I slept out here when I heard thunder?"

"No. But what were you thinking when you did it? Were you thinking of the jolt that would go through two travelers, hearing that pounding at four a.m., in something akin to the Bates Motel?"

He shook his head slowly, and I could see his mind working, trying to make sense of this.

"Well?"

"I . . . thought it was funny," he said, his eyes twinkling once before fading out. "Make a grand entrance . . ."

"Do you see what I'm saying? You were thinking about *Justin. Justin* is not the center of the universe."

"Well, neither is my brother!" he yelled, and banged on the tree with his fist.

"No, he's not," I agreed. "But who in your family is going to be the first to break the I-I-me-me cycle before it continues to spread all over town? Who's the strongest?"

I'd sensed since he'd approached the tree that his racing mind was defeating the effects of the dulling weed. He went on almost too quickly to think of something this clever: "Do you mean between the drunken, bipolar mom, the druggie, bipolar kid, the autistic man incapable of getting emotionally involved in anything, or the whips-and-chains punk?"

My grin returned. "And don't forget the brother who's a vacuum . . . with the suspected hint of autism."

"How could I forget *him?*" His eyes filled up, which I wasn't sure was such a bad thing.

I was hoping Justin might find moderation, quit going for the energy-charged manipulation tricks, and maybe give his brother's return up to the Higher Power.

But Justin hadn't been in rehab very long. He should not have signed himself out, I suddenly became aware of again, as his determination slipped behind some blackened, pent-up rage that maybe I should have been more prepared to see. Bipolars can jump to outrage quickly, according to some website I'd scanned for class. He screamed loud enough to draw RayAnn up to me again, both hands on my shoulders, all but propping me up.

"It's *not* going to be me this time! It's *always* me! I'm the one stuck doing *everything!* You have no idea what I have been through, you dumb-ass! I hate you!" He popped me in the chest with all ten fingers, but I was too numb to feel it. "I don't know why I wanted to come home to help you!"

"Justin—" I watched helplessly as he turned and ran off toward the path.

"Chase him—" I said to RayAnn, then held on to her hand in case she tried to. He might accidentally hurt her.

But RayAnn's fingers were dug into my shoulders, and I sensed she was looking in another direction.

"We've got other problems," she murmured.

Justin turned back and shouted, "It's *me* people ought to be writing about! Not my stupid, runner brother, you stupid—"

Suddenly he froze, too, looking past my shoulder, where I sensed RayAnn was looking. I turned, somewhere in my mind hearing her cell phone camera clicking away.

It was like lightning coming up from the ground, as if a bolt of lightning were buried and trying to make its way out.

The corpse I saw last night thrust itself to the front of my brain, and in the flashes of light I saw it across the field, standing straight up, its jaw unhinged, its teeth bared in that forever vacated smile of the dead.

"Darla—" came out of my mouth, and I fought to keep from swaying as Justin came up behind me again. The light was gone now, almost as if it had fulfilled its purpose and imploded into some mysterious black void. I thought I saw a line of smoke lingering, then decided it was my imagination.

"Did you *see that?*" he demanded.

He ran as far as the swampy area, probably loaded with snakes, and then stopped. His body slumped as he leaned his head in his hands. I forced myself to stay put, to not run to him, and to hear what RayAnn had to say about this.

"Are you all right?" she asked.

"I'm great," I said, though my breathing was out of control, like a whizzing firework on the Fourth of July. "What'd you see?"

"You just said the name Darla," she said with a tone implying that it was crazy. I didn't know how to answer. Hallucination? No, Justin saw it, too, and I'd never dropped acid—

She stuck the camera under my face, though it was hard to notice all the details of her fifteen shots while Justin was screaming, "Chris! Chris! I see you, man! Come out!"

RayAnn's iPhone could take HD images. I watched as

she flashed them, illuminating beautiful flashes of lightning, crystal clear in the tiny frame. Jolts, forks, no skeletal remains, and certainly no Chris Creed. She watched as I did.

"I only saw lightning," she said. "That's it. Same as last night."

Justin was still screaming, *"Chris! Come ba-ack!"*

"What do we have here?" I stumbled. Because I was thinking of Torey Adams's mom saying, "These woods make a body see . . . what a body wants to see . . ."

SIXTEEN

JUSTIN CHARGED ACROSS THE SWAMPY PART of the lightning field to get to "his brother," deaf to our screams of warning. Saltwater swamps in Jersey are snake pits, and though he appeared to get all the way across to the woods on the other side, we were not manic enough to try it.

So we did the five-minute walk to the car in maybe four, drove into a few cul-de-sacs on Route 9 before getting the right street, and parked on the other side of the lightning field. I took Lanz this time for his good sniffer. There were five trails, and when we finally found the one that backed up to the lightning field, there was no sign of Justin—or any-thing, for that matter, except woods and a foundation of what appeared to have once been an old farmhouse.

It was, by then, after four o'clock. I tried not to worry about Justin, but it was hard. I wanted to kick his hairbrained butt—his first and then his mother's for trying to manipulate him home for his much-needed dose of medication.

Let him go, I told myself. He'd found his way to rehab; he'd found his way home many nights before, sometimes far more loaded than he was now. To search for him any further would be to become part of his family's illness.

I felt frustrated as RayAnn and I looked down the list of townspeople we'd hoped to contact, including the princi-pal and the mayor. Now it was probably too late. Our flight took off at eleven tomorrow morning, which meant we had to be at the airport at nine, had to leave here by seven to re-turn the car, etc. It was a tough decision: Do we run around trying to get people to talk to us, or do we stake out the Adams residence? I felt pretty sure that Adams might eat dinner with his family, but he would probably go out at some point to visit the Richardson clan, meet Ali, or at least go to CVS for something he forgot to pack. I could approach him nicely and see if I could sweet-talk him into an inter-view. We decided on the stakeout.

We got "shorties" from the Wawa, this miraculous hoagie Adams had written about, for which there was no counterpart in the Midwest. Starved, we sucked the juice of onions, provolone cheese, and maybe four different types of ham while parked at the edge of a patch of woods that separated the Adams house from the road. I couldn't see if his mother had returned from the airport, as they had a garage without windows and were orderly enough to keep the cars behind doors.

As the sun set, woods loomed before me in all directions.

"Okay. So what *was* that?" I asked again as we sat in the car.

RayAnn stared out over the dashboard. "I surfed for strange lightning occurrences last night until I was cross-eyed. I need my hard drive at home. I need my password vault so I can get into specific databases. *National Geographic* would be a start, though my family subscribes to maybe twenty different scientific journals."

I nodded dejectedly. None of that would do us any good right now.

I picked her iPhone up off the dash for the fourth time and clicked again through the series of frames she'd taken. RayAnn and her sisters were rife with whatever electronic toys would help them study, but her iPhone amazed me. The special camera add-on she had could take fifteen frames in a second. Numbers seven and eight of the strange lightning images made me pause yet again. The way the lightning flash twisted around itself, you could possibly believe you were looking at a skeleton. But lightning flashes so fast that your mind can't process it in real time. So the effect is a "*What* did I just see?" almost while it's still happening. Strange, very strange.

"It's very understandable, Mike," she said, dropping her sandwich and staring into the dashboard. "But we're two levelheaded people. Justin is out of hand. You saw a skeleton; he obviously saw his brother. I'm wondering if it was a horrible idea for him to leave rehab."

I knew that I was doing the right thing to ignore my worries about Justin, but it was ripping my chest open nonetheless. I tossed my hoagie down on the sandwich paper and I laid my head back and shut my eyes.

RayAnn dropped her hand in mine and squeezed. "Mike, you are the most courageous person I know. Whatever it is you're thinking, don't torture yourself."

All I could think to say was "You're not too bad yourself."

She was actually pretty close to perfect in my mind. I tried switching tracks, focusing my thoughts on finding any bad behavior from RayAnn today, and the only thing I could come up with was speaking French in front of Justin.

It had sounded arrogant. I joked, "You were being kind of a snob today."

She laughed immediately, as if I had hit into her thoughts. "I was being rotten, but not snobbish. Reality check: I'm three days past sixteen, and I go to school with a bunch of very smart people who are tons older than I am. I am low man on the totem pole. Where would I find room in my life to have snobby thoughts?"

Good point.

"Just for the record," she said, "if you hear me speaking French? It means I'm scared. I'm blurting in a panic because I don't know what else to do. And I didn't want Justin to know what I was saying."

Learn something new every day. I opened my eyes and found hers. They were laughing now, but her face was red—and young. She looked vulnerable.

"You were scared of Justin?" I asked, reaching over and picking up a strand of her rusty hair. I was used to thinking of RayAnn as being *my* age, but she was *his* age. "He's a ball of energy right now, but I don't think violence is his MO either. I'm just going on instinct, but I'm not the least bit afraid of him—"

"It's not just him . . . it's this whole place." She leaned her head on my hand, soaking up my sympathies. "You're always talking about energy. It's like the energy of all these depressed people hangs around out there, gets caught up with the . . . the remnants of the lightning charges, or something. Steepleton really does seem like it's under bad frequency . . . if there is such a thing. So much has gone wrong here. I know there's good kids everywhere and there's mean kids everywhere. I'm not naïve. I wish I could find the right words for Justin and his friends. They're just a little . . . edgier?"

"Eat," I said. "You need sustenance. You're running on zero fuel and only slightly more sleep."

She reached past Lanz in the back seat and struggled until she had her laptop. "I can look up those articles now on the cancer rates and the car accidents."

She put her feet in my lap and sat sideways so she could fit the computer in her lap without it banging the steering wheel. She surfed with one hand and ate with the other.

"Here's the one about the cancer," she finally said. "The nature of the article is that North Jersey has all the New York City suburb populations, but they should not suffer health insurance rate increases that South Jersey gets to sidestep. More people doesn't mean more problems in this case."

She read, " 'The state's highest cancer rate is Steepleton, a mainland suburb of Atlantic City, nearly eighty miles south of Exit 125 on the Parkway.' I take it that Exit 125 is some sort of a landmark separating the north from the south of the state," she finished.

I ate slowly, feeling slightly off balance in connecting this straight-on, news-diction report with the twisting bramble of legend evolving out of these woods.

There were actually three articles about the car accidents—one for each accident. RayAnn couldn't find any article that tied them together in some sort of weird, ethereal relationship. But one car had smashed into a telephone poll on Leeds Point Road. Two others were overturned—one in a ditch and one in a creek that ran close to the sides of back roads leading through the woods down to the bay. In all cases, all parties died. That made seven fatalities in three years, and yes, that is a really high mortality rate for any small jurisdiction. I didn't think Randolph had more than two auto-related deaths in the past ten years.

"The only weird thing in my mind is that there's no mention of what caused the accidents. They all just say people died. Was it ice?" I asked.

She jumped from screen to screen. "One was in May, two years ago. Others might have been."

She shook her head slightly while sipping Diet Coke. "Obviously, we're not presuming that the Jersey Devil jumped out into the middle of the road, spooking drivers to amuse himself."

"I think not."

"Nor is Chris Creed doing that."

I meant to sigh, but it came out as a long moan. I was clueless as to a next viable step. Hence, we sat for almost another half-hour, going through notes and writing leads in our heads, until a car came down the road and turned in to the Adamses' driveway. It was totally dark by now, so we stepped out of the car and pulled back some bramble to get a view of the person.

A tall guy with short brown hair stepped out into the house's floodlights, slamming the door of an old Buick.

"My God," I said. "That's Bo Richardson."

He went to the door, and before he could buzz the bell, it opened. I got a glimpse of Adams wrapping his arms around the guy's shoulders and slapping him affectionately on the back before they both stepped inside and closed themselves away from us again.

"Dang, but to have that Ring of Power Justin mentioned last night," I whispered, in awe.

"You want to risk getting near an open window?" RayAnn asked.

I admired her spunk, but a lack of training had prompted the question. "If they were suicide bombers, the public's right to know might merit eavesdropping. *This* would amount to tabloid gossip-mongering."

We got back in the car. I felt so restless, I could have clawed the ceiling, but my instincts told me that Richardson, being part of the grieving family, wouldn't stay here all night.

RayAnn reopened her laptop, if just to have some light, and put her feet back on me. She scratched one foot with the other until I reached down and rubbed the arches of her feet through her socks.

"Tired?" I asked her. "We've been chasing around quite a bit, what with three trips to the Lightning Field."

"Nah, I'm good," she said. "I love moments like this."

"Like what?"

"When I feel like I have you all to myself."

I grinned at her, a little perplexed. But then, it did seem that when we were together it was often in a clutter of either people or paperwork—half-written stories and half-finished papers for classes, Claudia hanging over our shoulders, other reporters banging around in the office.

"We spend a lot of time in my dorm room," I noted, then quickly added, "when Stedman isn't there."

"I don't mind Stedman," she said. "He's sincere and likable."

If I'd had any sort of judgmental or selfish roommate when I had my accident, I might not be in college right now. I had to agree, though I noticed a click in her voice.

"I'm sorry," I said, awkwardly. "I feel like I'm always tied up, distracted."

She said nothing, only continued to watch me, and I knew that "tied up" and "distracted" were choices—like everything else in my life. RayAnn's presence simply hadn't changed those choices. A good part of me wanted to go full-throttle ahead into this relationship, but I was poised at the edge of a cliff and couldn't fall into that dive to the water far below. I simply couldn't relax. *Right person . . . wrong time?* How could I make it the right time? *Aren't I in charge of my own destiny?* If I couldn't get it right with RayAnn, could I expect to fare any better with the *New York Times* in two years?

"I have dragons to slay," I said.

"What do you mean?"

"I mean, it's like you're the fairy princess and I have to slay the dragons before I can truly have you."

In the light of her laptop, I could see her head falling and rising, like she understood me.

"Well. If I'm in it, it has to be a modern-day fairy tale. In other words, the princess gets to fight the dragons, too."

She took my fingers in hers, brought them to her lips, and kissed them. Her devotion wafted up my arm and into my neck, giving me flash images of boa constrictors. I reached my hand into her hair again, trying to ignore this latest scary imagery, but feeling sad.

I said, "But the dragons aren't after the princess."

A bit of shifting light from the Adamses' house revealed the front door opening, and Richardson came through it. Adams remained in the doorway, though they exchanged words as Bo walked backwards to his car. I rolled down the window quickly. We were more than a stone's throw away, but the driveway was far from the house, too. For once, we got a little lucky.

". . . can't get away until eleven, probably," Richardson was saying. Then I heard the words "Ali" and "ten" and "right now . . . find Justin."

That was it. I didn't bother asking if RayAnn heard something more. My ears had gotten ten times more acute since my accident, and sure enough, as Richardson jumped back into his car, she asked, "Did you get any of that?"

"Ali's arriving in town about ten, but he can't break away from his family until around eleven. Right now he's going to find Justin," I said.

She whistled long, impressed. "He's going to Justin's house?"

We watched as his car came out of the drive. Steepleton would be to his left. The Lightning Field would be a right. He made a right.

SEVENTEEN

As WE PULLED UP TO THE TRAIL leading to the Lightning Field, RayAnn confirmed that Bo Richardson's car wasn't parked anywhere around.

"Damn. Maybe he decided to go home," I said, frustrated. "Obviously Justin comes first, but I thought I could talk to him, get him to influence Adams . . ."

"What do you want to do?" RayAnn asked.

Going to either the Richardson or the Burden household was above my level of expertise as a journalist, and I couldn't even fathom it. I thought of calling Claudia for a fast lesson, but I felt too restless.

"We're here. Might as well go see if the boy is back at his home away from home."

There were no cars parked where RayAnn left ours, but as we walked the trail for the fourth time in twenty-four hours, I noticed shiny bits of metal in the little scenes I could take in. There were about ten bikes stashed in the bushes along the way. Word must have gotten out that Justin had come back.

The moon was so bright that I didn't need to hold on to RayAnn's arm, though we had left Lanz in the car. My instincts were telling me to leave him in case somebody else pushed me tonight and he decided to play guard dog and bite. RayAnn didn't appear nervous this time, and I guessed she was getting used to the place.

It took us a long time to navigate the field, but we heard laughter and music coming from down by the water, and near the rock pile we saw fire. Someone had brought two of those flame torches you can buy for summer barbecues, and they were lit on either side, throwing an orange glow onto a couple of faces I could spot. There also appeared to be a bonfire going on closer to the water.

"There's thirteen that I can count," RayAnn told me.

"You see Justin?" I heaved a sigh of relief as I suddenly heard him singing along with music coming from a boom box. *Not bitten by a snake . . . not super depressed.*

We found Justin in the same place we'd left him, but now he was surrounded by six or seven girls. I spotted Taylor Hammond, but not Mary Ellen right off. It was smoky. Cigarettes and marijuana. I didn't let myself cough this time.

"It's the journalism jocks!" Justin said cheerily as we came around the rock and into his view, all signs of his earlier hate for me gone.

"Are you all right?" I asked immediately, finding his face. He was smiling as if the whole thing this afternoon had never happened, but he put a finger to his grin in a secretive way. I gathered he didn't want to hear a load of grief over how he'd interpreted the strange bursts of light, though I had no idea whether he still thought he'd seen his brother. He looked stabilized, which made me wonder if he'd taken his medication or something in lieu of it.

"Meet . . ." He said maybe six names, and other kids were laughing and talking behind us, down by the bonfire.

"This is my harem," he concluded, with a healthy sweep of his arm.

I heard some *eff-you*s and sensed some sign language flipped at him, but none of these girls seemed to be moving away. He did look a little like a modern King Solomon, plopped in the middle of this group.

"You guys want chips?" he asked. "We got chips. You want a beer?"

I shook my head and don't know what RayAnn did. This impromptu party was certainly no eye-opener compared to living in a dorm, but I could tell she was uncomfortable.

"Do you want lawn chairs? We have lawn chairs." Justin jumped up and sprang over the rock pile, and we heard him calling, "Kobe! Give up those lawn chairs."

"Why?"

"Because I said to. We have out-of-town guests. Get the fuck up."

"Oh! Are those reporters back?" Mary Ellen's voice rang out. I spotted her shooting up out of a lawn chair that Justin was all but jerking out from under her. She and Kobe followed him as he dragged back two chairs.

Taylor was sitting close to me, and considering all she'd told me at the crime scene last night, I mumbled to her, "Is he behaving himself?"

"Well enough," she said with a sigh. "He's drinking a beer. *That* we can deal with."

I rolled my eyes, feeling helpless. Mary Ellen scooted around Justin and grabbed my arm, announcing to the harem, "This is Mike. He's blind. But he is very cool. Be nice to him or I will knock you senseless."

"Why?" asked a girl who was smoking with one hand and studying her nails on the other. "When was the last time you saw me be nice to anybody?"

"Last time I kicked your ass."

Unfortunately the girl took Mary Ellen's threat as a challenge. She got up, put her arms around my neck, and stroked the back of my head. It was pure sarcasm. She reminded me of Julia Stiles in some evil-chick movie role.

"Should I be nice to you?" She had snake eyes, full of bluster.

I felt RayAnn lose it beside me, sink down into a lawn chair, and mutter, ". . . like an episode of *Women Behind Bars*."

I turned and found her eyes. In high school RayAnn had spent many a weekend going mountain climbing or hiking or skiing with a crew of a dozen or so homeschooled kids. But she told me she'd found herself at only three or four parties like this in all of her pre-college years. She'd said she preferred being in an outhouse with the door shut to the smell of stale cigarettes and stale brew. I had been at even less. One, I think. We'd been a coupla dorks. But once you get to college, it's all history, I tried to remind myself.

"You're on your own," she said hotly, *"si tu vis a rester ici avec ces perdants."* If you really must stay here with these creatures.

I didn't feel like I had a choice at the moment. I unwrapped the girl's arms from my neck, realizing I could get her claws in my face next, but I was doing my best to hunt for where Justin was.

Behind me. He shoved the lawn chair into the back of

my knees until I sat. The girl sat in my lap. "I don't understand why I should be nice to you," she said, flipping the
bird in my face, probably something about Mary Ellen saying I was blind.

She was jerked up so quickly that she screamed. "*Ouch!*
Tear out my hair, why don't you?"

"You want me to?" Justin twisted her arm around until
she sat down on the rocks, cussing a blue streak. "Don't be
stupid, Deanna. He's got a girlfriend here. He wants you as
bad as he wants an STD. He *can* see, and he just saw what
you did in his face. C'mon. Do it in *my* face."

"Just leave it alone," I suggested to him, seeing that he
had probably scared the girl half to death.

Having Justin Creed in your face could be a bit shocking,
but to my amazement this Deanna girl put her head on her
knee and started crying, rubbing her sore and shocked head. I
seemed to remember from high school that the meanest girls
are the first to fall out when someone is mean to them.

Justin started explaining his behavior to me, though he
rubbed her hair. "Ooops. I'm not watching again. Remember I said the counselors always told me I don't watch people?
Not good with the details. Deanna, I only got about six of
your hairs wrapped around my fingers! Here . . . you want
'em back?"

She gave him a good piece of her mind, until he took

both of her cheeks in his hands and kissed her on the forehead. "You're right about everything. You feel better now?"

He crawled back up onto his throne. My next problem was Mary Ellen, who didn't sit in my lap but knelt beside me and threw her arm around me like we were best friends.

"Mike got me to turn over a new leaf!" she announced loudly. "I'm not going to be a bitch anymore."

A thunder of clapping and laughter sounded off, and I realized we were surrounded by at least a dozen people.

"How'd you get her to do that?" Some guy raised a bottle to the moon for a swallow.

I didn't get the impression that these people found Mary Ellen especially mean. It was just one of those funny, mutual punch lines that everyone thinks of at once. Still, I sensed that a part of her wanted to be serious.

"Mike is a great listener. And he asks good questions. He made me realize that I have an evil side. And I don't want to have an evil side. So, I don't have to."

"Ooooh, let's test her out!" I recognized Kobe Lydee's voice and a sound like a steel-toed boot kicking a sneaker sole. He cracked up laughing, but it was way too hard a kick, and Mary Ellen screamed in pain.

I found Justin's face, the balls of his hands to his temples. "Children . . . children!" he let go and yelled. "Apologize, Kobe, you moron!"

Kobe simply fell over on his side, howling with laughter at the sky.

"You broke my ankle, fool!"

"Let me see it!" Justin beckoned to her, and she skidded away from me up the rock until her foot was in his lap. "*Who* threw this party, eh? *Who* paid for all these refreshments, brought out these lawn chairs stolen from his own backyard, and lit these stinky torches?"

"You did . . . you did . . ." voices chimed.

"Because I can take all my refreshments and buzz on out of here and end this thing as quickly as it started." The mood dropped from a twelve to about a four. "Why did I bring you all out here tonight?"

Nobody answered right away. He was looking down Mary Ellen's sock, asking her to wiggle her toes. He took her word for it that she could, as her foot was in a sneaker.

"It's a bruise," he said, rearranging her jeans back down over her sock and patting her calf. "You'll live."

"But it hurts!"

He stared around at everyone, opening his arms, and she fell into them. *Smooth, smooth. Who would have ever thought Chris Creed's brother?* These kids were well into whatever brew he had packed away down by the water, were dangerously unstable, but he told them to simmer down and they simply did it. *He got what he expected.* When he was among this many people, his mania made him seem like the leader, the life of the party. It appeared like a plus instead of a minus.

"I want everyone to have fun, but why are we here? Why do I need my friends around me right now?"

Nobody said anything.

"Hel-lo?" he tried again.

Mary Ellen finally answered. "Because some of us have been seeing lights. Across the field. Out in the woods."

I sensed heads turning, and I turned slowly to find the place that had lit up this afternoon.

"They're all looking at that same spot," RayAnn murmured. "Definitely we're not the only people to have seen it. There's nothing over there now."

"The foundation is still there," Kobe said, nudging me, "of the house where the Jersey Devil was born. The infamous home of Mother Leeds and her thirteenth child . . ."

"Did you *have* to bring him?" Justin asked Mary Ellen. "Dude! There is no Jersey Devil, and you are so lucky I'm so unsober. I will break *your* ankle later."

"I'm entitled to my free speech," Kobe said in a disarming voice. I didn't get the feeling either of them was looking for a fight.

"I saw the light this afternoon, and I have two witnesses." Justin pointed emphatically at RayAnn and me. I felt a lot of eyes on me and heard RayAnn saying "We did see a light."

There were some *oooohs* and claps of approval, as if we had expertise of some sort. I didn't sense RayAnn bringing out her iPhone for further explanation, and that was a good thing, too. It occurred to me that Justin's friends had come to love him when he was slightly manic like this. His confidence was huge. It gave others confidence, not understanding that he was walking a tightrope.

"You know what *I* think that light is. Today I was totally positive I saw my brother over there, waving a lantern. I ran over and by the time I got there I was, like, doubting myself. What did you guys see?"

"It . . . was weird," I said, and let it be. I felt torn, wanting to show him the frames RayAnn took and explain, but also wanting to protect him from devastation in front of his friends.

"I have good reason to think it is my brother. If my brother comes walking out of those woods tonight, I will need my friends around me, so they can tote me to the hospital when I have my heart attack. If my brother *doesn't* come walking out of those woods tonight, I will need my friends around me because I will be super depressed, and you can stop me from throwing myself in the water, okay?"

"What makes you think it's your brother?" one girl asked.

I took it some of these people did not have all the inside scoop, because she asked seriously. Nobody who had the inside scoop laughed.

His jaw bobbed a couple times, and out of his mouth finally came "Because I tried quantum thought to bring him here. And then I get these two e-mails, and then people start seeing lights out in the woods. You can say quantum thought is not real all you want. But nobody can argue with how this happened. *He's out there. I can feel it.*"

He gazed at the spot where we'd seen the light, invisible to me now, over my left shoulder and across the field. I rolled my eyes privately.

"Can we . . . go over there and search around?" the same girl asked.

"If you like water moccasins," Justin said. "I got lucky today, but I'm not trying it again unless we see those lights."

"What's a water moccasin?" RayAnn whispered to me.

"Poisonous snakes. Indigenous to New Jersey," I whispered back. I could tell she was staring at me, but I was staring at Justin.

"I understand there was a torrential downpour yesterday when I was still up at rehab. The field on that side of the woods turns into a swamp, and unless you've got army boots, you're likely to get an ankle full of venom."

"What are you going to do if you see him?" the girl asked. Good question.

Justin said, "If I see my brother, then I will know that quantum thought has worked. In that case, I will wish protection all over myself from the water moccasins, knowing I will receive it, because I got it the first time. I will simply run the hell over there."

I could hear Kobe mumbling under his breath, and this time Justin picked up on it.

"Look. Whoever thinks I'm loony tunes, go the fuck down by the water and get out of my personal space. I'm not kidding. I'm not laying a hand on anybody; just go. I don't want people's doubt mixing up with my belief and tainting it. Not tonight. If you're a doubter, I will be able to single you out if you hang around. And then I will knock the shit out of you."

It took about ten seconds for a couple of jackets to rustle, and maybe four or five people went down by the water, including Kobe. The rest stayed.

"So, what do we have to do now?" the same girl asked.

"Nothing," Justin said. "It's all been done. Just wait. Believe. Have a party. Cavort and—"

Justin didn't get to finish. What was suddenly shining from that spot across the field was a large, very real flashlight, in the hands of a male. A silhouette was moving this way, water moccasins or not. A bunch of girls screamed so loud, I thought Lanz probably went deaf way back at the car.

EIGHTEEN

J USTIN WAS GOOD TO HIS WORD, rising from the rocks and sprinting to a point about fifty feet closer, but then he stopped dead in his tracks. We all moved to him, and I got locked in a clatter of shoulders, unable to find RayAnn.

"It's not my brother . . . go back . . . not my brother," Justin was saying, though I was unclear on how he knew that.

"It's *alive*," another girl added, and I hoped to God it wasn't the cops. Chief Rye would not likely share anything further with me if he found me out here partying with the underworld again. A flashlight beam shined in all our faces, so I couldn't see who it was until he was almost on top of us. I should have guessed.

Richardson stopped in front of Justin, who was swaying dangerously.

"Oh my God, Bo. You scared the life out of me."

"Return my texts and e-mails, and I won't have to chase you down." He clapped Justin on the back of the neck and pulled him close. Justin embraced the guy, who was tall and strappy and lean—typical army recruit. I was actually shocked. I expected someone a lot bigger. His eyes were big and black, but sad. He made an attempt at a smile.

"Jeezus, this place has changed. Used to be a boon hangout." He kept his arm around Justin, talking to everyone as we made our way back to the rock pile. "Only, back then, we hung out on the north side of the field and this side was water moccasin heaven. Amazing how a few northeast storms will change things. And back then, we had more trees. I know a guy, says he was out here the night the lightning struck in . . . what? Thirty-five places?"

We reached the rocks, but Justin didn't sit down this time. The kids were riveted, and the girl with all the questions finally asked, "What does he say happened?"

"He usually doesn't. He sits in the house taking meals through a straw. It blew all his teeth out. Now, there's one rumor that's probably true. Anyway . . ."

I heard some whispers behind me, to the effect of "Who is this guy?" It seemed Justin's relationship with Bo was separate from his school friendships.

"What's up with you?" Richardson asked him, holding the back of Justin's neck and kind of pulling him backwards, away from him. "You look like shit. I never expected you to turn into the stellar athlete Matt is, but what is this I hear blowin' on a breeze? You're not turning into a junkie. No way, my man."

"No . . . it's complicated." Justin kind of collapsed into a sit at the edge of a rock, and Bo sat beside him, his arm glued around Justin's shoulder. "Sorry. You just scared the hell out of me, that's all. I thought you were Chris."

"You thought I was *who*?" Bo did a double take, checking the path where he came from, then eyeing Justin suspiciously.

"Never mind . . . long story," Justin said.

"I ain't got time for long stories." Bo looked around at the crowd, finally making an introduction. "Hi. I'm Bo, Darla Richardson's brother. I used to party down here, too. You mind if I give you some advice?"

Nobody said anything.

"This is a place you should come on, like, the Fourth of July. And maybe Memorial Day. That's it. *Get a job.* Go ring up a cash register somewhere. If you're old enough to smoke weed and get laid, you're too old to be saying to your old lady, 'Ma, can I have twenty bucks to go out?' Get. A job."

Bo hadn't changed much in his speech-giving ability since Adams had written about him. He made me smile. I listened through the silence to see if RayAnn was chortling, but it was deadly quiet.

"Now buzz on out of here. All of you. I gotta talk to Justin in private."

They all moved away, hot insult and disappointment ringing through the air, but nobody crossed him. I guess you don't cross a dead girl's brother, not with rumors flying that Justin knew her pretty well. To my amazement, Justin grabbed the leg of my jeans, pulling me closer to him.

"This is, uh, Mike," he said, sounding half dead all of a sudden. "And his girlfriend, who doesn't like us much . . ."

Bo reached up and shook my hand, looking me in the eye with a gaze that had lost most of its hardness. He looked like a normal guy. A sad, normal guy.

"Mike's a writer. He's from Indiana," Justin said. "He's my new hero."

"Let's call it a mutual admiration club," I said, shuffling slightly, but Justin wouldn't let go of my pant leg.

Richardson shook RayAnn's hand, looking warily at me.

"You're not supplying him, I hope," he said. "What's with the dark shades?"

"I'm . . . visually impaired," I said.

"You look like a drug runner."

"Nope. Never touch the stuff."

"And you, you look like you're about fourteen years old."

"Nope," RayAnn said glibly, and I rolled my eyes. "We write for a newspaper. Visiting from out of town."

"You're not here about my sister," Bo said with dread.

Justin still didn't let go of my pant leg. "They're writing about my brother."

Richardson looked back and forth from RayAnn to me and finally laughed, with something like impatience. I could imagine that Chris Creed would be the last thing on his mind right now.

"I don't want no newspaper people around while I'm talking to you," Richardson said, and I shifted into emergency gear. I wasn't leaving.

I turned to RayAnn and said in her ear, "Why don't you go down to the station and see if Rye left us any updates?"

She pulled back and looked at me, stricken. She glanced down at a suddenly very deflated Justin and a complete stranger. She looked all around at these woods.

"Go," I encouraged her, ignoring my own nervous feeling. "Grab some street interviews."

I pulled my cell out of my pocket and held it up with a shrug. "You got yours."

She finally backed away with uncertainty. I didn't even want to risk walking her back to the car, though I wasn't quite sure what I expected to get from this. I needed a tradeoff.

I toed Justin's sneaker, and he read my mind. "Mary Ellen!"

She was walking away with a bag of chips and a six-pack under her arm. "Walk RayAnn back to the car and don't let anything happen to her."

Mary Ellen swept an arm around RayAnn's shoulders, and they took off together. I gripped my cell phone and forced my mouth to open.

"I'm a reporter, but I'm not right now, okay? I'm just Justin's friend. See? No pens, no paper, no recorders."

"What are you guys doing, being friends?" Richardson asked warily. It must have looked like a strange mix.

Justin sighed. "It's a long story. He's from a family like mine, with a mom like mine. He relates to Chris totally, so he's . . . filling in a brotherly gap for me."

Richardson blew past it with a shrug, saying, "I got nothing to say that's private, but I don't want you flippin' in front of your fan base. I can't stay long. My mom is flippin' with guilt right now, and if I don't get back to her, she's gonna be next to wander into the Promised Land. Listen. All I want to say is this is not your fault."

I sat in the lawn chair as Justin finally let go of my pants to sink his eyes into the balls of his hands, elbows on his knees.

"Honestly," Bo went on. "A couple of Danny's better friends were at the house tonight, visiting Mom and the kids, waiting for me. They said you haven't felt right about her being gone, you felt it wasn't something good, and you felt you should have looked out for her better. I guess a lot of people thought something was amiss. I mean, the neighborhood ain't the same without her mouth going off every five seconds. If I ever thought you would take it so seriously, I would never, ever have asked you to look out for Darla."

"I'm obsessive sometimes," he said mysteriously, alluding to his recent diagnosis but not mentioning it outright. I didn't suppose that Bo needed to hear it right now.

"It was just . . . a saying. Because she was so ape shit all the time. I said the same thing to, like, ten different people. You were the only one who took it that seriously."

"I take everything too seriously," Justin continued. "But I'm getting over it . . . hopefully."

"Well, I appreciated that and all. I felt okay, you texting me every couple weeks, telling me what she was up to. It was never anything good, but if I expected you to be able to control my wild-ass sister, I would have asked you to do something about it. Did you ever hear me saying anything but 'Thanks, man'?"

Justin kept staring across the field, probably at the place where that trail came out, where people had seen lights. Bo jostled him around.

"And what's all this I'm hearing? You picked up a hefty drug habit lately?"

The way Bo said it, I wondered for the first time if the two things were related. I had no clue what Justin knew about Darla's death, and I didn't think Bo was putting the two things together. But there being a relationship between the two things was just a sudden gut instinct. I watched Justin stare at the ground, his hands on his chin.

"I-I don't know," Justin stammered. "I was in rehab, past two weeks. I'm going back. I just came home for . . . you and her."

"So, look. I know you had gotten friendly with Danny, but my feeling? Go to Darla's service now that you're here, and after that, you gotta go back to rehab and let go of the situation. Look at what you're doing to yourself! This is hard to say, her being my sister. But am I surprised?" He stood up, paced a few steps in front of us, staring at the water. "Darla's been twice in juvie, once in rehab, and she terminated a pregnancy when she was fifteen. She had three car accidents in two different cars since she started driving a year ago. Did I really expect my sister to live past the age of twenty? Not unless she calmed down, quit using, and really decided to change her life. I was off by a year. She was on a suicide mission. Somehow, she sucked Danny into following after her."

Justin raised his head but simply stared, zombified.

"I don't know when Danny's funeral is yet. But I only got three days' leave this time, and with Adams having to untangle his life to get here, my family agreed to have Darla's memorial service Monday morning," he said. "After that, go back. It had nothing to do with you, Justin."

I cleared my throat uncomfortably. "Um, I don't think Justin was aware of Danny's death before now."

Bo turned, staring. "Where have you been all day? With your head in the sand?"

"Out here," he muttered. "Where . . . what happened?"

"Your friends didn't tell you? It's been all over the news."

"My friends don't watch the news."

"Get. A. Job," Bo repeated. "You're all dangerous. Danny was found dead out in Las Vegas." He turned and sat down again, tossing his arm around Justin's shoulders. "He wrote a long, long note to his folks and brother that never got mailed, and supposedly it said that Darla committed suicide, and he was wiped out, blaming himself, and he jumped off a balcony at—" He said the name of a big casino.

"A better kid was never born than Danny Burden. My sister, dude, she started this. It's hard saying, but you know

I always tell the truth, right? I believe what Danny wrote down. We all do."

"So . . . who buried her?" Justin asked, gazing off in a zombified way.

"I'm figuring that out. Your cousins, Mack and Ozone, claim to know nothing about it, but it just smells like the Brownie's Mafia, a half-assed job with the best of intentions, okay? It was probably started by somebody who believed Danny would get blamed, trying to help out, that's all. However, the Brownie's Mafia lives down by me. They're a lot closer to my family than the Burdens. They wouldn't have done it unless somebody paid them to take a risk like that. I'll figure it out. Don't worry."

"So . . . when did Danny, um . . ." Justin asked.

"Just a few days after Darla."

Justin shut his eyes, his breath rolling out. "That's why I never heard from him. I sensed it was something awful. I always sensed it."

"Well, now you know. It's done. There was nothing you could have done to stop it. People make their own choices, and sometimes those choices suck. If I could bring either of those two kids back, I would. But I can't. So, we're gonna go forward. You're gonna get back to yourself. Quit with all this shit about bringing your brother back. I'm sure it's a great distraction from whatever you were sensing about Danny and Darla."

"My brother has nothing to do with this," he said, and I was surprised at how much conviction he could bring forth without his fan base there to believe in him like he was Peter Pan. "And he *is* coming back."

"I don't doubt it," Bo said with a shrug. "He'll get his act together, realizing your mom is not King Kong and the people here are just your normal, small-town butt-wads. As soon as he's been to enough places to see that places are all the same, he'll show up."

I didn't agree that all places were the same. I thought Steepleton was more ominous, and maybe if Bo stuck around for some extended leave, he would feel it, too.

I was staring down at the ground when I felt the energy around me pierce through with something not good. There was no sound. I realized Justin had stood up without making any noise at all. He was looking over the top of my head at the spot he could never stop looking toward.

"In fact . . . he's here," he breathed.

I turned, scanned, and this time the break in the woods wasn't hard to find. It was drumming silently with orange light, like light from a dozen orange bulbs that weren't screwed in tight enough. A mist had risen over the puddles, so I couldn't tell if it was coming from the ground or above it. For a moment I saw what made the most sense given the shape and the mist and the orange: *A lantern slowly swinging back and forth . . .*

No, I told myself, but unfortunately my brain had another brain for company . . .

"Chris?" Justin jumped practically over the top of me and ran, shouting, "Chris? Chris!"

NINETEEN

BO JUMPED AFTER HIM, and I managed to catch Bo by the back of the jacket, almost pulling myself to the ground.

"I need to come," I said, and he seemed torn.

"Snakes around there," he muttered. Then, "What the bloody hell is that light?"

Bo moved pretty quickly without running, and I just fell into his footsteps, listening to each heavy step a split second before aiming my foot in the same place. He had a flashlight and military boots on that could ground down a snake, and I tried to focus on that rather than what if water moccasins could fling themselves up my pant legs.

After a day of sun, the path to Justin was more mucky than watery, and the mist was invisible when we were right on top of it. Bo slowed about halfway across the muddy swamp land, saying, "Is he crazy, or does he really have some reason to think that his brother's over there?"

"Well . . ." I was out of breath, hardly knew where to start to a guy whose sister had just died. "Some of the kids have been seeing strange lights over there."

"Say no more," he muttered, pulling me up beside him and shining a flashlight beam on the ground. "They got some episode of *Night of the Living Dead* going on, no doubt. It's one reason I was glad to get out of town. Me, Adams, and Ali . . . we're trying to believe the guy's alive, but all the younger dudes were coming into high school, making Chris out to be the Jersey Devil's latest sidekick. That is so not cool for Justin and Matt."

Bo threw the flashlight into my hand and sprinted ahead of me by the light of the moon. "Justin! Don't touch that, man! Don't go any farther!"

I could make out the two of them ahead of me, but no flashing lights.

Justin was calling, "Chris! Chris!" into the dark woods, but Bo had him by the hood of his sweatshirt and wouldn't let him go into them. I tripped into a pile of bricks at my feet, shining the light onto them, deciding they were part of a foundation that went maybe ten feet in either direction and was in tatters, with bricks maybe five layers high in some places and only two in others. Inside the foundation was mucky water, like a stone floor was keeping water in it, with watery plants and murky rivers and bricks. I thought I saw something slither away from the light, and my stomach flip-flopped.

"Follow the trail around to your right," Bo was saying. I stepped back onto higher, firmer ground, found the path with the light, and simply put one foot in front of the other while they argued.

". . . know it was him!" Justin was saying. "He just didn't come out because of you guys! He heard you—"

"Yo, Chris!" Bo hollered. "It's just me. Your old pal Richardson. C'mon out of there."

I sighed silently, thinking how Bo did not need this. As I finally came up to them, they were sniffing the air.

"What the hell is that smell?" Justin asked.

"Something . . . burning," Richardson answered.

Something did smell scorchy, but it was hard to separate it from the smell of standing water, which was putrid.

"It's a lantern!" Justin guessed. "He was swinging it, but kind of low to the ground."

"Nobody was swinging a lantern, Justin," Bo said impatiently. "That's the mist. It can fool you."

I said nothing, letting him go on with what seemed to be the most sanity of the three of us. "If anyone was out here, they'd have a good old American flashlight. What the hell century are you in?"

Justin sniffed the air again and groaned, as the smell itself was kind of painful. *Dead bodies?* I had no idea what death smelled like, but it couldn't be much worse.

"So, what's burning?" Justin finally countered. "Flashlights don't make a smell. Maybe it's, you know, a Coleman lantern . . . one of those camping-out things."

"Dunno," Bo said, staring into the dark woods, looking for lights. "But I ain't going in those woods. On this side of the field, they're half underwater. You stick your foot on what looks like solid ground, you sink up to your knee, and a water moccasin bites you in the kneecap. And I just saw a water moc slithering through that disgusting foundation behind us."

Justin took the flashlight from me and shined it on the flooding inside the bricks. His voice was tight when he said, "Lydee tries to tell people this is the foundation of the Jersey Devil house."

The silence hung thick. None of us was going to repeat that story aloud. The Jersey Devil dines on chickens, house pets, and occasionally a small child in the Pine Barrens, if you listen to some. It leaves tracks in the woods and lurks in pine trees, staring down at you with red eyes when you walk back here alone. One week in 1908, there were so many Jersey Devil sightings across South Jersey that schools and all industry closed for a day.

And now Christopher Creed hangs out down here with the Jersey Devil, tale compliments of Kobe Lydee.

"Justin, don't listen to that garbage," I said.

He picked up a brick and hurled it into the watery foundation, and ripples curled outward. I imagined a skull floating to the top with the eyeballs still intact, and turned my face away as Justin started examining the trail with the flashlight.

"Any footprints?" Bo asked.

"My God. Lydee would have a field day with this," Justin said after a minute of flashing the light on the ground. He meant *no footprints.*

"Gimme that," Bo said, and took his flashlight back, shining it on the slithering water and then behind us in the woods. "Justin. There is nobody over here."

"So what made that light, then?"

"I . . . don't know." Bo sounded tired and frustrated when he sighed. "It could be a lot more modern of a foundation, or it could be the foundation of a home that is as old as this foundation looks, but it could have been lived in twenty or thirty years ago, which would mean it had electricity. It could mean that we're standing near a shorted wire that's buried or something. We need to get out of here."

"Short wire—that's bullshit!" Justin kept it up. "To have

any electricity, the place would have to be hooked up to the electric company. See any wires?"

He hollered his brother's name a few times, but it just echoed back to us. He turned defensive. "I've got e-mails from him!"

Yeah, two e-mails on his hard drive probably sitting ten feet from his mother. How badly did I want to see them? Badly. But I wasn't about to go running over there and have the woman accost me yet again.

"Justin, shhh. Look, I got family to take care of. And I don't have a lot of opinions on things like where dead people go, but I got this opinion: It's something electric making that light and that smell, and it's probably dangerous. There is nobody out here. Now let's go. I'm taking you home."

"So many people think he's dead," Justin said with a flicker of fear in his voice. Obviously he did battle with that possibility, but it was the closest to a confession he'd given us. "To know that he's not dead . . . that's just something I need right now. I need something good in my life."

"Don't we all, buddy." Richardson patted his back. "Let's go."

We walked back across the field in silence, watching for shiny circles indicating a deep puddle. My feet were wet but my ankles stayed dry. Justin took one last longing look over his shoulder at the far-off, darkened path.

Bo said, "Pack up your gear."

I folded the lawn chairs, but Justin just stuck them in the brush, saying nobody came down here except himself and his friends—and his mom. And if she could take off with his medication, she could lug all this stuff home, too. I shook my head, watching him make a mountain of the torches and chairs and beer cans I heard being shoved into some bushes, and we walked back to the trail. I felt bad because I was slowing him down, but Justin walked along beside me, muttering something under his breath that was indistinguishable, obviously something to try to ease his anxiety. Bo, in his army boots, navigated back across the swampy area to get his car, and he planned to pick up Justin on the road side.

I watched him for a long way, waiting to see if the ground across the field was flickering with strange lights. Justin stood beside me, saying nothing, but I knew he was doing the same. Bo disappeared into the darkness, and the only stir was the far-off sound of his car engine. We walked to the road, and Bo was already waiting when we arrived ten minutes later.

I got in the back seat like I belonged there, and Bo took off with us. I figured I would ask to be dropped off in the center of town, where I might run into RayAnn, if nothing better came of it. At least I could see the house that Bo and Adams and Ali McDermott had spied on from Ali's bedroom nearly five years ago, catching their first glimpse of the real Justin Creed, at twelve, calmly flipping the bird to his mother through his bedroom wall.

TWENTY

IN THE CAR, JUSTIN GAVE Bo a massive review on quantum thought, and it seemed to me that his mouth was now on autopilot, just blathering to keep other thoughts at bay. He was going on about each of us being a life force, an energy force, and what we think is a big part of that energy. Bo looked tired but interested, maybe enjoying a moment of distraction himself.

"There's a guy in my bunk who believed in all that," Bo said. "He kept saying he was using his thought energy to get an early discharge. Early discharges are nearly impossible, but he had filled out an application to Stanford and got a full ride. One of those math brainiacs."

"Did he get his early discharge?" Justin asked.

Bo laughed uncomfortably. "Well, the fact that he walked into the commander's office with this letter and stood up for himself once a month for four months in a row might have had a lot to do with it. It's not every day that someone from our unit got accepted to Stanford."

"So, he got it," Justin said, sounding victorious.

"So, he stood up for himself," Bo half argued. "I dunno, Justin. I just don't want to see you get hurt, my man. Get your shit together. You stink like a cigarette factory right now. Then come talk to me about philosophy, okay?"

"I will get my act together," Justin promised. "And then I will get back to you. I got a lot to tell."

In the rearview mirror I found Bo's eyes, which looked distracted and puffy, and I thought it was really decent of him to have left his family to seek out the truth in the Justin rumors and try to help him out. He was as true to Adams's writing as I could fathom. However, I didn't think he was fully understanding Justin.

His "I got a lot to tell" had nothing to do with quantum thought and a lot to do with Darla, I sensed. I could not shake the feeling that he knew more than he was telling. There was so much the cops could not tell us, what with the scene having been secretly cleaned up. Awful thoughts started running through my head. Why had Justin suddenly dived into drugs around the same time that Darla disappeared? *Could he have possibly been a witness?* And the worst thoughts are often the ones that are hardest to resist; to ignore them is to tell yourself to ignore thoughts of a blue elephant. All you can think of is the blue elephant.

Could he have accidentally killed her, and Danny covered it up? I tried to think of Danny's suicide letter and how it might have been lacking in sincerity, which Chief Rye had suspected from the beginning. But without RayAnn beside me to bounce my thoughts off, my mind was all over the place. It was that fear more than any other that made me not respond badly when Justin turned to me with a sudden blast of ideas.

"C'mon in and meet my mom," he said, his tired grin charged with a sense of purpose. "I think we decided this morning that it would be good practice for you."

I responded more calmly than I might have if I weren't so distracted. "Nah. I'm honestly and truly phobic. There's no word in the Oxford Dictionary for 'matraphobia.' I've often thought of writing them a letter."

"All the more reason," Justin said. "If you had a fear of snakes, a shrink would tell you to handle a snake. The non-poisonous kind—well, she's nonpoisonous. I swear, she won't do anything to you."

"I gotta get back to RayAnn," I said.

He persisted. "Don't be a wimp. What are you afraid of? She's not going to bite you, I promise."

I was basically joking when I said, "I'll go in if Bo goes in." I meant that Bo was a burly guy who could knock her out if she started yelling and bossing us around, but I forgot about his tie to the Creeds.

"I am *not* going in there," he said. "That woman hates my guts to this day. Besides, I'm with you, Mike. I would not go in there with my entire unit. I'm trained as a sniper, which hopefully I will never need to be. But I can pick off a man at three hundred yards, given the right trap. Ladies, mothers especially, are beyond the scope of my power." He laughed, but in a distracted way.

That settled it.

At least, it did until Justin turned just as Bo pulled up to a curb. "Honestly, I want to do something good for you, Mike. I can cure you, I swear. Look. This is the last time you will ever see me. You're going back tomorrow morning, right? C'mon in."

Last time I'll see him. I put my hand on the door handle, feeling like I was about to attempt to push through a brick wall. But it was an autopilot move, and to distract myself from phobic willies, I addressed Bo.

"Listen . . . I know you've got a lot on your plate right now. But I sold my last belonging to come out here and write about Justin's brother. If there's some good word you could put in for me with Adams . . . Trying to get an interview with him is like trying to interview the Beatles. Right now, it's probably easier to get an interview with Paul McCartney, and, well, I'm not *Rolling Stone.*"

Bo groaned, shaking his head. Justin nudged him pleadingly, or he might have simply said no.

"All I can tell you is this. Adams is a down-home guy, not looking to get his name in lights about Chris Creed. And the way he was muttering tonight—about agents and labels and tours—I don't think he's supposed to talk about his music until one of those important people says to open the floodgates. I got no power over any of that. But I'll tell ya what . . ."

He slapped Justin's hair affectionately. "Adams and I are going to Brownie's for a couple beers around eleven, just to get me out of my house. Ali might be there. If you happen to show up and sit on the other side of the bar and not come near us without being asked, I will mention to him who you are and let him choose for himself. But you have to promise: If he doesn't come to you, you won't invade. Does that work?"

"That works," I said, feeling more hopeful than I had all day. "Thanks, man."

I reached my hand up to him. It was awkward, to shake hands from a back seat to a front seat, and I don't know why

I did it. But he shook with me, and a charge went up my arm, the same charge you might get if you shook hands with the lead in a Broadway show at the backstage door. I'd combed Adams's website probably fifty times over the years, and it can be pretty amazing, talking to people whom you've read about until they are legends.

Which is not to say that I was at all prepared to meet this next legend. I called RayAnn on my cell. I got her voice mail, which concerned me, but I left her a message: "It's nine fifty. Pick me up in fifteen minutes. No later . . . I'm at the Creeds." I handed the phone to Justin, who gave driving directions from the center of town.

I must have looked pretty stricken, because Justin was laughing at me.

I could not for the life of me put this scenario together in my head. He had a mother wicked enough to video his computer space so she could see the password changes on his keypad. She'd stopped me cold this afternoon. Yet he was walking into the house after being away for two weeks and had no fear that she would chain him to the radiator or sink her fangs into his head. I'd had a million nightmares of going home, and they always featured my mom in dragon ensemble of varying sorts, spewing forest fires at my head from years of pent-up outrage at being tricked by me and left powerless.

It made me watch Justin as he climbed the front steps,

tiredly but fearlessly. I knew I was going for one reason only: I wanted to see him in action. That much was therapy, along with a chance to finally see these alleged e-mails from his brother. It was like I didn't have a choice.

The front door was unlocked, and he simply pushed it open, grinning at me over his shoulder. "My mom hasn't locked the front door since Chris left, thinking if he ever comes back, she wants him to be able to come right in . . . *and get the enormous beating that's coming his way.* I'm joking, I'm joking!" He grabbed the sleeve of my jacket and pulled me in behind him in case I was having second thoughts.

The lights were off in the living room, but he put one on, and I followed him down a half flight of stairs to the family room, where I could hear the television going softly. The ten o'clock news was on, some talk about the body found in Steepleton, which did nothing good for my nerves. I put myself in journalist mode, watching, detached, aloof.

The Mother Creed was sleeping on the couch, wearing a sweatshirt and shorts. I noticed this time how thin she was. I could see her knees, which were kind of knobby. *Too thin.* At one time, she had been a fighter pilot in the navy—muscles and more muscles. No more. She was sleep breathing deeply.

Justin grinned at me, then stood right over her and said in a normal tone of voice, which under the circumstances sounded like screaming, "Hi, Mom! I'm home!"

She barely stirred, said something unintelligible, and conked off again. Justin picked up her arm and let it drop to the couch, still grinning. He did it again for effect.

"Really scary, isn't she?" he asked.

Officer Hughes popped into my head saying that the Mother Creed never left the house after three. Definitely, that was now the start of cocktail hour, rather than after the kids are asleep, or even five o'clock. Alcoholism, I knew, doesn't get any better without help. If my own mother hadn't gotten help . . . *What in hell had I done to the younger kids?* I don't think Justin was aware of the measure of guilt that was coming my way. He was simply carrying on some nightly charade, which I could tell filled him with sadness, but he was handling it with aplomb, with humor, even, pulling her up to a sitting position by one arm. Her chin fell onto her chest and her breathing remained the same.

"Dangerous, eh?" he repeated.

I wasn't sure what five years could do to my mother; there was no timetable given by the counselors. But this was slightly more horrifying to watch than what I had at first imagined. My imagination had simply included Justin having to defend himself with chairs like a lion tamer. He climbed up onto the couch, straddled her until her body moved forward and he was sitting behind her, holding her upright with one arm around her ribs. He let go, and she flopped forward. He wiggled down further, one leg on either side until her back leaned in to him.

"So, Mom. Who took out your contacts while I was gone?" He did some maneuver, pulling her eye sideways with one hand until something dropped into his other palm. He did the same to the other eye. He laid the two contacts on the end table beside him.

She muttered something. It was pathetic, awful, worse than hitting your mother, seeing one in a condition like this. No kid should have to see his mother like this. Mothers are huge.

He stood, pulling her up with him. She flopped into his side, half staggering, half being carried around the coffee table.

"Get her other arm," he told me.

I stood frozen. "Why . . . don't you just let her sleep where she is?"

"Because I just took her contacts out. She has allergies and she'll wake up with her eyes on fire if I don't. But without them, she'll fall down the stairs on her way up to bed when she starts coming to. Believe me—it's happened."

Something shot through me, a desire to help, maybe—some twisted desire to return all the kind gestures that mothers try to make, regardless of how bad they can be at it. I broke through my wall, sending invisible bricks flying all over the stratosphere, as I put her arm over my shoulder and the two of us walked her up the stairs.

It was clunky, as I had no vision down as low as the stairs themselves. We turned at the living room, and I counted the next steps quickly as they came into view in frames. It was my usual trick for ascending in a hurry, but my tunnel vision was deepening the way it could when I was under stress. *Eight steps,* I thought.

It turned out to be seven, so I staggered into the upstairs corridor, almost flinging her over my head. She stirred slightly, slurring out, "You're not allowed t' bring friends . . . !" and she was out of it again.

It was a last-ditch effort to dish out orders, and Justin chuckled quietly, taking all of her weight to let me get ahold of myself. Suddenly I was chuckling, too. He was right about one thing. There was nothing to fear here. I'm not sure I would have wanted my mom to be reduced to this in order to rid her of power, but if it had happened, it would be a result of her choices, not mine.

We approached the bed and Justin threw back the blankets. She collapsed on her pillow, opening her eyes only once. As it was as black as pitch to me in that room, I lifted my glasses, if for no better reason than to get one last clear view of the Mother Creed without her power. Eyes reflect the light, and what little poured in from the hall allowed her and me to exchange glances. The chill it sent down my back was, fortunately, short-lived. Her eyes rolled almost as quickly as they had locked with mine, and she was asleep again. Justin made a big deal of tucking the blankets around her, which I suspected was not part of his nightly ritual but a drama-fest to drive home the idea that she was stone-cold dead to the world and nothing to be afraid of.

Still, I was almost catapulted out of the room by my own phobic energy, and before I could exit the house via the front door, Justin pulled me down into the family room once more.

"You want to see those e-mails, don't you? Your girl-friend isn't coming for another ten minutes at least."

That all of this could have taken less than three minutes was amazing to me. It had seemed like an eternity.

"Sure," I said, huffing, trying to sound like I wasn't.

He sat down at his computer and put a towel over his hands as he typed.

"What are you doing?" I whispered.

"Told ya. She put a hidden cam in this room somewhere to see what my passwords are. I'm changing my password."

I looked all around.

"Don't bother," he said, watching me look. "It's one of those cameras that's the size of a grape seed or something. I found a receipt for it about two months back. I was already suspicious and downloaded some spyware to see if anyone was using my terminal when I wasn't. She's got her own laptop, but the test came back: affirmative. After finding that receipt, I started putting a towel over my hands to change my passwords daily, and the spyware altered its message to the effect that someone was *trying* to use my terminal but was unable to."

"Good for you." I chuckled, starting to calm down, though I knew I wouldn't be totally calm until we were out of this house.

He found the e-mails, printed them out, and handed me the copies. I studied one as best as I could by moving over to the light.

It was from a CCRider. It read: "want 2 come 2 u. How mom? DON'T TELL HER don't tell anyone." The second was the same sender, only, "I let u know when I come. Look 4 me everywhere."

This person couldn't even punctuate, let alone spell. It smacked of fraud, and I remembered that Justin had posted a couple of times on Adams's website. That would have drawn clicks to his e-mail address. In fact, he had just posted five months ago, back when Adams said he wouldn't be posting anymore. Justin had posted to thank him for all he had done to try to find Chris. The dates of these e-mails were more recent, a little more than two months old. But any cruel joker could have seen that post. Yahoo e-mail address . . . I was amazed that he'd received only these two.

I wished he had my investigative reporter training. He needed it, considering he was so inept at watching the details of people. This was a cruel joke by a cruel person.

I didn't want to derail his train totally. I said, "Justin. Wasn't your brother, well, very articulate? Didn't he speak sort of like your dad?"

"I thought of that," Justin said. "And yeah, my brother was obnoxiously well-spoken, my dad all over again. But he would be afraid my mom might see, and he was trying to disguise himself, to try to *look* like a fraud."

"Did you reply?"

"Yeah. Right away. I told him that I hung out at the Lightning Field and to come there. But this is all I got. And you can't trace Yahoo."

Very convenient for a prankster. I was speechless, but he didn't need my approval. He didn't seem to notice my tight face. He was a bull in a china shop, bursting past people's actions and emotions without them even registering. He only noticed what he wanted to, what he was able to, given his racing mind.

"I think it's my brother," he said, "because of the timing. You know the meditation rituals I started with the lightning trees? It looks crazy, but I've never been the type to care what things look like. Most people are crazier than I am. Most people are crazy enough to accept what's popular without ever questioning it. It's popular to say things are impossible. Well, fuck it. Ya know why? For more than four years, I don't hear from him. Then, I start sending up vibes using the lightning trees in February. And all of a sudden, these show up in March."

"Did you . . . put out any Internet posts and stuff around the same time?" I asked.

"No. I swear on my life. All I ever did was touch those trees."

I thought I heard a floorboard creak upstairs, followed by a gust of wind outside the window. The house was still making me nervous. I needed to get out, get a breath of fresh air, and be with RayAnn's calming effect.

"I have to go," I whispered, starting up the stairs.

"Wait while I check my e-mail. It's been a while. Then I'll come out with you. Say a proper goodbye. I will miss you, man. I'm sorry I lost it on you today. I get like that sometimes . . . I just pop off."

Speaking of which . . . I asked, "Where do you think your mom put your medication? You take two doses a day, right?"

He was busy clicking the mouse, but finally answered. "Well, that could take some finding. One time, maybe a year ago, the school counselor sent me for a formal diagnosis of bipolar disorder, just because I couldn't stop acting up in class. It was mild then, but she was smart enough to see it. My mom wouldn't let me go to a shrink. She said I didn't need any medication and there was nothing wrong with me."

"Jeezus," I groaned. "Being a control freak ought to be a crime in some cases."

"My guess?" he went right on. "She didn't want to admit there was anything wrong with *her*, and all of that would have come out in therapy. That's an alcoholic's thinking. They think everything they're doing is a gosh darn secret, when the truth is that everyone in town suspects what's wrong. Medication . . . let's see. First place I'd look? Under her pillow. Second place? I don't know. I'll think of it when you're gone."

She was boiling my blood, blind to the fact that her own son's high-energy mania needed to be leveled out.

"What happens if you can't find it?" I asked. "You've missed one dose already."

"I'll find it," he assured me, but looked distracted with his printer. "I've been warned. It takes a while to build up in your system, but it doesn't take nearly as long to start feeling it if you miss."

"Are you feeling anything right now?"

He grabbed the first page, smiling at me. "I smoked weed today, and tonight I drank a beer. I have no idea how I'm feeling."

I headed up the stairs to the living room level, figuring I needed air badly enough to wait for him out on the curb. I couldn't understand why I hadn't heard from RayAnn, but I pulled my cell out of my pocket, gripping it for security.

I never felt it coming . . . I never heard anything. Something beyond sound, maybe beyond energy, made me look up those stairs where we'd laid the Mother Creed. I caught her wild, angry eyes, not much more. She was standing there at the top of the stairs, towering over me like some dragon from my own nightmares, and something came out of her akin to "GET OOOOOOOOOOO . . . VER HERE!"

And the next second she was toppling me to the ground, screaming syllables and nonsense and jabbing her nails in my face.

"*Justin!*" I screamed, covering my eyes to protect them, and I could hear stomping and him hollering.

"Ma! Get off him! Get up!" I could feel him tugging at her, but she was tugging back insanely, actually pulling him on top of us.

Something scratched my cheek, and I thought it was her nails, but then realized it was her tongue. She was either licking me or trying to speak with her face pushed against mine. With my own hollering, I still managed to make out the word "Chris."

"Get her off, damn it!" I screamed at Justin.

"Oh my God, she thinks you're my brother," he said with gritted teeth, struggling to get her arms pinned down. I did not appreciate the fact that he was still giggling. *Manic, stressed, half stoned. What in hell made me agree to come into this nut factory?*

I spat out something pasty—the woman's drool—and that was the last straw. I closed my eyes and pushed, sending both her and Justin into the dining room table. A chair fell over—I heard it, but could not see a blessed thing. I counted to five slowly as my tunnel vision returned and I heaved a sigh of relief, which was momentary, as her little horse whinnying filled the air.

"My Christopher . . . my baby . . ." she sobbed, her hair wet with drool. I stayed perfectly still, afraid to breathe for fear that she would catch sight of me again. It was animal instinct, like playing possum.

Justin pulled her up, took her under one arm, and led her back up to bed, saying, "He's not here, Mom. What is up? You gonna start having nightmares every night, too? I'm a school kid. Gotta get my sleep, you know."

I jutted to the front door, fumbling first with the doorknob until the door swung inward and cracked me in the nose. I got to the curb and was sitting, trying to figure out what the hell had happened to my cell phone, when suddenly the garage door thundered opened. Tires screeched and a car pulled up beside me. The car door flew open.

Justin was grinning insanely from behind the wheel. I could not fathom what would put me in the death seat beside an underage driver in an expensive luxury car if it was not what had just happened in that house. I dived for it, and Justin took off as I was fumbling to shut the door, almost spilling me onto the asphalt.

"You're bleeding," he said, tossing something wet into my lap. Paper towel. He tossed something else. My cell phone.

I put the paper towel up to my temple, my hands shaking until I exploded. "What the hell was that all about?"

"Dude, I am so, so sorry. Nothing like that has ever happened before. She's totally harmless. I mean, she *was*—"

"Oh, yeah, *I can see that!*"

"She thought you were my brother come home. I can't think of anything else that would—"

"I don't care if she thought I was the prince of darkness!" I hollered, holding out the paper towel so that I could see a spot of blood the size of a golf ball on it. "She could have blinded me! I have enough problems to overcome without your goddamn insane mother taking my eyes from me! Do you have any idea how much money has gone into my vision? Just so that I can *work* someday?"

He groaned and said nothing, which was a smart idea. He might find her amusing, but I wondered how many days it would be—how many months or years—before I stopped spitting the woman's froth out of my mouth.

After a while, he asked softly, "Where we going?"

I dialed RayAnn's phone number, and this time somebody answered. Somebody not RayAnn. A guy's voice.

"Where's RayAnn?" I asked.

"Oh! Um. She's not here. *Ha*-ha."

My skin started to crawl and my arm grew weak to the point where the paper towel flopped down off my bleeding temple. "Where the hell is she? Who is this?"

I could hear people laughing in the background, and he was trying not to. "She left us, but she forgot her cell phone."

"Lydee, is this you?" I didn't wait for him to answer. "She never forgets her cell phone. You'd better hope to God nobody did anything to her."

I heard a click and her cell went dead. They might be dumb-ass kids who needed a job, but they were strong and, as RayAnn had observed this afternoon, mysteriously edgy. Her background was different from theirs. *Differences can make packs of animals attack each other.* I wondered, as my gut spiraled even further, if the same was true for people.

I imagined my own cell phone, the one time I heard from somebody I dreaded, tumbling through the air and plopping into a duck pond. I imagined hers tumbling through air somewhere, then being bitten through by the jaws of a water moccasin.

"This place is a nightmare," I said. "My worst nightmares are coming out of the woodwork. Take me to the motel. You better hope she's there and in one piece, or I'm going to set this town on fire and laugh while everyone in it burns to death."

TWENTY-ONE

WE GOT TO THE TWILIGHT INN, and I was running, which makes me totally blind, but I held on to Justin's shoulder with one hand.

"She's there," he said. "Or at least the door's wide open."

I stopped to catch my breath until the orange glow of the room came clear through the open door. A man was standing in the doorway. I recognized him—the owner, whom we'd gotten out of bed to check in last night.

I could see RayAnn behind him for a brief second as she moved from the bed deeper into the room, and her suitcase was up by the lamp. It lay open.

We entered and Justin muttered, "Bloody hell . . ."

"What's up?" I pushed him aside, stepping past the owner.

He said in too nice a voice, "Your friend has had some problems. I've been standing here until you got here—just giving her a little company. Looks like she got in a cat fight."

I found RayAnn's eyes popping as she stared at the man in disbelief. "I was *not* in a cat fight. Great. Is this what school was like, Mike? One kid hits another and they both end up in detention? Something like that?"

I'd been in *lots* of detentions, and that explained just about every one of them.

Her lip was puffy, had been bleeding, I thought.

"Tell me what happened," I begged, making my way over to her. There was stuff on the floor, and I stumbled past her empty laptop case.

She didn't move toward me. She shook her head, her swollen lip trembling. "Mike, I am not prepared for this story. This place looks sweet, until you get into the middle of it." She burst past me, flopping the laptop onto the bed and shoving printouts in her suitcase. "These kids are mean."

"What'd they do?" Justin tried. "Who hit you?"

"My lip is thanks to the car door, which I slammed on myself trying to get away fast—after Kobe Lydee had me by the throat, threatening me for a good two minutes. *Au mon Dieu.*"

Justin decided it was appropriate to lecture her on how to defend herself against a bully, but although I waved my arm to shut him up, he didn't pay me any mind. His mother's leap out of the dark seemed to have triggered a burst of energy. He didn't shut his mouth until I found his jacket and half shoved him off the bed.

RayAnn jammed things into her suitcase. "Six of them had ridden on bikes and handlebars to get out to the Lightning Field, and the ones who didn't bring bikes all piled into our borrowed car without asking. I figured, fine, I'd just drop them off where they wanted, even though they stank. Pot and beer breath. They were okay at first . . . as sweet as people can be when they've got a gang-up vibe and a we-hate-you tone."

"Why'd they hate you?" Justin asked. "Were you talking French at them?"

RayAnn nodded hard with mock understanding. "Gee, that's a great reason to steal somebody's car—even if I did. It's what I do when I'm nervous, and your friends were whispering and glaring—while I was giving them a ride and had answered all their background-check types of questions in the nicest of ways."

"What set them off?" I asked.

"They had a lot of questions . . . found out I didn't go to high school and that I was their age. That didn't sit very well, I guess. That's when they went from curious to frosty. I should have figured they'd 'get even' with me for being a little different. They talked me into taking them to Dairy Queen before dropping them at Mary Ellen's. We were eating ice cream in the car. I hadn't been to the bathroom since around noon, so I really had to go. They asked me to leave the keys so they could keep listening to the radio. I came back out . . ." She trailed off, rearranging a couple pairs of socks, as if she'd forgotten how to fold.

"Oh my God," I said.

"Yeah. No car. And in the car was my cell phone, my three-thousand-dollar laptop, and your priceless dog."

I glanced around until I saw her laptop on the bed. *Lanz* . . .

"They . . . probably only took it for a ten-minute joy ride," Justin guessed, and we both turned to glare at him.

"I don't know how long it was, because I use my cell phone to tell time. I think it was more like fifteen. I was two seconds from calling the cops when they came back, all laughing. They'd done at least one donut. There's gravel all over the back of the car, and there's a tremble when you drive it, like one of the tires isn't aligned anymore."

"Oh, great," I said. *Drunk stoners, joy riding in a borrowed car.* I was afraid to ask about Lanz.

"Kobe Lydee was driving. They got back all laughing, and couldn't understand why I was so pissed. That's when I was screaming French. *Obtenir un emploi, vous stupides, paresseux imbeciles!*"

Get a job, you stupid, lazy morons.

"I guess Kobe Lydee got scared I would tell the cops. So he threatened me—with everything from gang rape to being thrown in the snake pit out at the Lightning Field . . . the one in the house foundation."

My anger roared and mixed with guilt. I could see she was really shaken up, even though she was trying to hide it. *After everything that happened to me in high school, how could I not have guessed that something like this would happen to her?*

"I already called Glenda up at Rowan and told her what happened with her car. She's rightfully pissed, but not at me. She's driving down here with her boyfriend to get it. We'll have to pay for the damages if—"

"*I'll* pay for the damages," Justin said quickly, and I wondered if he was suddenly manic enough to imagine himself a millionaire, though he added, "I'll find Lydee, and we'll make *him* pay for the damages. I got the goods on him in so many ways. I'll blackmail his spoiled ass—"

We could think of that later. "Where's Lanz?" I finally got the nerve to ask.

"Still in the car, but he puked all over the back seat. Probably scared."

More guilt.

"I cleaned it up already . . . Mr. Stillman gave me a bucket, Lysol, and some rags." She pointed to the door, where the motel owner stood looking outside, pretending he wasn't listening to this.

"Better get him out if you're staying. If you're coming, my dad got me on the red-eye out of Atlantic City. It's a seven-hundred-dollar plane ticket, but he did it, no questions asked. That was the deal—if I felt uncomfortable, he would get me out, NQA. He says he'll loan you the ticket money if you're coming with me."

I wanted to run to Lanz, but I went to her first, trying to hug her. But she ducked under my arm and kept talking.

Justin's voice finally sounded a little contrite. "Just so you know, that was all talk, RayAnn. Kobe Lydee is a hot-air bag, and okay, he's a morbid loser, but he's not a rapist. Kobe Lydee is not going to do anything to you."

She dropped to her knees in front of him and stared up at the ceiling. I followed her eyes at first, and then, realizing nothing was up there, I saw her neck. Bruises were forming where Lydee had grabbed her. The bruise on one side was the size of a thumb. There were four small bruises on the other side.

"Just let me kill him," I said. I was dead serious. My insides were on fire, leaving me swaying.

A car pulled up outside with music booming out the window. A car door opened, and a shadow crossed our doorway. A kid who looked vaguely familiar stood on the other side of the motel owner. Someone from the Lightning Field, and from RayAnn's gasp, I gathered he'd been in the car.

"Here," he said, and tossed something. RayAnn's cell phone landed in the middle of the bed. He ran off into the parking lot, laughing. A couple of other voices laughed, and the car gunned away.

"See?" Justin said in disgust, as if kids returning her phone instead of throwing it out the window or selling it made all of this okay. Bad frequency is subtle sometimes. Still on fire, I couldn't believe it when Justin continued on with a shrug. "You got no sense of humor, that's your problem—"

"Justin, shut up!" I exploded. "You talk too much. He tried to strangle her!"

"She bruises easily," he said, which I'd known almost since I'd known RayAnn, but I didn't need to hear him defending Lydee and mean kids, and it was the last thing I'd wanted RayAnn to experience.

She yelled, "If their sense of humor ends up costing us eight hundred bucks to have Glenda's car repaired, are we supposed to think that's funny?" She turned to me with a sigh, more of disgust than fear. "They know where we're staying. I don't think they're going to ax murder us in our sleep. But they might spend half the night trying to make us *think* they would ax murder me . . . for what? For not going to high school and for starting college early? For not seeing the humor when they took off in our car for fifteen minutes and popping a three-sixty? Why am I not surprised they'd pick on me? I mean, this is the home of Christopher Creed, one *truly* different guy . . ."

Justin went mute for once. He plopped down on the bed, staring off into space. His jaw bobbed a few times before he settled on "RayAnn, if you can believe this, I promise you, this is a pretty nice place. I don't know what's come over them lately."

She zipped her bag shut, pushed on it for effect, then stood straight, hands on her hips.

"You know what? Torey Adams would not have been at that party tonight, Justin. *Your* little party. Do you realize that?"

Justin stayed quiet. Torey Adams had been really popular, in other words, and yet he wasn't this wild. He wasn't *mean*—

"Are you coming?" she asked me. "I'm not missing this flight."

I moved to my bag to pack up what few things I'd left lying around between last night and today. But I felt numb, like a person who's been kicked in the ribs but is still waiting for the pain sensations to run upstairs to the brain. RayAnn needed me right now. And I needed her. I couldn't stay without her as a guide.

The old man in the doorway had his arms crossed and was looking out over the parking lot. I didn't know what to say to RayAnn, and my frustration was backing up, so I unloaded on the man.

"You ought to be embarrassed, living in a town like this." I plopped my suitcase down on the mattress with a bounce, and I heard him say only, "Lately, I'd say I am . . ."

Nothing further. I just shook my head in disgust. What had Adams walked back into? I thought of my lost interview with my main man, and I wanted to heave. Justin started to babble, following on my heels.

"Mike. You don't have to leave. I can take you around. I can deliver you to the airport."

An underage driver suffering from manic-depression—*yuh-huh*. And his word had been so good about his mother being painless. I walked away from him, rescuing yesterday's jeans and socks from the armchair.

"Mike . . . Say you'll stay. Don't go now. Stay with me until the funeral Monday!"

RayAnn ignored him, full of her own power to the point where she probably didn't feel an argument was necessary. She finally noticed the side of my head. A laugh blew out her mouth as she came up close beside me.

"Who got *you?*"

I shut my eyes, trying not to swallow my own spit. I spat into a wastepaper basket I knew was near the desk. "The Mother Creed."

"You gotta be kidding me!"

The mattress crunched as Justin sat back down. He said, "She was just . . . she was just . . . she was just . . ."

"She was drunk," I finished. RayAnn's eyes darted from my temple scratches to my eyes, to my scratches to my eyes. They finally stayed on my eyes.

"Pack up," she said. "You're coming with me. I will help you pack."

"I don't need help," I said, on autopilot. It's what I always said at Randolph when people tried to help me.

"Fine. Just get moving. We'll miss the plane."

RayAnn's thinking was right, but her tone was all wrong. She was out of form—shaken up, scared, and desperate—so she was doing the one thing she probably would have guessed under normal circumstances would propel me away from her. She was dictating my movements. She was telling me what to do and saying to *get moving* about it. You don't do that to a matraphobic who has just been scratched in the face by an evil troll mother. You don't say that to a guy who left his mom to prove that he could make it on his own.

I didn't freak out on her—it just changed the direction

of my thoughts. *You don't have to see the whole staircase. Just take the next step. Dr. Martin Luther King Jr.*

The next step for me had to be to prove to myself that I could get around in my life without someone always telling me where the rut in the concrete was. I couldn't walk into the *New York Times* with another body holding car keys. I had known that for a while. Yet, I didn't know where to even begin to address my inability to drive.

Just take the next step.

"I think I . . . need to stay," I told her. "Not for Justin. For Mike . . ."

I heard Justin sigh in relief anyway, and she cast him a look that was about as hateful as a person could give.

"For *what?*" she demanded.

For my independence. For the perfect story. For a chance to interview Adams, even if it never happened. I didn't say it aloud but didn't have to.

"You're beyond ambitious, Mike," she said, reading my mind yet again. "You're obsessed. You're choosing between a goddamn story—one that is not very uplifting, by the way—and me."

It was a punch in the gut, hearing the truth aloud. But there was even more truth banging around here in the silence, things I had felt but had not been able to put into words before. I had to prove I could make it *without* her . . .

in order to *deserve* her. If I went with her now, it would be like going home . . . going to a woman who was smart enough and strong enough to run my show. Nobody would win until I could run my own show . . .

"RayAnn, I am sorry you had to defend yourself against an angry drunk and his likenesses. But I see that you came out of it okay. I would have wagered no differently. I wouldn't confuse your innocence with weakness."

She didn't get it. She spun her head from me, picking up her bag and dropping it to the floor with a thud. I knew she had turned to keep me from seeing her cry.

I'd talked to Justin today about people having different needs. RayAnn needed me. I was no good to her—not yet.

A car pulled up outside, and the motel owner said, "It's your cab."

RayAnn cranked up the handle of her carry-on bag and flung her laptop bag over her shoulder. "If you really need a lift from the airport when you get back, if Stedman or Claudia can't bring you, then call me. If not, I won't be around."

I held my arms out and flopped them down. She wasn't finished talking yet.

"I've got this thing. It's called my streak of pride. I have never chased any guy before, and I'm tired of chasing you. Call me if you need a ride." She looked me in the face. I heard keys rattling and the motel owner mutter he would wait outside for Glenda and her boyfriend to show up. RayAnn had tears in her eyes but pretended she didn't, and smiled pretty big. "But somehow, I don't think you'll need me for a lift. I don't think you'll need too much of anything from anybody."

Right person . . . wrong time? A person raised more normally might have felt that the loss of her was inconceivable. I found myself in a place that was thorny, but because I was so used to being there, it bore out certain twisted sensations of comfort. It's a place called *alone*.

I could have insisted on a kiss goodbye or could have built myself up for her final memory by explaining myself better. But I let her walk off in a blaze of glory while I stood at the door, watching her get in the cab and drive away.

I was scared shitless.

TWENTY-TWO

JUSTIN THOUGHT HIS COUSINS would be at Brownie's, and he wanted to go with me so he could pay a visit to Mack and Ozone while I hoped and prayed to talk to Torey Adams. It created challenges for me if Justin's cousins weren't there. I remembered my deal with Bo. If Justin was with me, Adams might be more likely to approach but there was less chance of it being a good interview. Justin could mess this up by failing to be quiet, and his speech seemed to be getting more zippy by the minute. He had walked Lanz without asking me while I was sorting out papers I wanted to take, and he put Lanz in the back of his mom's car, talking to the dog the whole time about cats, rabbits, and his own personal problems. His voice floated in the open door and unnerved me further, but I needed a ride. And we had decided jointly that if his cousins weren't there he would hang around outside or nap in his mother's car. He kept saying he was really tired, but I just couldn't see it.

I left with him, in a somber mood, missing RayAnn more than I ever dreamed possible. And it was more than just having a stable person to drive me around. It was her mentally clicking with me, our ability to communicate without words that made everything go smoothly.

He blathered the whole ride to Brownie's about how I should interview Mack and Ozone just to get a decent picture in my mind of the boons. It was as if this whole thing between me and RayAnn had not just happened, or as if she were just some annoying babe we had managed to get rid of. Manics refuse to see the downside, I'd read, and I had no choice but to hope for the best.

Justin turned the talk back to his mom as we pulled into a half-full parking lot.

"She's very responsible, actually. All day long, she's great. She's gotten quieter since Chris left, though people'd never know that. You ever seen a house as immaculate as ours? Anyway, she has to act out in public still; I don't know what's up with that except pride runs big in my family. At night she gets quieter, gets withdrawn unless something digs her out of it, and she eventually passes out. My life has been a nightly ritual for the past year or so. Honest."

He pulled into a parking space, swiping dangerously close to a souped-up old car beside us. Lanz staggered sideways in the back seat. To say I did not have a good feeling about Justin chauffeuring us around is an understatement. Grabbing the door handle numbly, I merely said, "It'll get worse before it gets better, if she doesn't get some help."

"I know, I know."

"You see Bo's car?"

"Not yet."

I sighed, feeling exhausted from all this. "You're going in the back door to look for your cousins."

"I don't see Ozone's truck either. I'll just crash out here."

I couldn't picture him being tired enough to sleep. But I went inside, taking the place in frame by frame. There was a long bar, which could probably seat thirty people on three sides, but maybe only ten people were sitting there. Light from a second room shone through, and I could hear billiard balls cracking and a few voices. I could see why Bo might have suggested that Adams meet him here. I took it from the drive up Route 9 that it was a lot closer to Conovertown than Steepleton. It was less than half filled, and with people who would not have known Adams and would not have any interest in his music. Country was blaring out of the jukebox.

There were a couple of booths, and by the window I found one where a little lamp shed extra light. It was perfect, and I slid into it. Leaving home at a young age creates a few stray bits of courage, and I had never minded eating alone. I brought my recorder out, put the earpiece in, pulled out a looseleaf notebook, and rewound to my earliest interviews in Steepleton. The first contained the Mother Creed's obnoxious outbursts, which I managed to float through, and I tried making notes on Tiny Hughes's initial comments about the copycat disappearances.

A waitress came, and I ordered a burger, fries, and an iced tea. Diet Coke would have reminded me too much of RayAnn. Looking suitably busy and preoccupied was not difficult, as suddenly I was working with a double physical challenge. I had to transcribe my favorite quotes with a pen, which was a lot slower than typing, and in the light of the booth lamp, everything looked blurry. I hoped to God that that devil woman had not done something to my eyes, and it was hard to concentrate.

I finally saw Bo and Adams come in, and even though this bar was not a place where he would be easily recognized, it was hard to miss Adams. He was surprisingly tall, possibly six one, which meant he was one of those bizarre people who grow at least four inches after their junior year in high school. The Steepleton football pics on the website floated to the front of my mind, in which he was nowhere near close to the tallest. Now he was an inch taller than Bo. I only recognized him from the ponytail. He had on a bright red ski jacket and shades.

He and Bo went around to the other side of the bar, and I simply looked down at my papers again. It was something else I had to get over, the feeling of being more comfortable around papers than people. I often did this at college when I was lonely—went out to a bar with a stack of paperwork or my laptop or a book. But in a college town there were many others who did the same. Here, I would have stuck out like a sore thumb if the place had been more crowded.

Give the guy some breathing room, my instincts said, and I forced myself not to look. I heard Bo order a couple of drafts, and when I finally scratched my head and did a fake stretch, I saw Bo pulling darts out of the bull's-eye on a target. Adams still had his red jacket on, which enabled me to pick up on him quickly.

Bo was good on his word. He whispered beside Adams's head, and Adams turned suddenly and studied me. I ducked my head to look as though I were writing. I was actually scribbling and looking back at him, something my shades allowed me to do.

Adams mumbled something to him, and they started playing darts. *Shit.* My burger came, and I studied some web printouts, pretending to read, watching their dart game kind of acridly. I knew this was often a journalist's life—being an outsider, assuming the bystander role on the sidelines. In some ways it suited me perfectly, but at the moment my awkward past backed up on me.

I didn't completely give up, because I noticed Adams look over at me every now and again. He probably wished I would disappear, not bother his conscience: *Hey, we all have to make a living, Mr. Rock Star.*

Finally, out of the blue, he turned and stared dead at me. I laid my pen down, decided to be brazen, and just stared back. His shades versus my shades. It was a long, "shady" moment, making me think of Todd Stedman. My roommate was in the artist's track at school, and he could stop what he was doing at a moment's notice and just stare as a thought took hold of him. Adams had written on ChristopherCreed.com about doing that himself. I could only guess where his thoughts were taking him, but he stared long enough that I started to feel luck coming my way. Richardson nudged him and gave him a handful of darts, and he turned back.

He missed the entire board with his first throw. *Let his almost-famous conscience get to him,* I thought, glancing down at my papers, imagining a lightning tree and pretending I had my hand on it. Stupid image, but . . . when I looked again, Adams had turned. He came my way slowly.

He fell into the booth across from me, not saying anything at first. I had a mouthful of food. I groped for the napkin, which he handed to me, and I wiped my lips and chin, taking my time downing it with iced tea, enjoying my victory with as much aplomb as I could muster.

"Mike Mavic," I said, holding out my hand, which he shook. "Thanks for coming over."

He finally laughed awkwardly. "Sorry. I hear you're a friend of Justin's and a writer. It's just that you caught me in an awkward period. Professionally, that is. It took me a while to figure out what I could and couldn't say to you."

I just sat back, watching him talk as if I were such an utter stranger—which I was, but it seemed weird. I knew his life so intimately well. I felt a little let down by his formality.

"My agent has this game plan . . . it's not so uncommon, but it's all new to me. He wants my first interview to be *Rolling Stone*. That's coming in August. But the magazine wants an exclusive, and it will only be published if nothing else appears in print first."

I found my voice. "Okay . . . that's interesting. I'm kind of new to this myself."

"And this is *not* a time in my life to have things coming out in print about, um, Chris Creed and me. It's just so . . .

dark. It was a part of my life I'm really looking to lose now. There are still some stray characters in this town who think I helped kill the guy."

I hadn't heard that version of things since my arrival here, but considering it was the Rumor of Steepleton High School four-plus years ago, I gathered I simply hadn't banged into the few remaining gossip-monger morons.

"I don't need that rumor to start appearing like crazy on the Internet, just before . . . you know. I don't want to sound selfish or overly ambitious or anything like that. I mean . . . if Chris needed me, there isn't anything I wouldn't do. But obviously, he's known where to find me, at least online, so he must be doing okay. Therefore I'd like to launch my album without . . . that part of my life holding me back from a great future. I hope you understand." He sounded sincere, and sincerely apologetic. Nice guy.

"I understand. Totally." I really didn't know where to go with this, as I hadn't thought of the complications. It led to more silence. He finally lifted his glasses, stuck them in his jacket pocket, and glanced nervously before locking in with me again.

He had some combination of pain and peace in his gaze that wasn't there in his younger, Creed-writing days. He looked worldlier than he did in the pictures mired in my brain.

"For Justin, I'll take a risk," he said, smiling awkwardly. "You just have to promise to let *Rolling Stone* come out before you quote me directly on anything about my career. As for Chris, well . . . only use what you think would help *him,* okay?"

I don't write stories to help—or hurt—anyone. He didn't understand newspeople very well. I flipped over my pad and laid my pencil on top, folding my hands as the only hint of the letdown I felt. First the Mother Creed attacks me, then RayAnn leaves me, then Torey Adams gives me fifteen reasons why I should not interview him, all of which I should have thought of myself.

I was about to fold the interview, then proceed outside to throw up.

But he dropped a hand on top of my wrist and said with a good deal of mysterious encouragement, "You look like a trustworthy guy."

I watched his hand, thinking of how it had warmed up a few stadiums of ten thousand people already. And now it was resting on my wrist, in a hick bar in a hick town. I don't know why I fixated on that, except that doing so was easier than dealing with all these writing parameters.

"Let's go over this again," I said, my will to succeed returning. He smiled. He wanted me to succeed. Nice, nice guy. "I can't quote you . . . on *anything*, it seems. At least, not until

August. Then, I can quote you about your music, but not about Chris. Or . . . you don't want to be quoted about Chris, unless you think it will help *him*."

"Well, yeah. I guess that's it." He laughed awkwardly.

I felt myself nodding. I would find the passages through once I got settled in back at the newspaper.

TWENTY-THREE

I HANDED MY PLATE TO THE WAITRESS as she flew past, and picked up my pen, saying, "You said I look trustworthy. As I'm visually impaired, I hold to certain beliefs, such as that you can read a person's conscience without him giving you his life history. It's . . . some sort of energy."

"I can do that sometimes," Torey agreed. "Generally, I look into a person's eyes. There's this saying I've always loved: 'The eyes are the window to the soul.' I can read things in eyes. Greed. Lust. Happiness. Inner peace."

"Me, too," I said. "I can even tell what drugs people have been doing."

He was watching me still, and I got the feeling if I didn't let him find my trustworthiness by looking at my naked eyes, this interview might be short. I raised my glasses, but I felt overexposed. I talked about my accident, my surgeries.

"If you look closely, you can see that my pupils are no longer entirely round. It's scar tissue, but my girlfriend says my pupils are flower shaped." He looked intensely into my scar tissue. I finally dropped my shades again and he grinned, sufficiently convinced that I wasn't hiding a viper's personality behind my glasses. "My eyes are a rose garden. What can I say?"

"You're pretty amazing. I've heard of singers and musicians who can't see. I've never heard of a writer."

"And you're famous. What's that like?" I got into it.

"I'm not famous," he corrected me. I got the impression from his confused grin that he found his recent life mystifying. "I mean, I would *like* to be famous. I mean," he stammered, "I hope this album will bring a lot of people a lot of happy moments. To me, that's famous. But I'm in this passage when everything is set up so that I *could become* famous, and I'm about to go on tour, and people who know me think I *am* famous. Things can get comical, especially where money and fame meet up. Because the big checks don't start rolling in until the close of that tour, and so while crowds are applauding and cheering me on, I'm still scraping it together for a one-room apartment sublet in Santa Monica."

I smiled. This stuff would work well on the page eventually. I made sure to jot down only abbreviated sentences so he would feel confident that I wouldn't quote him. I could swing back around to his music later, but I was dying to ask some Chris-related questions.

"Where do you think the man is?" I asked.

He looked down, spinning his beer glass around and around on the table, biting at his lip. He finally said, "I have no idea. That's the beauty of the thing, isn't it? A troubled guy says, 'Fine, if you want to pick on me so much. I don't need you. I'll make my own way.' And off he goes into the sunset, and the people who were so grand—grand enough to laugh at him—don't even get a postcard. That's how little he remembers, how little he cares."

"There's been a lot of talk over the years that one early post to your website might have been Chris himself."

He downed his beer, then signaled the waitress with the empty glass. "Again, I don't really know. Again, that's the beauty of it."

"What's beautiful about unanswered questions?" I asked.

The waitress dropped another draft in front of him, taking a crumpled five-dollar bill he'd pulled out of his pocket.

Crumpled five from the pocket. I had to smile again at Mr. Almost Rich and Famous, and he smiled back. Torey Adams was a combination of what guys would think of as a marble statue and girls would call adorable. I'd have to work on that before I wrote it, but I was getting the gist. He would turn heads anytime he entered a room—and not just girls' heads. Some people have a born-to-win aura, and his was radiant. But up this close, you could see his frailty. He looked perplexed and greatly amused as the waitress walked off with his crumpled five.

"See?" he asked. "Do famous people mooch five bucks off their mom before heading out for a night?"

"You should have gone for twenty," I chided.

"She tried. Moms, you know? If you took all the nights I spent in my house over the past five years, it would probably string out to be less than four months total. But hardly a day goes by that she doesn't call about something. I . . . don't know what I'd do without that."

I cleared my throat, wishing I knew the kind of life he was talking about. He watched me, sensing, I think, things I didn't want him to sense. I hated when interviews turned on me and I became the focus. He drummed on the table and mercifully jumped back to the subject.

"I guess unanswered questions are good because of how they feed people's imaginations. I think imagination is the most beautiful defense we have in a world that can be insanely cruel at times. Once all the questions are answered, the imagination runs out of fuel, has to shut down. We're back in skeptic mode. Everything's limited again."

It was amazing to hear Torey Adams's website wisdom pouring out of a mouth that happened to belong to Torey Adams. It took everything I had to keep from doing a victory yell at the ceiling.

"You like your questions served without answers," I noted with as mild a grin as I could form.

"Like good ol' roast beef, without the canned gravy." He let the silence run on for a minute, like maybe he'd done enough interviews to know that silence could be a part. But it went on too long. He suddenly asked, "What do *you* think happened to him?"

"I don't think he's dead," I said. "I think he did like he said in his letter to the principal. He *became* somebody else. He went after his happiness."

Adams nodded in agreement, then tilted his head to one side, obviously curious. "I've said as much myself. But I've always wondered . . . how do you do that? Does that mean his memories of life in Steepleton are gone from him? I had to take this boring Abnormal Psych class my freshman year in college . . ."

A laugh squirted out his nose as I raised my hand and

chuckled along with him. "I took it as a junior. My girlfriend took it as a freshman. We're all looking for the elective that won't be dull, and it turns out to be horrifyingly so," I said, my smile fading momentarily, wondering if I should still be calling RayAnn my girlfriend. I forced my mind away from it. "I think the word you're looking for is *repression*. As in, maybe Chris repressed all his memories."

"Thanks," he said. "Repression. But is that even possible?"

"Probably not," I said. "Not if he's sane. I'm going with the thesis that he's not sitting in some psych ward picking his toes and thinking he's five years old. I think it's more like this creative writing class I took this year. We started out writing in first person—*I* did this, *I* did that—and in the end, we were writing in third person—*he* did this, *he* did that. I'd imagine he remembers his life here when he has to, but he remembers it in third person."

Adams grinned. "That's an interesting take . . . even if it's over my head."

I sighed, wondering how big a compliment I should give. I didn't exactly want him to know I was a worshiper. "I'd say a *lot* of tormented guys read your website and afterward were able to see their lives through your eyes instead of their own. You've got merciful eyes."

His grin turned to a smile, though his gaze was far off. "I've often had this daydream of Chris reading my pages over and over and at least getting it that he needn't see himself the way people saw him in high school. I hope you're right."

While I wanted to keep Adams all to myself, my eyes caught Bo hugging some girl who still had a coat on and a handbag over her arm. I poked his elbow and pointed, bowing to the inevitable.

Adams turned to look and quickly excused himself. He hugged Ali McDermott next, swung her around, and despite my horrible luck earlier this evening, I focused on this jackpot of potential quotes until I was chuckling softly, pounding my fist softly on the table. Adams hailed the waitress for her, then headed back my way, while Bo was embracing some burly guy with a crowd of other people waiting to hug on him. I wondered if he came down here for therapy. A lot of sympathy ran around, and a lot of people seemed happy to see him after what could have been a couple years.

Ali and Torey sat down across from me, and Torey introduced us.

"My God, Torey." She beamed at me. "You come riding into town with the newspaper chasing you down and everything. You're becoming Mr. Something Else."

They both snorted softly as if they knew otherwise. Their foreheads came together, and she laid an affectionate kiss on his nose. He merely blinked a couple times, then turned back to me, leaving me wondering what it would be like to have a female friend affectionately kiss *my* nose. I hadn't made that big a dent in anyone yet, except RayAnn, who was too young to give nose kisses. It was a sophisticated move. I would not have had the composure he did if I'd been on the receiving end. *So used to being loved . . . so mentally healthy.*

"So, what do you want to know about Torey?" Ali asked me, and her famed dimples showed up. She looked about the same as her high school photo otherwise. Some beauty can't be improved upon. "He's my only friend from childhood that I still keep in touch with. I can tell you he got caught cheating off me on a sixth grade science exam, and the teacher gave him an ultimatum. Go home and tell your parents you cheated, or take a zero."

Adams's eyes could have lit the room as he smiled. "A truly *low* moment in my history as a son."

Ali pinched his cheek and refused to let go. "I would have taken the zero. Around my house, who would have noticed? He 'fessed up to Mommy and Daddy. Awwww, so adorable."

Adams finally freed himself and sighed. "Okay, you can print *that*. You happy?"

"I'll give you the background scoop," Ali said, growing very loyal and serious. "Torey graduated Rathborne. *With* honors. Then he went for almost two years to the University of California at Berkeley in the music program. But . . . again, his genius exceeded people's abilities to amuse him."

"That's a very nice way of saying that I almost flunked music theory because I was too busy writing music," he said. "I felt burdened with classwork, dropped out during my sophomore year, found my current band a year and a half ago. I felt really lucky, because they'd been session players, professionals for a couple years, but they liked my songs, my right hand. We won a battle of the bands—held at Berkeley, ironically—and my current agent came up to me that night. Introduced himself. I've had an amazing couple of years. I don't think college is for everyone."

Everyone who dropped out said that, but in his case, who would argue?

"And where have you been?" I turned to Ali.

She nodded. "My only claim to fame was doing emotional damage to myself in Torey's web story. But I'm tons better. I'll have my master's in social work in another two years, and I want to work with runaways. I'm engaged. To another MSW."

She held out a ring, not a big diamond but sweet-looking. I raised my glasses to look at it, congratulated her, and I felt a plop beside me. I slid over for Bo, and he settled in, sighing contentedly at his two friends.

"So, boys and girls," he said, looking at the two of them. "Here we are. How long has it been?"

"A year and four months for me and you." Ali pointed

at Bo. "And a year for me and you." She pointed at Torey, then looked at me. "Bo came up to my engagement party in Boston the Christmas before last. Though he wasn't happy."

They had been an item at the most climactic points of Torey's web tale. Obviously, they weren't now. She grinned at him teasingly, and he pointed a finger in her face. "I told you I would beat you up the aisle. I so wanted to beat you," he said. His tired eyes mixed with his smile and told me he was looking for a conversation to distract from Darla.

"Do you have a girlfriend?" I asked him.

"I wish. There's nothing in this world I want more than four or five kids. And I'm a hopeless romantic underneath these blasts of solid manhood." He made a firm muscle with his bicep. "Unfortunately, Kenai is basically a giant forest, and the Kodiak bears are friendlier than the women in my unit." He shuddered. "Change of subject needed. Go on, Ali. Tell him when you saw Adams."

She went on with enthusiasm. "I went out to see Torey play in Anaheim. It was amazing."

I wanted to add, *Yeah, it was.* But I didn't want Torey knowing I'd sold almost everything I owned to get to his first big concert—or that I was the journalist he wouldn't let backstage because I wanted to talk about ChristopherCreed.com.

Bo asked, "Were you born without eyes? I mean, vision? You know . . ." He shifted, with a nervous laugh. "I don't know what I'm asking tonight."

"I only needed reading glasses like everybody else until I got hit in the head with a baseball two years ago. But I try to steer conversation away from it. I honestly don't feel different than anybody else, until something happens . . . I get jostled in a crowd and then can't see at all for a couple moments. Then, I get annoyed. Other than that, I can almost forget about it."

"So you were a baseball player," Adams said, trying politely to turn the conversation like I'd asked them to.

I couldn't resist. "No. If I'd been a baseball player, I'd have moved a hell of a lot faster."

They followed my lead, grinning after I did, watching me like crazy. I sipped iced tea, stunned at how calm I was with my three foremost web heroes staring.

Bo finally said, "That's amazing, man. You're blind, and yet you're just going for that writer thing and college. What's your big secret? What's the difference between you and my sister? Were you rich or something?"

"No," I admitted. "Small-town boy. My dad wasn't in the picture . . . I left home at seventeen."

"So why do some people make it and some people don't?" he asked.

He was still making a comparison between me and his sister. I didn't feel it was my place to answer, though I could have spoken for hours. He didn't expect an answer, I guess.

"And . . . what is up with Justin? Is he a druggie or are

my ears catching things wrong? People out in the boon-docks are talking up a storm."

Ali looked stricken, and he said to her, "He's been do-ing everything shy of crack from what I hear."

"Oh, damn . . ." she said, resting her forehead on her fingertips. "I'm learning about this in my classes right now. How siblings are often coeternal opposites."

"And here's what's worse." Bo leaned over the table. "You ready?"

They said they were.

"Justin thinks his brother is out in the woods."

"His . . . brother Matt?" Ali asked, confused. Adams froze in a way that, I guess, only I could understand. The weirdness strikes you hard enough to freeze you only if you spent an inordinate time thinking about the kid.

"Not Matt," Adams guessed when Bo didn't answer.

Bo sucked in a deep breath and blew it out again. "There was a whole crew of kids down in the Lightning Field after I left you, Adams. I stopped by to check on Justin like I said I would, thinking maybe I'd lecture him, give him a few needed swats on the head. There must have been, like, nine-teen of them . . . all brewed out and smoked up, all waiting for Chris Creed to show up across the swamp."

"Do we . . . have any reason to believe that Chris might actually be around here?" Ali asked, casting a cautious glance at Torey, who suddenly looked depressed. He could never stand the way kids created a circus out of Chris's disappearance. He said nothing. He just stared into the table, thinking God knows what. I wished he would blog it so I could read it tomorrow.

"Come on, Ali," Bo said, shifting impatiently enough to bounce me once. "Look at the reality of it. If Chris were coming home? Chris would *go to his house*. He's either twenty-one like us, or he's close. He'd go see what was up with his family. He's not going to show up at the Lighting Field to juggle balls of fire for the loadies. Jeezus. I should have known I'd come home to something like this."

"You think it's Justin's drug use that's making him think this?" Ali asked with a grimace. She obviously had liked the kid.

Bo jerked his head my way and his eyes landed on the napkin on my plate. "Mike would know better than me."

I was back to my journalistic conundrums. Was Justin an interview, and hence, did I protect his privacy? Or was Justin a hurting person and these people might help him?

I felt my heart melting, my career choices turning into sludge yet again. "Uh . . . Justin seriously needs to go back to rehab. But, as is sometimes the case, drug use is a symptom. He's been diagnosed as bipolar."

Ali said thoughtfully, "I've long suspected that about his mother . . ."

"The drugs, her alcohol—I'd humbly submit they're

self-medicating. He needs to work the shit out that's in his household. It's . . . pretty unbelievable."

"You saw his mom tonight?" Bo asked.

I shuffled around in my seat until the urge to spill left me. I felt proud of myself for not announcing that the woman had all but raped me. But I got an idea. I wasn't working on the dead sister angle. Without spilling, maybe there was something I could imply to Bo about his sister and my suspicions . . .

"Can I ask you a question?" I looked at Bo and laid down my pen.

He looked glazed. "Sure."

"Did your sister, um, write anything to you? About Justin?"

He chuckled sadly. "She IMed me, like, twice, and both times it was something like 'I love you, but stay the fuck out of it. Luv, Darla.' That was in response to my five dozen IMs to her, to leave Danny alone and shit. She knew I sicced Justin on her, which amused her greatly, and to get even, she threatened to come on to him also. Hey, wait a minute."

He leaned away from me, staring suspiciously, and I suddenly saw a streak of Bo's wild-and-crazy eyes from the myths in these parts. I put my hands in the air, showing they were nowhere near my pen.

"This isn't part of my story," I said defensively. "All this is off the record. I just thought it might help you . . . I just spent a good part of the day with your man Justin."

"What did he say?" Bo asked. "Something about Darla?"

I wished I hadn't started this. For one thing, my suspicions had not been confirmed by Justin. But I plodded on. "Actually, he talked a lot of stoner rot all day and refused to talk about Darla at all. Maybe that's my problem. He signs himself out of rehab for a funeral and he refuses to say one word about the deceased. It's, shall we say, odd, especially considering he's still slightly manic and talks a hundred miles an hour about everything else in the world. I'm just suspicious he knows more than he's saying—that's all. I don't know if that helps you."

Bo drummed on the table, his eyes growing wider and wider. He finally shut his eyes and said, "Oh my God. I just had a terrible thought."

The waitress came and gave me my check, and I sent her off with the money. It gave Bo time to collect his words, which apparently he needed.

He leaned forward. "You don't think . . . Darla actually came on to Justin? And maybe . . . one of those two guys shot her in a jealous rage?"

Ali's hand flew to her chest, and her eyes darted heavenward. "Welcome back to Steepleton," she said.

TWENTY-FOUR

TOREY CONTINUED TO STARE at the tabletop until Bo ran his fingers over his buzzed army hair, saying, "I'm sorry, you guys. Ali, you're engaged, and Tors, you're almost famous, and you have to come back here for my games of the dark side."

"No, man, that's what we're here for." Torey came to life, reaching across and laying his million-buck guitar hand on top of Bo's arm this time. "The truth'll set you free. You know? You can't help your sister this time around, but you can find out the truth."

I took it Torey's fascination with truth had not changed.

"Oh, God," Bo said. "I don't want to see Justin wind up in jail . . . for *any* reason." He turned his agonized face to me. "Did he say anything today that would imply, you know, he was ever 'with' my sister? Romantically?"

I shook my head, and somehow sensed that could not be right. "Have you seen the suicide note?" I asked.

He shook his head. "I was at the Burdens' house earlier tonight to hug on Wiley some. The mister and missus said they weren't ready to see it yet."

I pulled my copy out of my notebook and laid it in the middle of the table. "Don't say who showed this to you. But I think it implicitly denies that Justin could have shot your sister."

Bo read it aloud for the first few paragraphs, as Chief Rye had, then gave it to Torey with a shake of his head. "Damn, that Danny was a worse writer than I am. How'd he expect to pass college English?"

Torey picked it up and slowly and patiently took over reading Danny's tale of grief aloud. It reminded me of him pouring over another letter, once upon a time. *I wish to be gone . . . therefore I AM.*

Torey got to the bottom and handed it back with slow respect, maybe a few memories of his own.

"You think it was a ruse?" Bo asked. "Danny writing this to protect Justin?"

Ali shook her head. "He wouldn't kill himself to protect Justin. I think he was being sincere. I think . . . well, she killed herself, and he panicked after the shock of what he saw."

Bo sniffed. Angrily. Maybe in frustration. I didn't exactly want to be sitting beside him, given what I knew about his temper when he got mad. He seemed to have outgrown his outbursts, but I was still on edge. I'd already been beat on once tonight.

"Doesn't explain how she got six feet under out in the Pine Barrens," Bo said.

"Look." Ali reached across and rubbed his elbow some. He acted like he didn't notice. "We all know the loyalty of people out in the boondocks—though I understand we're not calling it that anymore."

"Conovertown," Bo said. "We're still boons at heart."

"Yeah, and those are pretty big hearts," she said. "I'm sure somebody saw what happened and tried to cover Danny's back. Whoever it was thought they were doing a good thing . . . a heroic thing. For the living. It's a shame it didn't work out, but let's focus on the intentions of people who really do care . . . beneath all their toughness."

"This stinks of the McIntyre brothers, Mack and Ozone," Bo said, unable to resist. When Ali's eyebrows shot up, he said, "Half brothers of Mrs. Creed, if you can believe that. We call them the Brownie's Mafia, though it's more bluster than anything. They're always threatening to kill somebody. Problem is, their aim is so bad, they couldn't drop a turkey. We all know it."

Torey smiled.

"If a body needed burying, they'd give it a whirl, I bet, without totally fucking it up. They could keep somebody buried for three months. That sounds like their work."

"How does Justin fit in to this?" Ali swung the conversation back around. "Do you think he's in some sort of trouble?"

I didn't tell them he had driven me here and was only about twenty feet away. I just had a bad feeling about it, given that he'd seemed even more manic after his mother came to grizzly life than when Bo had dropped him off. I thought his condition might set Bo off worse. "I'm not sure. But I will try to find out what he knows. He, um . . . he's taken a liking to me."

Bo nodded, watching me gratefully, probably remembering how Justin had wanted me to stay for their private talk. "Thanks, man. I don't need his monkeys on my back right now unless they need to be there . . . I got a lot to deal with. You'll see what you can find out?"

I said I would, this time doing it right, putting *Bo's* cell phone number in my phone. "I'll call you if I find out anything about him being involved."

"And do me another favor, too," Bo said. "While you're hanging out with Justin and trying to find out if he got caught up in my sister's shenanigans somehow, can you please try to find out something else?"

"I'll try."

"Find out why that twerp picks *now* to think that his brother is coming back. It doesn't have to do with how he knew *we* were coming back, does it?" His finger circled to imply Ali and Torey and himself, the inner circle of Creed memorializers.

"No," I assured him. "I know why he thinks his brother is coming back. It's probably nothing that would sound very interesting to anyone but him."

"So, it's nothing credible. Right?" Ali asked, looking concerned. "I mean, let's face it. Everyone at this table thinks Chris is going to show up someday. But when a time comes that he might actually show up, we're skeptical before we even find out the reasons why. You're saying that there is *no real reason* to suspect that Chris would show up here, right?"

I didn't know how to answer that honestly. My jaw kind of bobbed in a way that they misinterpreted. Bo and Ali sat straight up, staring for all they were worth.

I had only been pondering how I wasn't entirely dismissive of quantum thought influencing a brother's heart from across the miles. I hadn't meant to give them heart seizures.

"You don't think he's going to show up here in the next day or two. Do you?" Bo asked more directly.

All I said was "I'd be inclined to say no."

It sounded more hopeful than I'd meant it to. I thought of Chris as a forgotten chapter in their lives, but apparently he could be easily remembered, and with a lot of excitement.

"What do you know? Come on," Ali begged.

"Nothing," I said, feeling bad for having accidentally led them on. I stumbled, "I'll tell you what . . . your guess is as good as mine, okay?"

"Since I have no reason to believe he will show up while we're in Steepleton, my guess is no," Ali said, watching me, as if I was supposed to add to it. I let out a sigh of frustration.

"I'm a no," Bo said. "I ain't even so sure he's alive anymore, poor kid."

Adams had been pretty quiet throughout the back end of the conversation, leaving me to think that he got a lot out in writing and maybe had become the type of person who didn't have a whole lot to say. And I sensed he kept his words concerning Chris at a minimum. Maybe out of respect.

He had his chin on his chest, his eyes shut. At first I thought it was dislike of the conversation. But Bo nudged him. "Yo, Trancelike. What are you doing? Reaching for that gift of ESP you got? The gift that found you a dead body in the woods, once upon a time?"

"I didn't find that body via ESP," he said quietly, without opening his eyes. "I found it via a psychic who told me I was going to find it."

In Adams's tale, he and Ali ended up at a psychic's, who told him he would find "death in the woods." He thought it would be the body of Christopher Creed. He actually did stumble upon a body, and Adams wrote a compelling passage near the end of his story. He marveled at how accurate the psychic actually had been, even though she was a chain smoker living over a garage, and had some game show blaring on the TV in the background when she announced her "death in the woods" prediction.

Adams pulled himself forward, leaning over the table. He was smiling and shaking his head, as if he was undecided about something.

"I shouldn't tell you this," he said.

That's the last thing you should say if you don't want to tell something. Ali nudged him and said, "Don't do that to us!"

He wouldn't have started if he didn't plan to spout. "I posted on ChristopherCreed.com yesterday when my mom e-mailed me they'd found a body . . ."

"I know," Ali said. "I still get e-mail alerts when you post. And?"

"There was something I didn't include. An attachment my mom sent along that was supposed to make me laugh. I guess it did . . ." He brought a piece of paper from his jacket pocket and unfolded it. "Since we're talking about that stupid psychic, remember how she was mooching a room over her niece's garage? Apparently, she finally got her own permanent digs and is doing well."

He tossed the paper onto the middle of the table. My fingers and Ali's slapped down on it at the same time, so we were both reading sideways. It was a .pdf file of an advertisement, and Mrs. Adams had been good enough to put the *Press of Atlantic City* dateline at the top from a week ago. I let Ali do the aloud reading.

"'Vera Karzden. Psychic. Criminal Investigations. Psychic Forensics. Cold Case Readings.'" Ali looked at Torey in disbelief. "Oh my God! I think you made the woman famous!"

"If so, I didn't mean to," he said quickly, and we all laughed. Miss Vera's prediction that he would find "death in the woods" had freaked Torey out so badly that he didn't sleep for nights. From his web passage about him and Ali visiting her, you would think he had never forgiven the woman for being so accurate.

He said, "Read on."

"'Miss Vera has moved her offices from Margate, New Jersey to Route 9, just two miles north of Steepleton—' and the address and phone."

They laughed a little more, thinking it was funny to hear something about Miss Vera so many years later. Margate was only about half an hour from Steepleton, so the move wasn't exactly strange.

Torey even added hastily, "A lot of people move from the islands because it's too expensive there now." But his tone implied he was offering explanations to keep from being freaked out by something.

"Her Margate offices . . . I wonder if that was her room above the garage!" Ali laughed. "Glad she finally made it!"

I was smiling too, though I felt tempted to say *More bad frequency.*

I supposed Bo had read ChristopherCreed.com, but probably only once, if that. I wouldn't have pegged him as a reader.

Ali said, "Remember when you stole Chris's diary, and Torey and I found in there that he'd briefly dated some girl named Isabella Karzden? Torey and I went to her house in Margate to see if he'd told her anything about where he was going. Remember this?"

Bo muttered, "Yeah, sure," but looked lost in thought. Obviously this had nothing to do with his sister.

"She hooked us up with her aunt Vera, the chain-smoking, Dorito-munching psychic who lived over the garage." Ali let out a snorty laugh, and Torey managed to smile. "She told Torey he would find 'death in the woods.' Torey ran out of there so fast—"

"Two miles north of Steepleton . . ." Bo recited, twisting the ad around so he was looking straight at it. He read off the address. *Bad frequency,* I thought, though Bo seemed to have a slightly different opinion. "That's somewhere between Steepleton and Conovertown."

Nobody could deny it. The silence pounded.

"So," Bo said, seeming to come to life after being lost in thought. "Do you guys believe in fate?"

Only Torey answered, saying, "Oh my God. Don't—"

Bo pulled out his cell phone, laughing but not smiling. "You guys want to know why I hardly ever drink more than one beer?" He tapped his glass, which only had an inch of brew left in the bottom. I think it was his second. "It's because I have moments like this."

He dialed. I felt the call would be a dud. It was close to midnight, and the woman probably had business hours, even if she was a psychic.

"Just be careful, man," Torey said quickly. "I hold no opinion on psychics. In other words, I was just showing you a weird and funny ad. If you're let down, I don't want it on my conscience."

Bo put the speakerphone on, and we put our heads together to hear. I was almost smiling, not believing the passage of great writing I'd set myself in the middle of, even if she didn't answer. But the situation got better than my wildest dreams.

A woman actually picked up. She didn't sound like she'd been asleep. It was a normal "Hello?"

"Is this Miss, uh, Vera?" Bo asked.

"Sure is," she said.

"Sorry . . . if I woke you up. This is not a crank call, okay? My name is Brody Richardson, though my friends call me Bo. You ever, um, take night visitors?"

I could hear something like the exhale of a cigarette. The woman replied, "Grief doesn't have hours. And I'm so sorry for your loss."

TWENTY-FIVE

OUT IN THE PARKING LOT, I found Justin snoring behind the wheel of his mom's car. He was sitting straight up, mouth open, as if the sleep had come on so suddenly that he didn't even have time to lie down.

Adams looked over my shoulder and whispered, "That your ride?"

Lanz stood in the back seat, wagging his tail. I nodded, then turned to smile at Torey. "Justin Creed."

Adams did a double take. "He was a little kid last time I saw him, and now he looks almost like a man."

I could see the kid in Justin, but knew what he meant. Bo and Ali were already in Bo's old bomb car, and he honked, which made Adams jump straight up, though Justin didn't even stir.

"Do we . . . include him in this?" he whispered.

"Uh, no," I said, using the same line of reasoning as I'd used to keep him out of the interview. He'd gab and dominate. "Let him sleep. He really needs it."

We took off down Route 9 in Bo's car.

Ali turned around to the two of us in the back seat. "Torey, are you sure you're okay with this?"

Bo added, "Listen, buddy. If visiting the woman freaks you out too much, I'll turn around now."

Torey straightened only slightly. But out of his mouth came more Torey Adams integrity: "Bo, I got a great music tour coming up, and you've had a death in your family. Would I deprive you of *any* means to get to the truth?"

"You don't have to come in," Bo added.

"I'll decide when we get there." He picked one thumb with the other and said under his breath to me, "I don't know which would be worse: going in and maybe being singled out again for gross and disgusting predictions, or staying in the car alone at midnight so the Jersey Devil can come along and make a snack out of me."

Bo added loudly, "I'm suddenly not so sure *I'm* going

in. What in hell am I doing, going to a psychic to find out who buried my sister? If the guys in my unit found out about this, they'd think I'd lost my marbles."

"You're responding to your grief," Ali said, rubbing the back of his head. "Nobody would expect you *not* to have dialed that number under the circumstances." She turned sideways in the front seat, so we could hear her musings. "It was weird, how she knew who you were right away. It was almost like she was *expecting* you to call her."

"Don't let's get carried away," Bo said. "You'll freak Adams out, and I don't want him puking in my car on the way home, lovely as it is." There was a rip in the fabric on the ceiling and it hung down. I had to keep batting it away from my face. "She read today's newspaper is all. Anybody, psychic or not, who heard the name Richardson today would think of that."

The house was right on Route 9 and had lights on in every window, so it wasn't hard to find. It was a cute little rancher with ground lights going up the walk and around the bushes—a step up from a room over the garage. As we parked in the drive and rang the doorbell, Torey stayed silently beside me, apparently having made his decision not to be eaten alive by the Jersey Devil.

I felt a sense of déjà vu, which was probably even stronger in him. In his story, he'd been amazed that he felt nothing entering the psychic's house and nothing as she made her predictions. Waiting for her to open the door reminded me of that. You'd expect to be overwhelmed with some feeling of creepiness, especially given the midnight hour. But we could see boxes in the front room, as if she still had a lot of unpacking to do.

She opened the door in a T-shirt that said IRISH PUB, and shorts and bare feet.

"Sorry—I was painting. I'm a nightowl," she said, standing aside so we could come in. The smell of paint was overwhelming, and through the doorway I could see the dining room walls glistening.

"Sit down," she said, and pointed to a long couch in the living room. There were boxes in front of it, but she pulled a folding chair over and sat facing us, using a box to rest her elbow on.

"You sure have changed." Ignoring the rest of us, her eyes rolled up and down Torey, who was next to me. As she'd spoken to him for all of about five minutes five years ago, it jarred me.

"Um . . ." He tried to smile politely, but his neck looked tense enough to crack. When she didn't break in with further commentary, he added, "And you've quit smoking, I take it?"

"Oh, no, I just don't bring them into my soon-to-be parlor. I just had one. You can't smell it?"

I smelled it but wasn't sure they did.

Adams shook his head once, studying his fingers with a nervous grin. "Guess I'm not very psychic."

"So, you found death in the woods," she persisted. "I read your website. The whole thing."

Torey scooted around in his seat, though the four of us were kind of squashed. "Yeah, well, I really don't want to talk about . . . that's not why we're here."

She looked immediately at Bo and kept her gaze fixed there. We hadn't introduced ourselves, so she could have easily thought *I* was him. Bo didn't pick up on that.

He laughed nervously and said, "Lady, I'll be frank with you. I'm a one-beer Charlie, and I was at the bottom of my second when I said we should come here. I guess you could say . . . I don't know what I'm doing here."

"A lot of people feel confused on their way through my door," she said easily.

He didn't look too comforted. "I mean, if Adams hadn't whipped out your ad and pointed you out as the person who was pretty accurate with him, I wouldn't be here. At all. I don't exactly believe in psychics."

She grinned, with as much victory as sympathy, I sensed. "But here you are."

"Well. Yeah."

I waited for her to say something like "So what can I

help you with?," but she just seemed interested in talking about his mom, his sisters and brothers, the Burden family, and how everyone was feeling. In telling all that, little facts started spilling, starting with Danny's suicide letter.

"Aw, the poor family," was her comment to that.

About Bo's mother thinking the whole time that Darla was in Vegas . . . "Mothers are sometimes the last to figure out the truth," she verified.

About what a nice guy Danny was and how he'd been sucked in: "Women are vipers," she said, shaking her head, and added, "I know my gender. What can I say?"

None of it was very psychic. But Bo jumped naturally one step closer.

"I believe Danny. I believe my sister, well, did herself in. I'd just love to know how she got in that grave. Because it looks like a murder now. It could become bad business for some innocent people out our way."

"Could be," she agreed noncommittally.

I glanced down until I found my watch. I had never dismissed Adams and Ali's psychic as a complete hoax, but she was going nowhere fast. I was worried that Justin might wake up, find me gone, and take off with my dog.

"There's these two guys out in Conovertown, called the Brownie's Mafia. I'm thinking maybe they did it. Buried her, I mean." Bo had held up two fingers when he said "two guys."

She suddenly held up three fingers. "Three people buried her."

"Three . . . what?" Bo babbled.

"Three. I see three. Two male, one female."

Bo scratched his head. "Um . . . the *body* was a female."

Miss Vera went on in a normal voice, "The female's voice is saying, 'Haul ass, you goddamn lazy morons.'"

"Even *sounds* like my sister." Bo laughed unhappily, and I got an image in my head of two guys digging a grave and Darla's ghost standing at the top, mouthing off, while her body rested in a blanket beside them. It was surreal, but probably similar to what Bo was thinking, because he shuddered.

Miss Vera's next statement didn't gel with that image, though. "The female said, 'Dig deeper. I don't want to see her toes poking through come April showers.'" She swallowed in revulsion, making me stare. Like Adams, I'd been taken aback by her ability to just talk normally while telling things that are so abnormal. You *want* to think it's a hoax.

Bo put a hand over his mouth and laughed uncomfortably again. "That's disgusting."

"Yeah, sure is," Miss Vera agreed, looking more pensive than apologetic. "Who talks that way?"

"Darla," Bo confirmed. "Maybe some boon chicks who've been taking lessons from her. Well, let's say you're right. So, one of Darla's girl groupies got involved. Which one could keep her mouth shut this long? That's what I'd like to know. It would all come pouring out in the first snort of coke. Those girls never shut up. And it makes me doubt, suddenly, that Mack and Ozone are involved. There is *nobody* out there who would talk to *them* like that."

I thought Miss Vera might add some more intriguing details, but she merely reached across me and Adams and patted Bo once, decidedly, on the knee. "Look. You know it was a double suicide—that is correct. You know there's no bringing either of those kids back. Why not just . . . try to let it alone and move on?"

"Because we're back to old tricks," Bo finally said, "of thinking somebody is going to swing for a crime when they're innocent."

"Who's going to swing?" Miss Vera asked.

Bo shook his head, looking confused and suddenly weary.

"Because there is another key player involved," she said.

Bo watched her, his mouth hidden behind his fingers, which he drummed a little. "You mean the girl."

"No, besides the female. There's someone you haven't mentioned yet. Someone who wasn't at the grave. Someone who helped make some really important decisions just after Darla died."

Bo shook his head slowly back and forth. "You sure about that?"

She nodded, though it was maddening in its lack of detail. "Focus on the female and the male who wasn't at the grave. Find out who they are if you want all the answers. They're very close to one another."

"You mean . . . they're in love? Married?" Bo asked.

It made me want to ask Bo, "What is Mrs. Burden like?" Because she had a saintlike son, I'd been picturing a saint-like mother and father, but having studied so much of family dynamics, I realized how untrue that might be. I suddenly pictured the father cleaning up the mess in the shed, the mother burying the body with God knows who, and I wondered how tough the courts would be on a couple who merely buried somebody already dead. And, being that the girl was engaged to their son and no adult in town had liked her, it could look like a murder.

Bo must have been on my page, because after a long groan he said, "I can't picture anything worse than losing a kid and then being charged with a murder that you didn't commit of another kid. Who'd take care of Wiley?"

"You're thinking of the Burdens," Miss Vera confirmed. I figured she'd read the paper.

"Yeah. Except I can't imagine Mrs. Burden talking like that. She never even says 'darn.' But who knows what a situation like that would do to a pretty mouth? You can't see if it was them?" he said, forgetting for a moment he didn't quite believe in her.

"I see them in danger of being implicated," she said, and put a hand up in warning. "But where people's emotions run high, that creates cloud cover. I can't see if it's their fear, or just your fear, or if it's real. Sometimes I see things in my sleep. And I'll be able to see more clearly when your feelings aren't filling the room, creating cloud cover."

In other words, was it time to go already? I sighed and covered it with a cough.

"All I can do is ask around." Bo stood up. "Well, thanks, Miss um . . ."

"Vera." She stood up, too.

We all stood. The "session" had been short and brutal. I think Bo could have lived without that image of some mouthy female trying to get his sister buried deeper. It seemed he'd felt surer of things before he'd come here. He'd been confident then that Mack and Ozone had been involved, but these new images could make him doubt.

"You haven't asked about Christopher Creed," Miss Vera said, looking at Adams.

Tension rose off him. Ali finally said, "If Chris is dead, I think Torey would prefer not to know."

"He wasn't dead last time you saw me, and he's not dead now," she announced with a smile. She reached out and touched his sleeve. "Last time I scared the hell out of you, so I'm glad to say this time that I have some good news. *He saw you in concert*."

Adams's eyes finally rested on hers. It was a touching moment that made even me smile, in which all his doubt seemed cast aside for a moment of reward. His eyes lit with intrigue, as if he really wanted to believe her.

"He likes your music," she went on. "A lot. Your career will be a tough road, but eventually a rewarding one. And when you release that album, he'll be first in line to grab it."

Torey smiled hugely, and Ali fell into a sideways embrace with him. A part of me wanted to be doubtful of her, but I got a hot chill, the kind you get when you turn in a paper to class and the teacher writes "Brilliant!" across the top. The only doubtful energy was coming from Bo, who would now have to pay a session fee for a compulsive, beer-driven decision.

"You, uh, know where Chris is now?" he asked skeptically. "Maybe you could share that."

"That's not always as easy as it sounds," she said, defending herself. "As for my abilities, I see in frames. I see images. There's no sign behind a body saying, 'This is Farmer John's north pasture.' And sometimes I feel people's emotions—get half in their head and see what's there, though there aren't always words for what they're seeing. Somebody very close to Chris has been . . . praying for him? Using some form of prayer or meditation? It is powerful. And it will bring him back."

Whoa! Bo wasn't together enough to remember the

quantum thought conversation from the car tonight. I was stunned, rooted, until I got a quick dose of common sense. *Don't families always pray for missing family members?* It could have been an educated guess.

"When?" Bo asked, a little tersely.

"Soon," she said. "Very soon. In fact, he might already be here. He can see the full moon in the pines from where he is standing. And he's not a woodsy type of guy."

We left quickly, because I was afraid Bo would say, "That's crazy," or get on some inappropriate bender. His energy was sore. The whole time we were driving back to Brownie's, he shook his head over and over.

"If it's not Mack and Ozone, then I have no idea," he said. "But I can pry information out of any of Darla's girl gang—if it was one of them. Ya know what? I was almost starting to believe that lady. It was working pretty good—until she got to the part about Chris being close by."

"At least she didn't scare the hell out of Torey this time," Ali said.

"Well, we know she's wrong about that much," Bo said. "I ain't a gambler. But you don't have to be to know the odds of something like that. You guys, me, and Creed all come rolling into Steepleton at the same time, when we've all been gone for years? The chances are a gadzillion to one."

"Maybe . . . he came back because he heard about Darla's

death," Ali said hopefully. "I do think he's read Torey's website and would feel bad for Bo right now. Can you imagine if we actually got to see him?"

Bo shook his head. "It had something to do with meditating . . . somebody praying. Obviously not his dad—he's an atheist—and his mom's too drunk. What *was* that? What was that lady talking about?"

I let it go, didn't want to remind him of Justin's spiel on quantum thought at this time of the night. I was exhausted after the adventures of being molested by the Mother Creed, losing RayAnn, and going to visit a psychic with three legends. I'd have to be a lot more alert than I was to make the concept sound credible.

Torey yawned. "Even if he is here—my guess? It's not likely we'll get to see him."

"Why not?" Ali asked, turning to watch him in the seat beside me.

Adams looked pensively out the window. Over his shoulder I could see the moon out there, a full moon behind pines, and figured Adams was looking at it too and understanding something. He'd had deeper insight into Chris than anybody.

"*He* might want to see *us*," Adams said, ". . . see Steepleton, see his family, make sure that he did the right thing. I just don't get the feeling he's ready to *be* seen."

Ali reached back and patted his arm sweetly while yawning herself. She said, "Chris *wasn't* a woodsy guy, and I can't picture him sleeping on rocks near where a dead body was just found and peering out between the trees. He'd have to have changed a lot to do that."

I half smiled, thinking of Justin's visions of a swinging lantern and Kobe Lydee's visions of a spook. Behind all the twists of legend, an actual reality existed. Adams was most likely to understand Chris, though Ali looked disgruntled.

She said, "Torey, you've got jet lag, darling. I'd still say you need sleep."

TWENTY-SIX

THEY ALL LOOKED BEAT, but since they hadn't been together in so long, they wanted to do one for the road at
Brownie's. I felt so comfortable that I almost said yes to their
invitation to stay with them. My ease with three myths from
my reading life amazed me and made me wonder if all
my attempts to lose my bad frequency and loser behaviors
weren't paying off in a big way. I wondered if I wasn't like a
plant. You can never see a plant grow, but they do.

Then I did what I usually do when I start feeling too
comfortable. I started to feel *un*comfortable. It's just not

normal for me to feel comfortable. An alarm goes off inside, telling me all sorts of silly thoughts, like I am still a loser and will do something awkward in a moment if I don't leave—and I'm haunted until that comfort is blown. It's a demon I've yet to face down.

And it reminded me of how I'm always the first to leave. That's a trick I learned that keeps people coming back to me. *Always keep them wanting more.*

I told them I needed to find Justin but that it had been great meeting them—something I would never forget. I think Torey looked pleased by that. He waved as they went back inside. I forced myself slowly to Justin's car. Lanz was in the back seat, pacing around, and the doors were unlocked. Justin was no longer inside.

I walked Lanz in a woodsy area on the far side of the parking lot, hot under the collar that Justin had left my dog in an unlocked car in a parking lot that was now very crowded. Beyond that, I had no idea where he was, and I didn't feel like reappearing to Bo, Ali, and Torey with yet another problem. It would breach my comfort zone of remaining slightly aloof, and I wasn't in the mood.

Lanz and I walked toward the back of Brownie's. Although the music was loud up front, it was very muffled back here. I heard voices and thought one of them was Justin's. Lanz moved silently beside me, sensing my vibe, and we sidled up to the building, where I could hear pretty well.

Justin was arguing with someone. ". . . just know dead bodies don't get up and walk. They don't bury themselves in the woods."

"Around here, they do, kid. Did I ever tell you about the time when I was ten and I saw the Jersey Devil right outside the bedroom window?"

"Not funny," Justin said.

"I am not trying for a laugh. And that was *before* I started drinking—"

Another guy laughed, and the first one went on.

"Honest to God, kid. I heard something out my window that sounded like chewing. Like . . . giant bear teeth grinding up bones. I pulled back the curtain. And there was this horse face staring right at me."

"Maybe it was a horse," Justin said impatiently.

"With wings? It was flapping, my man. Had a wing span as wide as our double-wide—"

"Here's what I think," Justin cut in. "I think you guys know more than what you're saying. And I think you know . . . I was with Danny when—"

"With who? Where?" one man broke in loudly. I supposed these were his two cousins. With Danny . . . *when Darla shot herself?* I smacked my forehead to keep my chest from hurting. This was the last news I wanted to hear.

"Listen to me, Justin," the other said. "Don't tell us nothin' we don't need to be hearing. Just let it go. Let the wind carry it off to wherever the wind takes a problem. I don't know nothing about Darla and Danny, and neither does Ozone, okay? I'm sorry for whatever you went through. We all got our crosses to carry."

"But—"

"But just take it for what it is," Ozone kicked in. "Strange things have been happening in these woods since the Indians had them, since before the settlers took them. The dead move. The dead don't like to be buried."

"Ozone, don't fool with me now," Justin said.

Mack cut in. "Just leave it alone, give it some time. In another few years it'll be just another eerie tale of Steepleton. And that's all I know to tell."

"You guys, you *swear* you don't know anything?"

"On my life."

"On our mom's life."

"Okay, then. I believe you guys."

For all his drug taking and acting like the hottest dish in school, Justin was still burdened with his problem of poor observation. They *sounded* like they were lying, or at least weren't telling the whole thing. If they buried Darla, who was the female? Were the Burdens out of trouble?

I was afraid Lanz might whine, so I turned him slowly and we moved silently back between the rows of cars while I thought. *Justin was with Danny at some crucial point.* I knew my instincts had been dead-on, that he knew more than what he was saying and he'd been paying the hefty price of silence ever since.

Justin had gone around the other way and was standing at the car when I got back. It made me reconsider one thought, which had been to go back inside and let Bo know this.

He sighed in relief, seeing Lanz and me. "Thought for a minute somebody stole your dog. Whew. I just had to go off in the woods and take a leak." His voice was tight like an overstuffed box with the lid ready to blow off, and yet I had to marvel at how he was able to meet one challenge after another, all while his medication was being withheld from him.

"You see Adams?"

"Yeah, he's in there. Ali McDermott's in there, too." It occurred to me he might want to rush in and say hi, and they could question him themselves. He wasn't as symptomatic as I'd imagined he would be. His conversation with his cousins hadn't been at rapid speed.

His eyes, studying the car keys, looked exhausted, and he only said, "Where to?"

I could see the lights of the Wawa way down the road, little more than a sparkle at the end of a tunnel, and I sighed, thinking of RayAnn lecturing me about Justin not being Charlie and all of that.

"Let's get you something to eat. I got a motel room for tonight, paid for, if you want to take a steamy shower and crash."

He moved mechanically to the car, said he wasn't hungry on the drive, but I got him a breaded chicken sandwich, chips, an apple, and a Pepsi in the Wawa, which he devoured in the parking lot. He looked fortified and alert.

"Thanks, man. I gotta get my mom's car home. She knows I've used it . . . I think. But I haven't been caught in the act yet. I'll drop it off and walk back to you. It's only about a mile, and God knows, I don't think I need to be there when she wakes up tomorrow, not after . . . I just need one more night of peace, and I'm cake."

Juggling problems with more problems. The guy ought to be a circus juggler. He drove me to the motel.

"So, you'll be back?" I asked, to make certain.

"Yeah. Gimme forty-five."

I found my watch face. "That would be two o'clock."

"I'll be back at two."

I stayed awake until three thirty, but he never showed up.

TWENTY-SEVEN

Some people say bad things arrive in threes. Others say we have bad days—when we wake up on the wrong side of the bed and everything spirals until we hit the sack and try it again. I can attest to that "bad day" thing, except for me it's a twenty-four-hour period that has nothing to do with the sun coming up or going down. It seems to end around the same time my bad luck started, only a day later. This time, my luck had turned sour after sundown Saturday, when the Mother Creed was either trying to speak to me or kiss me or both and ended up spitting in my mouth. I should have known I was in for it until sundown on Sunday.

I awoke early and was on the phone by six forty-five, realizing I had no computer and no way to get the PayPal money Claudia had promised to wire me for the extra room. The cheapest flight change I'd ever heard of was seventy-five dollars. I called the airline, which said it could set me up for a Monday three p.m. flight and it would cost me ninety-five dollars. *Next step? Try being really bad in math.*

Innocently, I gave them my ATM Visa number, really just biding for time, waiting for them to say that the charge wouldn't go through. But somehow, it went through. I hung up, simply hoping the "insufficient funds" notice wouldn't get to them until I had boarded the plane and taken off.

Next. I needed to eat for the next day and a half, and I had six bucks on me. The last thing I wanted to do was to call RayAnn and tell her I was in a jam. It was time to finally start my diet anyway. RayAnn's favorite fruit in the whole world is Barnum's Animal Crackers, and I remembered there had been half a box of them in my carry-on bag, which she'd been pecking at on the flight. There were nine crackers left—a decent breakfast for a dieting guy. I ate them. *Next step taken.*

I fell back asleep again and woke up at nine. At this point, I had to accept that Justin had gotten his butt slung into some sort of mess with his mom, or maybe he'd even gotten pulled over by the cops and arrested for not having a license. He was unstable and might not be coming at all.

I didn't want to ring his cell phone for fear it was in the Mother Creed's clutches. Bad luck is one thing, but to have to answer some morning-after, groveling third-degree about where her son was, or who I was, didn't appeal to me in the least. I didn't want to call Claudia and tip her off that I was trapped in a motel with no ride out—not after I'd told her so vehemently to trust me. I would tell Claudia afterward— after I had solved my dilemmas. All of them.

I went around to the front office of the Twilight Inn, but it was closed and I didn't know where the owner was. The place seemed deserted, and I thought of that white church everyone in Steepleton went to that Adams had written about. Or maybe the owner was still taking Sundays off, him being the type of old man who, perhaps, had been doing everything the same way since the days when everyone took Sundays off. My room for Saturday night was paid for; he had no reason to be here.

Anything was possible; nothing was etched in blood except that I would have a hard time getting to civilization.

I sat in the room until one in the afternoon, writing out in longhand a story about Steepleton and what creepy behavior may or may not be related to a new dead body in a place that was "collectively depressed." That was a term I made up. I was proud of it. It wasn't the slam-banger story that I could send to Salon.com, but in case something happened, I had only to find a fax machine to actually meet a deadline. Claudia might raise an eyebrow about having to find somebody to type it into a hard drive, but it was Sunday and libraries were closed. By one o'clock, I was itching to find a way out of this motel. I was suffering images of having fallen into the Twilight Zone and I was stuck forever in this ghost motel with nobody ever coming except spooks.

I needed to fax this story to Claudia. Somehow. I had my cell phone in my hand with Bo's number staring back at me. All I had to do was dial. But the guy had funeral arrangements to make and grief to bear. I couldn't call him for a ride, couldn't call Adams because I desperately wanted him to see me as a professional and not some sort of loser who couldn't get his rides together, couldn't get his shit together.

Take the next step.

Lanz had overprotective energy as we stood at the edge of the parking lot, looking down this two-lane highway with no shoulder and only woods on the side. But twenty minutes or so into our journey, I stopped panicking every time I heard a speeding car behind us and simply took four or five steps to the right to be cautiously into the woods when it roared past.

I started calling this "good luck Sunday" just to spite the devil, and as we walked and dodged vehicles, I reminded myself of my good luck issues so I wouldn't give in to utter panic: My plane ticket change had miraculously cleared my insufficient bank account. I had a story in my backpack that I'd written under extreme conditions—no laptop, no Internet, no anything but a pen and tablet—and yet it wasn't half bad. I had dog food in my bag for Lanz in case we got stranded, and a bottle of water.

To ward off images of Lanz and me being flattened by approaching cars, I thought about my $6 million settlement that my lawyer felt he could get from Randolph, if I could just hang in for six more months of not being able to afford shoelaces. Even the $1.5 million settlement was beyond my wildest dreams, and thinking of a life of being able to afford someone to drive me around forever kept me bouncing down the road.

Justin's forty-five-minute walk took Lanz and me slightly less than two hours, but I stood in front of the city hall at ten minutes past three feeling like I ought to try Mount Everest next. It's this thing with how you look at circumstances—life is grand or life blows, depending on where you allow your focus to be. "The next step" was working, which was blotting out people in my history who had told me that blind people have no business leaving cities without either a trusted family member or an employee of Services for the Blind.

Next step . . . I was starved. I fed Lanz out of his Ziploc bag and gave him a long drink before heading into an Indian grocery store for a bag of East Indian chips. They tasted like corn. While eating, I started getting beyond steamed at Justin, then at his mother, and I told myself firmly, *Don't waste your energy on anger. You need your energy for you.*

I had to remind myself, after fighting off anger over having to make that long walk, that I was in a better way than those two. I'd rather be me than them.

Then I went over to the police station. Rye was there, even though it was Sunday, and he came out from behind the big glass window to speak to me.

"I'm going to Philly to pick up Danny Burden's body. The funeral director and I. I can't talk right now, but there's nothing new except that the crime scene has been wiped clean of evidence. We're getting a forensic specialist down here . . ."

Crime scene . . . they were thinking homicide. I tried telling myself that was out of my jurisdiction.

"It's okay," I simply said. "I was actually just wondering if I could use your fax machine. Library's closed and I'm not familiar with—"

"Sure," he said, opening the door and leading me behind the glass.

Claudia or RayAnn . . . Gut instinct again, but I went for RayAnn, speed-dialing her on my cell.

"It's me. Are you home or at school?" I asked.

"Home. Are you okay, Mike?"

"How are you feeling?"

"My lip resembles a nerf football but . . . *how are you?*"

She sounded completely worried, and I found myself grinning. "Great. Thanks."

"Are you coming home today?"

"Tomorrow afternoon. Listen. I know you're still in recovery mode, but if I fax you something, can you type it and send it to Claudia?"

"Your story?"

"Yeah. It's not the mother lode. But it will tide her over until I can think about the best way to . . . to put all this down."

"It'll keep my mind occupied. Sure."

"Your father wants to kill me, I suppose."

"Actually, he's more pissed at himself. Parents always feel responsible when something happens to their offspring. I keep telling him he's not a soothsayer, and neither am I, and who would have thought Fort Lauderdale in April would be safer than a quaint little Jersey town." She sighed. "My mom wants to come after Lydee and his passel of car-stealing friends. She says she spent years trying to create a life for her kids that circumvents what she calls school psychosis."

I'd been around the Spencers enough to make an

educated guess as to her meaning. "School psychosis: a lengthy list of horrors that schooled kids will commit upon each other when thrown together into one building, all day every day, with no parental figures."

"Bravo," RayAnn said, though her laugh was cockamamie, making me think her swollen lip still bothered her. But it was good to hear her laugh.

I felt better. "I've gotta be quick. I'm in the cop station."

"Give me the fax number. I've got something to send to you, too."

I found it on the side of the machine and repeated it.

"Oh. And Claudia called me," she said.

Fire of burning pride hit my cheeks, and I tried to stay calm. "Did you tell her you were almost strangled and our car got stolen temporarily?"

"I don't know her that well yet. She'll think I caused it. I don't like the way she looks at me. She thinks I'm a young-ster. She's got no respect."

"She doesn't warm up easily, but once she's your friend, she's a friend for life," I said, hiding relief. I couldn't blame RayAnn if she'd told Claudia the whole thing, but I wasn't ready to hear "I told ya so" from my editor in chief.

I asked, "Why'd she call you and not me?"

"She figured you might have trouble getting the money out in the middle of nowhere and wanted to do a direct de-posit into your bank account from the office. But she didn't have your bank account number. She has mine because I get direct deposit for my stories. She wanted to know if she could put the extra money for the motel room in there. I said yeah, we use the same bank, and I would transfer it by phone. That was early this morning, so there's fourteen hundred bucks in your account."

"How much?" I asked in amazement.

"Fourteen hundred."

"Why so much?"

"Because . . . once Claudia got a travel budget approved for your motel room, she was able to charge your plane ticket, too." I could read the huge smile in her voice. I could buy back my laptop. Getting to the airport would not be a problem. No wonder the flight change blew on through my bank account.

"RayAnn?"

"Yeah?" She waited in thick silence. I couldn't stop gulping.

"I'll, um . . . I'll tell you later." I hung up, guilty of using silence to sidestep opportunities. I told myself I could do this "take the next step" thing with my love life after I was done with my professional life.

Chief Rye was already gone by the time I got the last page through, but Tiny Hughes was at a desk, filling in paperwork of some sort. As I waited for whatever RayAnn was sending, I approached.

"Is there a local cab company?" I asked.

"Not really. There's Yellow Cab in Atlantic City. But it'll cost you an arm and a leg to get around with them."

"Mmm. I'm looking for the best way to get to the airport tomorrow."

"Oh. There's an airport shuttle that leaves from the Borgata Casino on the hour, weekdays. I think it's only around twenty-five bucks."

Bingo. "And what's the best way to get to the Borgata if you don't drive?"

He watched me long and hard, maybe trying to picture the life of a legally blind person, and his face grew concerned. "Any friends in the area?"

"Well . . ." I wondered if Bo and Ali and Torey would qualify now as friends. It was a nice feeling to wonder that. I added aloud, "They're all, um, detained with funeral plans."

"I'll get you a ride," he said, and picked up the phone. I started to object. I didn't want to accept gestures of kindness in my game of do-it-yourself.

I was surprised and confused when, after a moment, Tiny said into the phone, "He's here." Then he hung up again.

"Who was that?" I asked.

"A friend of yours," he said mysteriously. "Somebody who's been looking for you. Someone who called this morning and said to call back if you showed up here."

Well, obviously it wasn't Justin. He was the only person who knew where to find me.

Tiny must have liked my confused grin. He raised his arms in a dramatic shrug.

"Maybe . . ." he said, "it's Christopher Creed."

I smiled as I heard the fax machine ring and let that mystery take a back seat to this one. "I think this fax is mine."

The article RayAnn alluded to came through very slowly, the way only an old-fashioned fax in a small town can do. Before I could get too antsy, the door of the police station opened. Torey Adams came walking toward me. I framed out the red ski jacket from last night before seeing his face.

He smiled, then heaved a sigh, something like a sigh of relief.

"You're my mystery caller?" I asked.

"Yeah."

"Something . . . you forgot to tell me last night?"

"No. You didn't take anyone's number but Bo's last night. I had no way to find you. But considering what you were doing here, I figured you'd either call or show up here at some point today." He sounded awkward. It didn't exactly explain why he was looking for me, but I watched him look all around the place, as if maybe it was bringing back memories. His eyes stopped on two chairs outside the glass window, and then he pointed at it.

"This used to be all wall," he said. "Glass is new."

I just went along with his mystery appearance. "Everything changes, my man. Nothing stays the same."

"Nothing except . . . how this place creeps me out."

I turned back to my fax, smiling to myself. "You mean Steepleton in general, or the police station?"

"Steepleton in general," he said, then smiled, jumping tracks without further explanation. None was exactly needed. "Ali went with Bo and his mom to make funeral arrangements. I figured maybe I could help you out."

I was full of myself—full of a new infusion of confidence. I wanted to spend time with him, for sure, but not on those terms.

"Torey, that's nice, but I'm playing a game with myself. Today is officially 'Mike Is Not Taking Help Day.' It's a psych-out exercise, to exorcise all the demons I got from listening to all the people who ever said blind people can't live outside the city, can't hold professional jobs, can't can't can't. I'm actually doing very well."

We did a staredown of the shades for only a moment. He then laughed. "Oh! I don't mean that sort of help. The idea is very clear to me that you can do anything you set your mind to. I mean, well . . ." He held out his hands. "I'm a writer. A different kind of writer, obviously. But if I sit in the house for another minute, thinking of awful things and people in my past, I'm going to lose it. Maybe . . . you'd be helping me by letting me help you. "

I laughed. Torey Adams wanted to be my writing assistant. That was funny. Very funny.

"Well, we are kind of in the same boat," I said, watching a third page slowly plop into the fax receiver. "You talked to me last night about how you'll be posh after your tour ends. I'll be posh after I win a lawsuit against my school over the baseball-in-the-head thing. In the meantime? If you got access to a car, I'll put some gas money in it."

"I have a car. And my mom gassed it up this morning," he said. "Tank's full. Thank God she wasn't relying on me for that."

We laughed together. It felt great.

I pulled the fax out of the machine. I moved the paper around until the headline came into view. "'Natural lightning reservoirs maintain an electrical charge after being struck,'" I read. "It's from . . . a four-year-old *National Geographic*. My girlfriend, RayAnn—she's a research maniac."

"You got a girlfriend?"

Yeah, and we staked out your house yesterday. I decided to skip it.

"We had a recent blowout," I confessed with a sigh. "You got a girlfriend?"

"No," he said. "Not since I left Berkeley." He left it

dangling, leaving me with the feeling he didn't want to talk about his relationship any more than I wanted to discuss mine. "So what are we doing here?"

I passed him the pages, again shaking my head in disbelief that he was here. "Right . . . tell me if that's anything interesting."

He took the pages and read the article aloud. I walked into the outer lobby slowly, listening as he followed me while continuing to read. I sat my weary legs down in one of the two chairs. Lanz lay down at my feet, sighing contentedly at his chance to rest. It was a luxury not having to read the thing. He stopped halfway through and said, "I knew about this. I knew about lightning traps."

I turned and found his face, which looked hypnotized. "Do tell."

"Well . . ." He laughed nervously. "After finding a dead body in a limestone cave, I read up on everything limestone in these parts. My mom helped me. Let me see if this article contains anything I didn't know . . ."

Officer Hughes came out of one of the rooms down the corridor and stopped in front of us, having seen Adams. Torey breezed through the rest of the story silently, then handed the article to the officer.

"We think you might want to look at this," I said.

I could tell it was of interest to Officer Hughes, because

instead of simply scanning it, he sat down beside me and read the entire thing.

"Why did I never see this?" he asked. "Can I make a copy?"

"Why did I never post all my limestone findings on my website?" Torey asked guiltily.

I said to Officer Hughes, "I'm sensing that the concept of 'natural lightning reservoir' might provide the answer to a couple mysteries around here."

"Uh . . . yeah," he said, then laughed uneasily. "Nothing will provide answers to all the mysteries these woods hold—unless of course the industrialists come through and knock down every tree in the Pine Barrens and wipe the slate clean. But this might explain why sometimes people have seen strange lights flickering out on Doughty Road, and other places near the Lightning Field."

"Lights flickering in the woods . . ." I reached behind my seat, trying to remember where I'd left my backpack.

"What are you looking for?" Torey asked.

I told him. He disappeared and a minute later returned with my pack. I pulled out one of the pads RayAnn used and handed it to him. I pulled out my recorder—what RayAnn and I called double backup—and heard him click a pen. Officer Hughes went on.

"It's just something that happens maybe once or twice

a year. Someone calls in, says they think there's a fire in the woods, or with an unobstructed view, they say there's something that looks like lightning. But it's coming *up* from the ground, they say, and it's all very strange. When we get to the spot the caller points out, there's never anything happening. This has been going on since the Lightning Field got struck."

"Five years ago," I remembered from Mary Ellen's telling me.

"I remember that," Adams said. "I mean, I was avoiding everyone and writing my blog, but my mom told me about it. The spring after Chris Creed disappeared."

"Right," Tiny said. His laugh was even twitchier. "I don't think the two bear any relationship to each other, but lots of people like to keep their beliefs fun."

"I like fun as much as the next guy," I said with a grin as I took the article back, "but not at the expense of others. This article says that certain rocks and rock cavities are conducive to storing lightning charges."

He looked over my shoulder, intrigued. "Yeah."

"And one of those types of rock is limestone."

"Correct," he said.

I nudged Adams and said with due sarcasm, "And Torey. What do we know about limestone?"

He groaned. "Let's just say there's lots of it around here. There are lots of limestone caves, er, cavities."

"Exactly," Tiny said. "This might explain why that happens. Maybe I should call over to Stockton sometime this week. The geologists might be interested, might know how to detonate one—if that's what it is."

"Maybe you should do it sooner and with some urgency," I decided, pointing to a cutline under a picture: *The charge can be dangerous if it's stepped on, still containing enough voltage to stop a human heart.*

"Has there been something like this recently?" he asked.

"A lot of us saw something bizarre out by the north side of the Lightning Field," I said, "including me and my girlfriend, RayAnn, who has never done a drug in her life. But I think some people out there saw it, maybe a month or so ago, and twisted it into an image of one dead Chris Creed . . ." I laughed, fumbling for words because I didn't want to bust anyone. That wasn't my terrain. "And there have been a few other sightings."

"The north side?"

"There's a place that looks to be an entrance from an old path. It's got two trees on the right and one on the left, with smaller trees in the background. You know . . ."

I was fumbling, but he picked right up.

"That's not actually a path. It's the foundation, or what's left of it, of where some say the Jersey Devil was born. Mother Leeds had this thirteenth kid, and all the Quaker ladies heard her utter the *g*-word when she found out she was pregnant. They said she cursed the baby and it was born with a forked tongue and other, uh, menacing traits."

"Probably a Down's syndrome baby," Adams put in. I laid my palm out for him to skin. That's what I'd always thought too.

"You guys are ruining local lore. But yeah," Hughes said.

"And regardless of who that foundation originally belonged to, you might actually have a natural lightning reservoir near it. And with those kids watching for spooks every five seconds . . ." I didn't mention Justin's name in particular, but Hughes was watching me, concerned. I finished, "I can't say how long or soon it will be before a group of them goes to investigate."

Torey added, "I don't know much more than what's written here. Except I remember my mom telling me something that she might have gotten from the Stockton geologists. The lightning traps start 'puking' lightning when they're getting ready to die. You'll see lightning daily rather than weekly or monthly. That's a sign, but they generally die by explosion. It's a small explosion, she said, but I wouldn't want to be standing within fifty feet, and sometimes they start fires . . ."

Hughes stood up. "I'll search my Rolodex and call somebody today. I got a couple of the Stockton geologists on hand . . . had them ever since Bob Haines's body was found."

He moved quickly down the hall, and I held out a hand again for Adams to skin. "Glad you were here."

He skinned me. "Let's be glad when the thing is found and neutralized. What should we do now?"

I asked him to lead me to an ATM so I could have some cash on hand and so I could leave him some gas money, even if his mom had filled the tank. It seemed only right if he was going to drive me around for an afternoon.

"I see a bank a block away," he said once we got outside with Lanz. "Place has changed a bit. Bet there's an ATM there. You want me to get the car?"

"Nah, let's walk it," I said, not sure where I was going yet or what I'd be doing next. I just didn't want to lose his good company now that I'd lucked into it. I would maybe draw the afternoon out.

"Lightning Field," he said as we walked along. "That's another big change around here, I guess. I'd heard of kids hanging out down by the back bay. But we never went down there. It was mostly all boons back when we were freshmen."

"Bo gave us the lowdown on that," I said. "It's changed shape and the scenery's different, but it's still full of water moccasins, dead water, and, obviously . . . charges of lightning that the loadies are thinking is one Christopher Creed."

Torey was quiet for a couple moments, and then he started to laugh. "Some things never change. Do they?"

The ATM distracted me, and I didn't think an answer was necessary. I decided to withdraw a couple hundred dollars . . . gut instincts. I just felt like I might need it.

As we turned, a guy on a mountain bike pulled up beside us. I recognized the jerk that had tossed RayAnn's cell phone in the door and took off, laughing and burning rubber.

"S'up?" He smiled, watching Lanz, who made me a landmark.

I lit like a torch, amazed at how kids can do shit and then act like it was nothing the next day. I supposed, to them, it *was* nothing.

"Thanks for the phone," I said, my sarcasm cutting through.

"You're welcome." He bowed his head, kind of proud of himself, though his face turned red with heat.

"Anything else you want to say?" *Like "I'm sorry"*?

He stared at my counterpart. His voice sounded surprised this time. "Whoa. Are you Torey Adams?"

Torey reached slowly past me and shook the guy's hand, who said his name was Steve.

"Oh my God." He studied him with an astonished grin. "It's the legend himself."

I sensed Torey stiffen as he elbowed me slightly. "Um, I think Chris Creed is the legend. I'm just the tale teller."

"No, I mean your music and all. Did you know there's a huge display case with posters of you in Steepleton High School?"

Adams cleared his throat before saying, "Yeah, my mom mentioned that to me. That's, um, nice."

I felt it was very nice considering he'd never graduated from there. He'd been all but run out of town when people suspected him of being an accomplice in Chris's disappearance.

"And the newspaper has a column in it called *This Day with Torey Adams.* Did she tell you that, too?"

He didn't answer this time, and Steve kept going. "Honest to God. They got a picture of you playing some huge concert, and every week they run it and they call your publicist, and he tells them whether you were in the studio, or who you were jamming with, or where you ate. It is very cool. They did it, supposedly, so that us kids in school would read the newspaper."

"Yeah . . . I hope . . . it helps—" He stammered, sensing my anxiety, I was certain.

"D'you do autographs? Come on. My friends will die when—"

"I'm here for a funeral, so I'm not doing autographs, and what is it you have to say?" *Definitely* he sensed my anxiety.

The guy laughed sarcastically. "You don't have to get snippy. Jeezus."

"What's this about a phone and last night?" Torey confronted him, jumping to my defense so quickly, it left me stunned. He looked quickly from the guy to me and back again.

I wasn't above grinning acridly and saying, "He could probably tell you better, being that I left him and his friends to look after my girlfriend . . . I wasn't there."

"Look. We didn't hurt her." Steve's voice was loud, and he held up his hands defensively.

"She's got a fat lip and a handprint across her neck," I replied.

"That was Kobe, that wasn't me. I'm the one who brought her fancy cell phone back. I could have sold it," he said.

I lowered my head and stared at Adams's waist, laughing in disbelief. "Does any kid in this town know how to say 'I'm sorry'?"

"It's a long-standing problem," Adams replied.

I could only chuckle, which egged him on.

"Do you know what I mean?" Adams persisted.

"I know. My girlfriend is fine, but she left last night, kind of unglued. I'd be unglued, too, if someone threatened me with rape and murder after boosting my car." I wanted to see what the kid would do with that one.

"Kobe and Justin, man," this Steve went on with a red face. "They're kind of the center of things around here and they're on each other's nerves. Kobe's been losing it by looking for too many spooks, and Justin's losing it just because."

So this was Kobe's and Justin's fault.

He went on, "If you really wanted to keep your girlfriend safe, you shouldn't have left her with Kobe after spending a whole day with Justin."

"Oh. So it was *Mike's* fault." Adams jerked his thumb at me, so much on my wavelength that I skipped right over the intended moment of guilt and cracked up again. He was chuckling incredulously, too.

"Gee! I think I'll take a crash course in high school politics," I said without losing my glee. "I'll be such a wise person after that."

Maybe only the author of ChristopherCreed.com and myself as its most avid reader could get why this was so funny. The kid surely didn't get it. Torey pulled his shades up to look at me, and he'd been laughing so hard on the inside that his eyes were wet.

"Are you *sure* you want to write a story about Steepleton?" he asked. "Are you into self-abuse?"

"No, but I am wondering . . ." I sniffed and toned down my smile a bit. "Do you feel that Steepleton is *worse* than other towns, or are things the same all over?"

"I'd say it's worse." He chuckled. "But how much worse?" He moved toward Steve and put a hand on his shoulder, another hand on my shoulder.

"Steve. How long'd you guys boost that car for last night?" he asked, so seriously that I almost cracked up again.

The kid managed to say, "We were back in less than fifteen minutes." We ignored his defensive tone as Adams studied the sidewalk, nodding, calculating with pinched lips.

"In other towns, the kids might have driven across the parking lot. Maybe even around the block," he finally said. "Everyone else in the car would have been saying, 'No, no! Let me out!' Some girl would have been crying—"

"You don't know what went on in that car!" the kid said loudly. "You don't know that some girl wasn't crying. You weren't there."

Yeah, but if something like that had happened, he would have told us.

Torey tired of our half-serious game. He got a little snappish. "Were you looking for us for some reason, or just stopping to shoot the breeze?"

"No, I was looking," Steve said, jerking his head at me. "Justin sent me to look for you. He says he needs to talk to you about something. I don't know, man . . . He's acting strange."

"Where is he?" I asked with a sigh.

"At the Lightning Field."

I turned until I found Torey's eyes again. I raised my shades so he could see how I rolled my eyes, not amused. I dropped my glasses onto the bridge of my nose in disgust and muttered under my breath that he'd been a no-show today and I'd walked to town.

"Let me guess," I went on, my gut instincts firing off like crazy. "Is he talking at a hundred miles an hour?"

"Yeah."

"He mention his mom?"

"Yeah. But I couldn't make sense of it."

"What did he say?"

"She . . . took drugs off him or something? Says he doesn't need them?"

"Hmm." *She took his prescription and won't give it to him. He's manic, been through a stress, lost at least two doses, and . . .*

"He do any *other* drugs?" I asked.

"Just one line of coke."

Just. "Gee, that'll help slow him down," I said sarcastically.

I glanced at Torey's left hand, thumb stuck in his pocket, million-dollar guitar fingers dangling loosely . . .

"You don't want to go back there with me," I said. "It could be dangerous. You got a career to think of."

I couldn't see the look in his eyes because of his shades. I just know they didn't move off me.

"I'm not leaving you," he said swiftly.

I wondered if *rock star* would be good enough terminology for him. I wondered if he wanted to be nominated for sainthood. I just hoped this wouldn't turn out badly. I put Lanz in the back of Torey's mom's car and dropped into the passenger seat beside him.

TWENTY-EIGHT

WHAT DO YOU SAY TO A KID whose eyeballs can look in nine directions faster than most eyes can look in two? I did not know what to make of Justin, since my drug-taking history is only one episode deep. (I smoked pot with Stedman one night last year when the rest of the school was watching the Randolph baseball playoffs. We don't watch baseball on principle.) I can usually tell if someone has done a line or two of coke by the way their eyeballs dance, but this was like watching a fast-forwarded version of a high-speed chase.

Justin was circling a lightning tree, muttering something to it, or muttering to Mary Ellen, who was seated inside the hollowed-out stump, hugging her legs to her chest and glaring at us over the top of her knees. I couldn't see anyone else in the field. Lanz stepped forward and in front of me, sort of putting himself between me and Justin.

Adams was silent behind me, taking it all in, I supposed. He was like a calm non-presence. Justin was too wild and distracted to realize who this was, and Mary Ellen didn't seem to know. Adams's charismatic posters didn't reveal the normal-guy element well.

"I hate when he gets like this," she said into her legs. "He got like this a lot just before rehab."

He looked in five directions in two seconds.

"Can you *feel* anything?" He looked directly at me, but I supposed he was asking Mary Ellen.

"No! I honestly can't! I mean, I can feel that you're scaring me half to death," she snapped. She rolled her eyes toward me. "Back when I was trying to tell him he was bipolar, he wouldn't listen to me. Now he's telling us he's bipolar. My cousin Dwayne is bipolar and gets all twitchy like this. He tells me people talk to him through the walls when his parents are out—"

"Nobody is talking to me through the walls!" Justin insisted. "This is not the same as that! This is quantum thought. How dare you confuse me with a psychosis."

Um, it looked the same.

"Everyone who doesn't want to believe in supernormal powers says the people who experience them are psycho. What the hell kind of a world is this if all magic moments are psychotic? You think *I'm* crazy? What about the people who believe that?"

He caught sight of me again and proceeded before I could think of what to say.

"Magic grounded in science . . . Do you believe in quantum thought, Mike? Do you believe people's thoughts become things?"

I decided to take the high road. It might neutralize him somewhat. "I believe Edison really wanted to create a light bulb."

"And hence, he *did*." Justin stuck his fingers to the tree, looked at them curiously, and shook them out.

"But we went over this yesterday, buddy," I reminded him. "We decided people ought to think of the other guy. Especially the Creeds—"

"Why is it"—he stuck two fingers up to the crystallized trunk again—"that I can feel a charge coming from this tree? But nobody else can? I can *feel* it! I am not lying!"

Mary Ellen shook her head, watching me helplessly. "My mom says not to argue with Dwayne. She says he sees what he wants to see, feels what he wants to."

It seemed to me I'd heard something similar from Torey Adams's mom about anyone who hung around out here, and I didn't suppose these woods were helping. Nothing was helping—not his missing doses, not his drug consumption, not his stress levels.

"I am not 'crazy,' thinking my energy can reach my brother. What do you want me to do now that all those lights have been seen? Stand here and shout at him?"

The lights were not helping either.

His words had come out in quick, jerking sentences. He turned around and faced the north woods. *"Christopher Michael Creed! Come out here, fuckface! I need to see you, man!"*

"Maybe you're feeling an energy charge because you did two lines of coke in one hour," Mary Ellen suggested, and she sprang out of the tree trunk finally.

So now we were up to two hits of coke on an over-charged head.

I scratched mine, sensing the time wasn't quite right to make references to trapped lightning. He might stuff me into the lightning tree headfirst.

"If he's out there, he'll come when he's ready," Mary Ellen said, but I sensed her deep turmoil thrown into the stew. As Kobe Lydee's sidekick, she probably was very confused about whether she would see a spook come out of these woods, a live guy, or nothing.

"He has to come out of there before that funeral and I go back to rehab! He's playing with me! And I need him! *I need him!*" Justin insisted.

Steve came into view from the side. I hadn't noticed him here before. He was out of breath and must have ridden down here at ninety miles an hour. He looked back and forth from Justin to Torey and, I supposed, decided it was better not to distract Justin from what he was doing to say "Open your eyes" or some such thing. Maybe he'd tell Justin later, all, "Guess who was standing right beside you this afternoon?"

Torey stayed silent and still. Steve put three fingers up to the tree, then put his hand in his pocket without saying anything. I took that as a neg from him, too. I didn't bother.

I turned to Mary Ellen, who looked torn between watching Justin and watching me. Her eyes turned to mine, and she said, "Mike. I just want you to know that last night, I tried to get out of the car. I was screaming to get out. But they wouldn't let me."

I wondered aloud this time, "Are the words 'I'm sorry' too much for *anyone* in this town?"

Adams put his hand on my shoulder and said with dramatic seriousness, "I am sorry, Mike."

We might have laughed if Justin weren't sobbing suddenly and babbling incoherently. The only words I understood were "not fair, he can't just . . ."

And this Steve guy was all, "*This* is not Justin. He was a

great time until just recently. You important people should know that."

My class notes came jolting to the front of my brain—probably because I needed them. I knew bipolar disorder is often triggered in adolescence. *It can be triggered by a traumatic event. What had happened the last time Justin was with Danny Burden?* I looked at the menacing clouds rolling in overhead and went with my gut.

"Torey, can you get rid of these people? I need to talk to Justin in private."

He stared at Justin for a moment, then looked questioningly at me. He brought his car keys out like a good assistant, but turned to Mary Ellen. "Come on. Quit crying. Lemme take you home, okay?"

"Aw, me, too?" Steve begged. "It's going to rain on my head, man. I'll leave my bike in the bush."

I figured he just wanted to be in a car with Mr. Fame, and Torey was doing his best to set boundaries as they started off. ". . . guys *doing* back here? *We* never partied back here . . . clean up your act . . . stop crying, okay? . . . and stop touching me!" I got a blast of him pulling his shoulder away from Steve's paw. I wondered if, somehow, he didn't have a worse deal than I did.

Having gotten to town by myself with a completed story for Claudia, I was in a mindset of thinking ahead like I'd never been before. While waiting for Justin to calm down a little, I called Yellow Cab just in case. I didn't want to be stuck out here in a blinding rain storm where lightning liked to strike. They said they could be here in fifteen minutes when I gave them the road and the landmarks. If we didn't need them, they'd have a hard time finding me to give me hell.

Justin had slithered down and was sitting on the ground in front of the lightning tree. I lowered my aching legs beside him, but the trunk was not very fat. So, we were facing off in sort of different directions. I watched Torey lead Steve and Mary Ellen off, looking back at me every ten seconds with concern.

"Sorry I didn't come back last night," Justin started, refusing to look at me. At first. Finally he turned, sitting Indian-style and facing me. His eyes passed over me six times while he said, "Whatever, I'm not myself right now and all I can say is I'm acting like a scumbag loser."

I didn't deny it. "What happened?"

"Last night somebody gave me a vial of coke and some Seconal, which I didn't want, but I didn't give back, either. I just couldn't let go of them. I was manic those times I thought I'd reached my brother, the time I saw him at that cemetery, in that barracks-looking place. I can see that now. Manic has great energy, man! I suppose you think that sounds crazy, but it's true! I was adding coke to the thing. It was just in case I wanted to be even more manic, but after I took my mom's car back, I did a couple lines, and then I couldn't sleep, so I went over to Mary Ellen's and crashed out under her bed, and here I am. I have some coke left. Take it from me. Here. Hurry up before I change my mind."

I found the vial he was holding out, his hand trembling slightly. I flipped the black cap off and turned it over on the ground, but when I found his face again, capsules were going into his mouth.

"Jeezus, Justin. You're gonna . . . stop your heart," I said, with no actual clue what I was talking about, but it sounded right.

"No, now I won't. I'll be good in about fifteen minutes. Slow train coming . . ."

I handed him my water bottle out of my backpack for lack of something better to do and fingered my cell phone, knowing I could punch 9-1-1 without even looking.

"Just . . . give me a few minutes. Slow, slow train. Then I got something I need to tell you."

I reached out and put a hand in his hair, going, "Take it easy. Whoa . . . whoa . . ."

I had touched so few people over the past few years, outside of RayAnn. Affection in my life had been something one-sided, from one person only. It had been selfish and indulgent on my mother's part, and it brought me a dim view of touching for comfort.

The idea rode me that I could let RayAnn walk away

from me, but I could make room in my heart for someone with a drug problem. A couple times she had been really blunt with me: *I can understand about your mom, but don't you miss Charlie and Merilee?* I'd never answered her. I had made my choices, and there was nothing I could do about it. Now, suddenly, there was.

I rubbed Justin's hair and his back, which brought his head down into my lap, and he was crying at the ground. The clouds hid the sun almost entirely by the time he found his voice, but somehow the world felt dry as a bone. Dry and silent.

"Remember the night I hit my mom?" he asked.

I nodded. "You said you were trying to go out and she didn't want you to."

"I used to sneak out my bedroom window a lot. She'd catch me the next day, ground me for life and whatnot. But I never actually tried to push her aside so I could walk out the front door before. She's just so . . . unseeing. Any normal mom would have seen I was unglued about something and would have let me go, and maybe I could have explained later."

I started to put it together that he hadn't been lining up a drug deal that night. I guessed as much aloud.

"Hell, no!" He raised his head finally. "At that point in my life I had smoked one joint. It was the night Danny Burden called me. The night Darla died."

I wondered if he should wait until he was calmer to talk about this. But I kept a hand on his shoulder, which seemed to be calming him more quickly than the drugs.

"He said Darla had shot herself in this outbuilding on the back of his property and he didn't know what to do. He could hardly talk. Nothing was coming out except these . . . terrible wails most of the time."

"So, you hit your mom to get to him."

"I totally nailed her. When she was too bloody to hold me down anymore, I took off on my bike. The only thing I had said to Danny—the only thing that made sense—was 'Don't touch anything. Nothing. Don't go back in that building until I get there and we can figure something out.'"

"Why did Danny call you?" I asked. It seemed to me he'd have had better friends out in the Pine Barrens.

"Because I was the one he talked to about Darla. Because I took Bo so seriously and he knew I was trying to look out for her when they started going out. Every time Danny had a problem with her, which was often, he called *me*. We spent a lot of time together over at his house, riding his dirt bike around Conovertown. There was so much that I couldn't even tell Bo. For one, Danny'd caught her cheating. Sometimes he wasn't even sure the baby was his."

More intrigue. The girl sure could stir up trouble. "So, what happened that night?"

"She shot herself at around five thirty. Danny's parents and Wiley were at church. I got there around six. Danny had done like I said. He hadn't gone in the outbuilding, and it was a good thing. We had time to think. He told me he had yelled at her pretty loudly, and the neighbors probably heard it. She'd been threatening suicide for the umpteenth time and he said, 'Go ahead!' and a bunch of stuff at the top of his lungs or something. Mr. Burden had kept his gun in the cabinet above the refrigerator for years. Danny had shown it to her once—he'd held it quite a few times too . . . guy thing. He didn't want to hurt anyone . . . But his fingerprints were all over it. And somehow, after she shot herself, he had the good sense to think it could easily look like he did it. That's what he said to me over the phone."

I looked up at the sky, the clouds. He jumped tracks. "You know what dry rain is?"

"Yeah," I said, catching lightning trees in small frames. "It's when there's thunder and lightning but no rain."

"Feels like that right now." He put a hand up as if to feel the air. "It's dry. Nothing's left the sky. Nothing's on its way down. Where was I . . ."

"Darla and the gun," I said, to bring him back around.

He buried his head in his arms. "So, we went in there. I mean, we didn't even go in. We just opened the door. Danny had a flashlight. He shone it. She was lying behind the bike, but the way she fell, she was still sitting up. Her eyes were open. She shot herself in the right temple, but the hole in the left side of her head was huge, if you get my drift. It was totally . . . black. Her eyes were open. She'd been bleeding out her one eyeball, out her nose and mouth . . . These white globs were stuck to the wall. I'd swear it was her brains."

He choked and sobbed until I felt sure he would puke, and I was about to follow suit. I put an arm around him again, and he was shaking all over, though I think he would have been anyway, without the outside help.

"Dude, I never saw so much mess."

"Jeezus, Justin."

"Yeah. Danny was trying to rush up to her this time, and I grabbed him by the back of the shirt. I talked him into—this is the tough part—into simply going into the house and letting somebody else find her!" He banged the top of his head with one shaking fist. "We weren't thinking clearly. All we thought was that it could have easily looked like a murder, and I was thinking of Bo and how easy it is to blame kids out there for bad stuff. But I always loved those crime scene shows where the detectives figure out what's going on by one carpet thread. Danny hadn't been in there in months. He kept his dirt bike in the front garage. His family had an alibi—being at church. I had to find out if I'd given my own mom brain damage or something, so I left him."

"Always juggling," I muttered, but he didn't catch my drift.

"I never thought—neither of us thought—how clearly impossible it is to stay in a house when you know your girl-friend's corpse is at the back of your property."

"But . . . you went home?"

"I had to! I'd plastered my own mother! The cops were there. Said Mom was at the hospital, had a broken nose, and had charged me with assault. She had me arrested and told the cops to let me sit in jail overnight."

I remembered Taylor talking about that at the crime scene, saying Justin had reported it as the most relaxing night of his life or some such thing. Thin veneers can cover a mountain of problems around here when nobody's look-ing at the details.

"The cops had my cell phone, but it was turned off. And because they had no idea what had come down, they didn't turn it on, like, to see who might call me. They thought they were just doing a parent a favor or something."

"So, did you hear from Danny?"

"He had called that night, but when he couldn't get me, he sent an e-mail. Stupid, wow. I love that guy, but he was not the deep thinker of the hour. I got it first thing when I got out. It just said he was running . . . he couldn't stay in the house knowing what was in the outbuilding. He left a note for his mom that just said, 'Going to Vegas. Love you.'

I was all wrenched up about that, because if he ran it would look totally like he had done it. But he could never afford a cell phone, what with paying for Wiley's therapy. I had no way to find him, couldn't think of how to help him, unless I destroyed the evidence. And there was something bigger. Dude, you can't just leave a dead body. It just . . . isn't supposed to be done. You're supposed to bury the dead. Every human heart knows that."

"Yeah," I muttered in a praying way. "Justin . . . Did you bury her?"

"After I got out that morning, and nothing came up on the news or the Internet, like, *nothing*, I went back. I didn't know what I was going to do. I knew Mr. Burden had a shovel in there. I *could* . . . bury her, clean the place, anything to help out Danny. I figured I could get to a pay phone and make an anonymous call. I could have done that without going back. I don't know *exactly why* I went back. Except maybe I thought I owed myself a second punch in the gut because I'd left her there the first time. I just never thought a whole day would go by without someone finding her body. We had left the door open, thinking somebody else would find her. But then you have to think, do you want to put somebody else through that sight?"

"So, what happened when you went back?"

"I had a flashlight. I tried to prepare myself to see it all again. But first, the shed door was closed this time. I opened it . . . she wasn't in there. It was like the whole thing had never happened. For a moment, I thought I was insane. That night in the jail was the first time I stayed up all night with no desire to sleep whatsoever."

Onslaught of his illness?

"I still wasn't tired. But I wondered . . . was I sleep deprived? Had I imagined the whole thing? But I had that e-mail from Danny, which kept me from running straight to the nuthouse fast. I decided Danny must have done something, buried her in the Barrens, cleaned up the evidence in a state of panic before he ran. And yet I knew he wasn't up for something like that."

"No," I agreed, completely stumped.

"But I never knew for sure it wasn't Danny who buried her until Bo came last night. He told me about that suicide note and Danny being dead. And what am I supposed to say to him? I *left* your sister dead in the garage? I couldn't say that to him."

I agreed. That wasn't for Bo to hear.

"You gotta think of who is alive! Right?"

I didn't know what to tell him, but he seemed a little calmer having told this horribly confounding tale. I couldn't see exactly what he was guilty of. He hadn't aided and abetted a criminal. Danny hadn't done anything either. He was still shaking, but not so violently.

"So. Who buried Darla?" I asked.

He wiped tears from his eyes. "Maybe it was the woods themselves."

I could almost believe it, sitting out here under this dark gray sky.

"Strange tale," he went on. "And maybe that's the end of it. Except it's really not. Because I never shut my eyes at night when I don't see her one opened eye, all glaring, as we walk away. Because we left her . . ."

"Justin, she was dead. She wasn't looking at you," I said in horror.

"I know that much," he said. "Mike, I don't do spooks. At least, not for long. I just do guilt and depression and . . . now I do drugs. *Ha . . .*"

He needed to go back to rehab. Tonight. Before I could start in on that thought, he took up a different avenue. I was thinking the kid had no tears left, but his voice was in need of oil again.

"And it was just the nicest, kindest, sweetest thought . . . that I could bring my brother back! You know? Maybe, just maybe, this world wasn't such an awful place, if he could show up . . . if there was something in the lightning trees, or something in me, or something in quantum thought that could deliver me that one little smidgeon of a miracle. Are you going to tell me there's no such thing? That *all miracles* are manic nonsense? What the fuck kind of a thought is that!"

He was rambling, agitated, not really expecting any answers.

His voice revved up again. "That night Chris threatened to leave, the night he read Mom the e-mail he eventually sent to Principal Ames . . . I don't know what was wrong with me. I wasn't thinking, *Wow, he could be actually leaving, isn't that terrible?* All I could think was that he'd finally gotten his weenie act together and stood up to Mom. It was a picnic. It was comedy hour! I went to sleep that night laughing into my pillow. And then, when it happened, I kept thinking he would show up. A year went by, and I started getting all, *Jeezus, Chris, keep it up, why don't you? You're really milking this thing!* And then I got pissed, and then I got old enough, and used to Mom enough, where I could start to understand his side of it. I never actually thought of him as dead . . . until I saw Darla."

"Oh my God," I groaned for him. It made sense— why he'd become so obsessed with wanting to know *now,* needing to know *now.*

"Because I don't do spooks, Mike! I'm not Kobe Lydee, who loves to be morbid! For me, the alternative to my brother being alive is only one thing. He . . . blew his brains out and was eaten by dead squirrels and moles and hedgehogs, a huge gaping hole in the side of his head."

"Buddy, he's not Darla," I said, but he was on a roll.

"He's in the ground. He's bones and hair. He's part of

the roots of some tree out here, feeding those leafy buds at the tops of the trees with the carbon monoxide leaks from his intestines. Or he's at the bottom of some overpass in Wyoming, where he got his geeky self off at the wrong stop and tried to backtrack on foot. And he's now part of some sludge canal on the side of the road where a speeding semi hit him and never stepped on the break to realize."

"Justin, don't."

"And maybe, if somebody looked hard enough through the muck, they would see something shiny, his class ring, wrapped around one remaining finger bone."

"Justin—"

"And some ten-year-old would pocket that ring, not knowing what the finger bone was. And he'd be on his way. And that's the closest my brother would ever come to being discovered—that his class ring is floating around inside some plastic container of robotic Legos. And his hairs would float up and feed the butterflies. *That's* why I never went to a psychic, Mike. All this shit about the dead speaking? I can't bear it. My dad's a scientist, and I was raised with that stuff. That's why quantum thought is the first thing that ever appealed to me. It's about energy. It's about energy becoming mass—"

He stood and looked over at that break between the trees, probably one last hope that the lights seen were his brother. I already knew better. My skin was crawling with invisible worms and bugs and cesspool mire. I yanked him back down, going against my gut instincts, but what choices did I have?

"Justin!"

I hoped to get him to look me in the eye, stop with the eye-darting routine.

"Look at me!"

He was slowing down, but he was sniffing and hiccupping his defeat again. But he looked. I took off my glasses.

They say the eyes are the mirror to the soul. Adams had spoken that truth last night, and it was something I always believed. Eyes are what make people understand that actors and actresses in the weirdest of costumes are really who they are. If someone has gained seventy pounds eating hospital food and finding companionship in dorm food . . . if somebody has grown four inches . . . if someone has gone from longish blond hair to a dark buzzcut, his eyes will still be his.

If somebody's voice has changed from "I DID-n't DO anY-thing. It's no-O-t my fau-AU-lt" into a calm, normal man's voice, Justin Creed might need some help with that.

I said very slowly, *"I would venture to say . . . your brother mixes lies with truth sometimes to protect his identity. I would venture to say . . . he is alive and he still loves you."*

But Justin had not learned the value of seeing the

details. We'd had a dad who never said much of anything, and a mom who was so domineering and loud that you couldn't trust a single thing she told you. We had a grandfather who gummed the neck of an ol' sweat sock bottle nightly and an Aunt Dee Dee who—yeah—was pretty much of a commando herself, but she was more generous with her money and more trusting of children she didn't give birth to. There was nobody in the mix to watch, to listen to, or to trust.

And part of what came next was my fault. I had forgotten how literal kids are at sixteen. I should have just said it: *Sober up and open your eyes, fuckface. I'm your brother.*

But Justin was not observant, especially not now. He looked me dead in the eye, but his lids were half shut, and he was exhausted from grossing himself out over dead bodies while on Seconal. He said, "Well . . . if you ever happen to see him, tell him I love him, too."

He raised an arm dramatically with one finger pointed. "I'm riding my bike home . . . to sleep it off and take care of my intoxicated mother."

The "intoxicated" was very slurry, but he took off running up the trail, which meant Lanz and I couldn't follow him quickly. I hoped to God he wouldn't pass out along the road.

I watched him disappear, thinking maybe the truth would strike him before he dug his bike out of the bushes. But it didn't. He was drugged up, and in moments, he was gone.

I looked all around me, looking for peace. I'd often found it in nature, in being alone. But this place was creepy, and I just wanted out.

Step one: Admit you are powerless over your addicted relatives . . . I admitted it, silently, to the lightning. And I breathed easier, felt my head loosen a little.

I started to walk with Lanz toward the trail and decided I'd keep myself busy.

I called my lawyer. I punched in his cell number, as my case was considered huge.

"Tom, I want you to call Randolph in the morning. Tell them I'll take the settlement."

This meant a hundred thousand for him instead of six hundred thousand. "Michael. What the hell happened? Don't be impetuous, okay? That is a *lot* of cash, and I really think—"

"How many times have we talked about this? I know exactly what I'm doing." He called me Michael always. He'd known my real name was Christopher Michael since the second or third time we met. But he was afraid he'd forget that part and call me Chris in the courtroom, and my "family history" was not part of this case, he'd assured me from the start.

"Did you run into your mother or something?" He meant it as a joke. "Are you getting ready to run again?"

That wasn't really what this was about.

"We all like . . . money in the bank," he stammered. "God, *don't do this—*"

"Listen! There are some things more important than money," I said, and he sighed. We'd weighed out my options a bunch of times. "For me to take that six million dollars, it's like making a statement that I don't believe I can earn it for myself. It's a declaration of distrust in my ability to support myself."

"Can't you . . . hold out for the big bucks and still earn your own fortune?" he asked.

It just felt all wrong. "I don't know what I would be telling myself about myself . . . if I felt I'd let all that money be handed to me. It could be crippling. And I'm not crippled."

Not yet. I kept my eyes wide to make sure I wasn't losing vision from all this stress. Everything looked the same.

"I know, I know, I know." His singsong was not happy.

"When do you think I can get the money?"

"If you deliver Randolph that great a news report, I would imagine they would write you a check in a few days, just to make sure you didn't change your mind. Where will you be?"

"Just make that call and I'll let you know."

I called Claudia. She made it tougher by throwing me a surprise curve ball.

She saw my number in caller ID and got on the phone

with "You owe me fourteen hundred bucks if you're not coming back here."

I stopped dead in the trail, stunned. "What did you do? Open a budget to hire a psychic?"

"I had a long conversation with your little friend RayAnn. She submitted your story and called me because she wanted to submit one of her own about Steepleton. It doesn't read as well as yours. Well, that's why they have me. It's pretty good, though. I'm running a side-by-side. Anyway. She told me she doesn't think you're coming back."

RayAnn and her research abilities. Had she searched for a woman investigator who'd pulled bodies out of the Oklahoma bombing site and discovered that no women investigators had children our age? It turned out to be something much easier. "She was being a little cryptic, but I take good notes. Wait a minute . . ."

Claudia shuffled papers. Finally she said, "RayAnn wondered how you knew what Bo Richardson looked like when he pulled up to Torey Adams's house. She said there's no picture of him on Adams's website. And then she wanted to know how you knew that water moccasins were poisonous snakes indigenous to New Jersey. You're not exactly a walking encyclopedia of knowledge like she is, and that one struck her as odd."

When you become somebody else, it takes work, but

after a while, *you actually become somebody else.* When people talk about the person you were, you have a system in place to keep being the new you. That's not to say you wouldn't have momentary lapses, but they're few and far between.

"RayAnn also says she wants me to call the Mother Creed."

"What the hell for?" I asked. "Don't you give me up!"

"I wouldn't dream of it. Ethics, darling, though I might punch a hole in the wall before I'm done with you. Anyway. It's a series of interview questions she thinks is over her head." I listened to her printer go off. I took it they were doing some figuring in my absence. She rattled a piece of paper. "Ready?" she finally said.

"Shoot."

"Mrs. Creed. Had you eavesdropped on your son Justin—intercepting his e-mails and listening to his end of cell phone calls—the night of Darla Richardson's suicide? Did you follow him, see the corpse, and think your son would be implicated? Did you have Justin locked up in jail overnight so that your cousins, the McIntyre brothers, would have time to clean up the scene and bury the girl so that your only remaining child would not be implicated in a murder?" Claudia panted dramatically, as if she'd just sprinted a mile.

A blast of thunder struck and Lanz moved me on a

little faster, though I was busy smiling and trying not to trip at the same time. RayAnn was not exactly in front of me in what she could figure out, I told myself. She'd just been sitting and punching out words all afternoon while I was slaying one dragon after another.

"She'll deny the whole thing," I said.

"Whatever. A lie is still a quote."

"She'll threaten to sue you."

"Bring it on." When I laughed, she wasn't amused by it. "And you still owe me fourteen hundred bucks."

"I'll pay you back next week."

"So you're coming back, then."

I sighed. "It's more than a story, Claudia. Maybe it's a book or a website or—"

"You're not answering me, Mike. You're the best writer I've got. Don't mess up your education."

I laughed again. "Claudia, you're a first-year grad student. But trust me. I learned more from you than I ever learned in a classroom."

"Don't patronize me, even if it's true. Where the hell are you going?"

Dang. She was sincerely pissed. I tried not to think of it as I hung up.

I dialed Torey Adams.

"What's up?" he answered.

"Got another job for you after you drop those kids off, if you're up for it."

"The last one is just getting out of the car. What do you need, man?"

"How'd you like to drive my brother back up to rehab tonight?"

It wasn't a slip, calling Justin my brother. Torey suspected what was up the minute he did that double take at Brownie's last night. He was good enough not to bust me to Ali and Bo, guessing it's something you'd rather do yourself, and only if you're up for it. But he'd come around today, asking to play humble servant—that was rich. He and my mom, the only ones who'd gotten it right away, would always have had their antennae up.

I knew for sure he'd guessed the truth when his answer contained no surprise. Only: "Well. I got this full tank of gas."

We chuckled. My headache was gone. "It's about a two-hour drive, Torey. But he's seen a dead body. I thought you might be . . . a perfect person to drive him."

He asked, "Where?"

"I'm not sure. But he's on his bike, and he's going to pass by your house in about five minutes. He'll get you to the place if you cut him off."

"I'll find him."

"Do it fast, because he could fly over the handlebars or

drive into the meadows. He's not sober, but if you offer to drive him, I think he'll go back. Just take him and take off. Don't worry about me."

I could see the end of the trail coming up. Lanz was steadily moving us forward in spite of more thunder.

"Wait, Chris," Torey said. "Where are you going?"

"Hold on a sec."

A huge explosion had suddenly gone off behind us. I turned to see an orange puff of mushroom smoke rising above the Lightning Field. If my instincts were right, it came from the place where RayAnn had seen the lights. If Justin's friends had seen this, the stories would have gone on for centuries. With my overly keen ears, I made out the sound of an engine, a hose squirting water, and I half imagined a fire truck and some Stockton geologists detonating a natural lightning reservoir before it hurt anyone. If they were stupid and forgot to call the media about this, the stories of people having seen lights out here would go on for centuries.

I turned. Torey was panicking slightly, going, "Chris? *Chris?*"

"Don't worry about me," I said.

"But . . . will you be here when I get back tonight?" I could hear his voice rise, a panic in it that went through me like a hatchet.

I ought to stick around for Justin, a part of me said,

and I might have actually had the courage to do that if my mom was together. But with the two of them so problematic, I could only think of what I felt the Twelve Steps would say to me: *Let them pull themselves out of their messes. You can't do it for them. If you stay now, you'll return to your lamb-led-to-slaughter routine. You can return later as a reward instead of now as a supplement. You still need more healing to your vision. Preserve yourself first.*

Adams would have to straighten Justin out about who I was, but my gut feeling was that the truth would dawn on Justin somewhere between home and rehab if Adams just stayed quiet. I imagined it like that. Like everything else, Justin would understand what I'm doing in time. And whatever he had to say about where science meets magic, that would be fine with me, too.

"Torey, thanks, man. For everything." It certainly didn't do justice to the guy who gave me a fresh set of eyes in which to view my life, a set of eyes that helped me flip from first person to third person about who I was. Adams had probably kept me from winding up dead—yeah, under some overpass out west of Nowhere. For now, I let the click say it all.

We reached the end of the trail, and it had taken long enough that a Yellow Cab was there. I tossed my cell phone down, right at the center of the trail where anyone could find it. It was the first thing I'd intentionally done since leaving here to keep the talk growing. Some temptations are irresistible.

Lanz and I jumped into the back seat of the cab. With the slamming of the door, the rain started coming down in buckets. It was like magic. Two nights ago the cops worked all night on that corpse while it rained April showers like this. And as soon as they were done, the rain stopped. I had some thought of bad frequency in reverse.

"Where to?" the driver asked.

I pulled out my key ring and held on to the laminated goals on the plastic strip. I think you're allowed to change your goals, so long as it's for the right reasons. My reasoning lately had always centered on following that next great story, and what was I going to do with all this info? Where could I write this thing where nothing—not even something good—could interrupt me? Hawaii? Lake Superior? Maine? Key West? Paris? *Polynesia?*

"Just take me to the bus station," I said.